*"You know," Amanda said,
"I've never met anyone like you...."*

She was always so careful of her every move. But
now she didn't even think about what she was doing.
Curling her fingers over his forearms, she raised on
tiptoe to brush her lips over his cheek. His skin felt
warm to her touch, but she suspected that deep down
in his soul he felt very, very cold. "I think you're a
very special man, Joseph Slaighter."

She pulled back then, feeling a little self-conscious.
"I just wanted you to know that."

It was impossible to tell what thought brought the
swift flash of pain to his eyes in the moments before
his expresion grew shuttered. But there was no
mistaking the source of his relief when he pushed
himself away from her seconds later.

She didn't think she'd ever seen anyone so grateful to
hear the telephone ring.

Dear Reader,

Welcome to Silhouette **Special Edition** . . . welcome to romance.

Last year, I requested your opinions on the books that we publish. Thank you for the many thoughtful comments. For the next couple of months, I'd like to share quotes with you from those letters. This seems very appropriate while we are in the midst of the THAT SPECIAL WOMAN! promotion. Each one of our readers is a *special* woman, as heroic as the heroines in our books.

Our THAT SPECIAL WOMAN! title for this month is *Kate's Vow*, by Sherryl Woods. You may remember Kate from Sherryl's VOWS trilogy. Kate has taken on a new client—and the verdict is love!

July is full of heat with *The Rogue* by Lindsay McKenna. This book continues her new series, MORGAN'S MERCENARIES. Also in store is Laurie Paige's *Home for a Wild Heart*—the first book of her WILD RIVER TRILOGY. And wrapping up this month of fireworks are books from other favorite authors: Christine Flynn, Celeste Hamilton and Bay Matthews!

I hope you enjoy this book, and all of the stories to come!

Sincerely,

Tara Gavin
Senior Editor

Quote of the Month: "I enjoy a well-thought-out romance. I enjoy complex issues—dealing with several perceptions of one situation. When I was young, romances taught me how to ask to be treated—what type of goals I could set my sights on. They really were my model for healthy relationships. The concept of not being able to judge 'Mr. Right' by first impressions helped me to find my husband, and the image of a strong woman helped me to stay strong."　　　　　—L. Montgomery, Connecticut

CHRISTINE FLYNN

LONELY KNIGHT

Silhouette®

SPECIAL EDITION®

Published by Silhouette Books New York

America's Publisher of Contemporary Romance

SILHOUETTE BOOKS
300 East 42nd St., New York, N.Y. 10017

LONELY KNIGHT

Copyright © 1993 by Christine Flynn

ISBN: 0-373-09826-X

First Silhouette Books printing July 1993

Printed in the U.S.A.

CHRISTINE FLYNN

is formerly from Oregon and currently resides in the Southwest with her husband, teenage daughter and two very spoiled dogs.

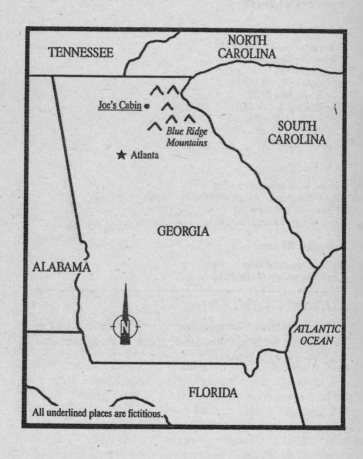

TENNESSEE

NORTH CAROLINA

Joe's Cabin •

∧ ∧
∧
∧ ∧
∧

Blue Ridge Mountains

SOUTH CAROLINA

★ Atlanta

GEORGIA

ALABAMA

N

ATLANTIC OCEAN

FLORIDA

All underlined places are fictitious.

Chapter One

He is a lonely knight, that prince of thieves.

—Robin Hood

He wanted to hit something. Hard.

Anger surged through Joe Slaighter's big frame, tensing the powerful muscles beneath his well-tailored suit. He was not a violent man. Nor was he prone to rash behavior. At least, he wasn't anymore. There had been a time when he'd led with his jaw, but it took a lot to make him truly angry now. It took even more for him to allow that anger to show.

A crowd of three hundred dignitaries, guests and reporters had assembled on the meticulously groomed lawn outside Georgia's state capitol building. In the shadow of its gold dome, the majestic pillars and buttresses of the noble structure lent a backdrop of staid credibility to the ceremony taking place. Twenty square blocks of urban blight were being dedicated to a huge renovation project. South-end Center, it was called, and judging from the model of the complex near the bunting-draped diaz, the upscale development promised to be as spectacular as all the adjectives the press had used to describe it.

The crowd certainly seemed impressed. Of everyone present, Joe was the only one who failed to applaud as the honorable mayor of Atlanta introduced Governor Clayton T. Jones, the man whose tenacity and dedication had finally made the the project possible.

His jaw clenched, his eyes as hard as the ebony stones in his platinum cuff links, Joe remained dangerously still as he glared at the dignified, silver-haired man stepping up to the podium.

Joe had never met the governor. Not in person; though he'd spoken with him on the telephone. A face-to-face meeting hadn't been necessary to know what kind of man Governor Jones was. Over the years, Joe had met plenty of others like him. Men who didn't care who they stepped on to get what they wanted. Men who hid behind the rhetoric of doing what was best for the public good, while they lined their own pockets or fed their own egos. Joe was far from being a saint himself, but at least he was honest enough to admit that he really didn't care about anyone's interests other than his own. Nobody gave a damn about "the public." Certainly, nobody gave a damn about the people this project was displacing. It was each man for himself.

The governor began to speak, his eloquent tones filtering through the warm April air. A light breeze blew, heavy with the scent of blossoms from the flowers and peach trees lining the grounds. Pulling in a lungful of that balmy air, Joe tried to quiet the anger; to push it back into the place inside him that felt nothing, that didn't care.

He couldn't do it this time. Not completely. It had been years since he'd felt the quiet rage that had once been so familiar, and he hated the way it made him feel. Or maybe what he hated was acknowledging the bitterness. Maybe he'd always felt it, but it had simply become so familiar that he only now realized it was still there.

Not liking that thought any better than the others, he sought to bury his darker emotions under his usual cool control—and told himself for the dozenth time that he should have listened to Bernie and stayed away from the dedication. There was nothing more he could do to stall this project. Bernie understood that. Even when she disapproved of what he did, she always understood.

He hated that he'd let her down.

The handle of his briefcase bit into his palm. Relaxing his fist, he eased his grip.

Since he'd ignored her obviously sound advice—something he did with predictable regularity—he figured his best move now was to head back to his office. What he really wanted to do was hit the gym and take his frustrations out on the weight machines. A five-mile run didn't sound bad, either. He didn't have time, though. His calendar was full for the rest of the day, and the dedication ceremony hadn't even been on it. He was here only because he'd seen the people gathering as he'd left a hearing. As if pulled by some invisible string, he'd found himself on the fringes of the crowd.

The same sense of inevitability that had brought him here kept him in place. Frustrated with himself, with the situation and with everyone involved in it, he watched the politician at the podium hold up his hands to silence the ovation greeting him. The screech of audio feedback from the microphone sliced through the air, silencing the remnants of applause while the governor waited patiently for an aide to adjust the mike. Basking in his constituents' approval, he smiled fondly at his stylish and well-born wife, acknowledged the dignitaries seated on the diaz with him, then began thanking everyone for supporting "his dream."

It was as Joe was thinking that one man's dream was often another's nightmare that he felt someone nudge his right arm.

"Excuse me. May I cut through here?"

The voice, soft and feminine, carried a trace of apology. It had also been barely audible over the oration coming through the loudspeaker.

Having either heard the request or been nudged, too, the man next to Joe moved aside to make more room. A moment later a woman with short blond hair, carrying a shoulder bag the size of a small suitcase, slid into the space between them.

The breeze picked up, ruffling the pale wheat-colored strands of her bangs and causing sunlight to shimmer gold and silver off the subtle shadings. Either out of impatience or habit, she brushed her bangs back, only to have them promptly fall right back into place. It wasn't the gesture that caught Joe's attention, though. It was the scent the breeze brought toward him. Her scent. A blend of something soft and powdery—and entirely too innocent to have caused the vague tightening in his midsection when she glanced up and smiled at him.

She had the face of an angel, or an imp, depending on how a man wanted to view the delicacy of her fragile features. Her smile was just as beguiling. There was actually a shy quality to it, yet she met his eyes without hesitation. Fascinated with the contrasts, he almost forgot about feeling like he wanted to rearrange someone's dental work.

Joe knew himself well. The sensation tightening his stomach was purely sexual, and not particularly welcome. His reaction to this lady had nothing to do with any special attraction, though he wouldn't deny that she was attractive—if a man liked the type. The cut of her sun-streaked hair, which was far too short for his liking, was as perfect as the understated shadings of her makeup, and she wore her pink silk suit with the studied elegance of someone bred to money. She was too genteel, too "society" for his tastes. He preferred women who were something more than a polished exterior; women who didn't want a man's pedigree before she'd consider sleeping with him. And this woman, despite the impish smile and the ridiculously oversize canvas bag weighting down her shoulder, had *elite* written all over her.

His glance narrowed. There seemed to be a vague familiarity about her, but he dismissed the thought as soon as it arose. If she looked familiar, it was only because, in many respects, she looked like many other society types. There was no reason he should know her—and no reason to think his response to her was particularly complicated.

He understood the quick heat for what it was. Frustration. Pure and simple. Any man who'd spent any time in a pool hall knew that if a guy couldn't get a woman, the next best thing to get into was a fight. The opposite, Joe figured, must also be true. Lacking an appropriate target upon which to vent his frustrations, his body was apparently channeling that energy in the other direction.

"Sorry," he heard her murmur, then watched her frown at the wall of people looming in front of her. It appeared as if she were about to slip on through. But instead of continuing to work her way forward, she hesitated, seeming to decide that she really didn't want to get closer, after all, and glanced toward the podium.

"This project has taken over a decade to put together," the governor was saying in his rich, Southern baritone. "I first conceived the idea when I was a young man in your legislature. As you know, it wasn't until I'd been elected mayor of Atlanta that the actual planning began. I've been fortunate to see that groundwork move forward through my first . . . and the beginning of my second—" he added since he'd been reelected last fall "—terms as your governor. It took the efforts of many good people to lead us to this day, and you can be proud of what they have accomplished. This area of our city has long been of concern to us all. Instead of abandoned buildings and tenements, which breed the worst elements of society, the Southend Center will achieve a new standard in urban living."

Normally Joe would have chalked off the glib phrases as so much bull. A freighter load of it. Now his frustration only increased with the expansive claims.

"Right," he muttered, as the governor proceeded to describe how crime rates would drop. "A new standard for anyone but the people living in the area you just condemned. You don't give a damn about them."

The woman at his elbow—the one with the smile that was half mischief, half seduction—glanced up at him. Her brow furrowed at his remark.

"Well, he doesn't," Joe insisted, though she'd said nothing to contradict him. In fact, she looked as if she hadn't the slightest clue as to what he was talking about.

He figured he might as well enlighten her. "Not all of those buildings are vacant. There're still people in at least one of them. He didn't bother to talk with anyone living there, though. Does that sound like he cares about them to you?"

Joe now knew without a doubt that he should have listened to Bernie. He hadn't done himself any good by coming. He'd been here long enough to see that the project was going to go ahead on schedule and to work his blood pressure into the ozone layer. Now he was defending to a total stranger a remark he'd meant only for himself and challenging her in the process.

Under any other circumstances, Joe would have extracted himself without pushing the issue. He wasn't the type to make a scene in public. Or in private, for that matter. He preferred more subtle means of vindication. But something in the woman's expression invited him to stay right where he was. His words had brought concern to her eyes and a kind of guileless interest in his question.

The jolt of familiarity was back. Stronger this time. The nagging thought that he knew her had nothing to do with her expression, though. If anything, the concern so evident in her eyes didn't fit with whatever it was he remembered about her.

It took a moment, but as his glance came to rest on her very full and appealing mouth, he finally realized who she was. The instant he did, the reason for her concern became apparent—and he was certain it had nothing to do with injustice or inequities.

"Have you spoken with him about this?" she asked.

Joe's glance swept boldly down, then lazily returned to her face. She had incredible eyes. Limpid, long lashed and a warm golden brown. Bedroom eyes. "You're his daughter."

Another round of applause began, followed by another feedback screech and the flash of photographers' strobes. Joe barely noticed. He noted only that her concern became guarded.

"If you mean that I'm Governor Jones's daughter, yes, I am."

"Amanda. Right?"

She apparently saw no need to confirm what he already knew. Her expression never changed. "And you're . . . ?"

"Slaighter," he said, then expanded it to, "Joe Slaighter," in case she mentioned his name to her father. If she did mention to the governor that she'd run into someone who was less than impressed with his little project, he wanted the man to know exactly who he was.

In his left hand he gripped his briefcase. He didn't bother to offer his right with the introduction, wondering even as he pushed it into his slacks pocket what she was doing among the masses instead of being up on the diaz with her parents. He knew she wasn't camera shy. Amanda Jones had entered Atlanta's social circle by way of the obligatory cotillion about the time Joe had paid off his college loans and bought a car that didn't already have a hundred thousand miles on it. In the seven or eight years since, while he'd built a clientele of many of those same rich cotillion patrons, her photograph had popped up in local newspapers and magazines every time she'd graced some event with her presence. He particularly recalled an article about her engagement party last year. The story of the obscenely expensive blowout at the governor's mansion had made the front pages when one of the guests had driven his Jaguar into the swimming pool.

"So, Joe Slaighter." She said his name gently, her voice surprisingly free of defensiveness. "You didn't answer my question."

"I spoke with him" came his terse reply. "Twice."

"And?"

It was hard to carry on a conversation with the crowd clapping at every other word coming over the PA. Now it was the sound of a cork popping near the microphone that signaled the crowd to applaud as the governor cut the ribbon draped over the model. Within moments, the official part of the ceremony over, the hum of conversation spread as people shifted toward the refreshment tables.

Joe remained right where he was, his eyes fixed on the face of the woman waiting for his response.

Amanda met his unyielding stare with studied calm. It wasn't in her nature to deliberately provoke. It wasn't like her to back down, either. She truly wanted to know what he was talking about and why he was so convinced that her father was disregarding the welfare of the underprivledged. She didn't believe for a moment that her father would do such a thing. But this Joe Slaighter didn't strike her as the typical activist bent on disrupting a public function to further his cause. And he certainly wasn't one of the unfortunate people he was so concerned about.

With much more subtlety than he'd employed, her glance swept his impressive frame. His dark gray suit had the impeccable fit of a fine tailor and the briefcase he carried bore the subtle-but-unmistakable embossed logo of a famous designer. His tie was raw silk, his shoes looked suspiciously like Italian leather, and she wouldn't have been her Aunt Helena's favorite niece if she hadn't noticed his hands. A woman could tell a lot about a man by his hands, her outrageously candid aunt had once explained to her; and before Joe Slaighter had so deliberately pushed his right hand into his pocket, she'd noted with some relief that he didn't indulge in manicures. As her aunt would say, his were hands that would hold a woman as if he knew what to do with her. And to Amanda, his broad, blunt-fingered hands had indeed looked very...capable.

The man was the picture of financial success; a broker, she guessed, or a lawyer. One with rich clients and expensive tastes. Not the type of person to normally exhibit the extraordinary fierceness she could see in his eyes over injustices to the less fortunate. But then he was rather extraordinary in other respects, too.

She could almost feel the tension radiating from him. Tall and brooding, his darkly handsome features were sharpened by an underlying intensity that spoke of passion, power and a definite disregard for proprieties. By the way his glance had raked down her body moments ago, he'd as much as said he was the kind of man who didn't play games. Not by anyone else's rules, anyway. Now, his unnervingly frank scrutiny had changed from approval to censure, and he wasn't bothering to civilize that, either.

"What do you know about this renovation project?" he wanted to know.

"Other than it means a great deal to my father, I know very little." She didn't add that she preferred it that way. She hated politics and just about everything connected with it—which was why she avoided functions such as these whenever she possibly could. "Why?"

"You don't know about the shelter in the old book depository?"

"The shelter?"

"The homeless shelter," he said flatly. "In the old District 9 warehouse. It's been there for two years."

From her hesitation, Joe could see that she wasn't familiar with either the shelter or the area. Not that he found the lack particularly surprising. She'd probably never set foot inside of a public schoolroom, much less spent time familiarizing herself with one of the most notorious areas of the city.

"There are over thirty people living there. Women and children," he added, so she'd understand who was being hurt the most. "Little children who have no place else to be while their mom's are out looking for jobs or working at minimum wage trying to save enough for a place of their own. The shelter isn't much, but there's a day school in it for the kids and someone to watch out for them when their mothers can't. The bulldozers are scheduled to start leveling the entire area in less than a month and the government, your father," he emphasized, to place the blame where the power rested "wouldn't postpone it. In less than a month, those women and their kids will be back on the street."

"My father wouldn't let that happen."

"He just did."

"Then he must not know the whole story. If you—"

A muscle in his jaw jerked. "He knows."

Amanda's chin edged up.

Joe cut her off.

"With this little show today, he just closed the shelter and the school without giving the people in charge half a chance to relocate. The block the shelter is on wasn't even part of the renovation plan until a month ago. Now it's one of the first blocks scheduled to be cleared. That's all the notice they were given. One lousy month. The contractor decided he needed more space to store his equipment, so the city topped a pending bid to the owner for the property. The lady running the shelter didn't stand a prayer."

Amanda's eyebrows rose so subtly that anyone else might not have caught the movement. Joe caught it, though. He'd been watching for her reaction, wondering if, like her father and his staff, she would blow off the matter as something she could do nothing about. Or worse, couldn't be bothered with. Instead of anything he'd been prepared to see, she looked very much as if he'd just provided some clue *she'd* been looking for.

He didn't like the feeling that he'd just given something away. Especially when he had no idea what that something might have been.

"Can she move it someplace else?" Amanda wanted to know, wondering if the "she" to whom he'd referred might be responsible for his passion. "Perhaps to some temporary facility until other arrangements can be made?"

He looked at her as if she hadn't been paying attention. "That's what she wants to do. That's what she's *trying* to do," he said, then lowered his voice in deference to her maddening calm. "It takes time to find a facility that will hold that many people. I tried to tell your father that on the telephone. Twice. Both times he told me he understood the problem and that he'd have his people look into it. Well, his people never did a damn thing. No one even bothered to go down to see just what it was we were talking about.

"Ah, hell," he muttered, pushing his fingers through his hair. "I don't know why I'm telling you this. You're no more interested in those people than your father was."

Amanda felt her shoulders stiffen. She hadn't been prepared for the disdainful dismissal. She should have been. Not for the dismissal, necessarily, but for the possibilities that arose anytime she stepped beyond the carefully constructed borders of her own little world. She wasn't just Amanda Jones out here. Over the years she had gone from being Representative Jones's daughter, to being the mayor's daughter, to being the governor's daughter. She was an appendage of a politician, a public figure by default. For a moment, caught by the force of Joe Slaighter's fervor, she'd actually forgotten that inescapable reality.

It was even more disconcerting to realize that she'd forgotten to protect herself.

Wary now, the public mask slid into place. Rather than defend herself, which she'd long ago learned never did any good, anyway, she was preparing to tell Mr. Slaighter that he was free to believe what he wished when a bulky shadow fell between them.

"Excuse me, Miss Jones. Sorry to interrupt. Will you come with me please?"

Even before Amanda glanced over to see Ruben Howard adjusting his horn-rimmed glasses, she'd known who to thank for her rescue. Her father's aide had a voice that sounded like gravel being rolled in a can. He also never smiled. It was against his religion. Or so it was said by those who'd known him long enough to realize that his moods were betrayed only by his varying degrees of somberness.

The purpose of his intrusion explained why his expression looked particularly pinched now. "Your mother wishes to speak with you. She's waiting with the governor. On the diaz.''

Where you were supposed to be, he'd probably been instructed to add, but being a gentleman, he didn't.

"Don't let me keep you." Slaighter's glance swept over Amanda. "I've taken enough of your time."

Including them both in his nod, he turned on his heel, his departure remarkably civil considering the dismissal behind it. Yet, just as the suit he wore failed to civilize the leashed power in his body, the veneer of politeness hadn't diminished his anger. It clung to him as he moved through the people milling about and headed across the open promenade. Or maybe, Amanda thought, what she sensed now was simply her own irritation.

"Was he bothering you, Miss Jones?"

"No," she said, when in fact the man had affected her far more than she was prepared to admit. "No," she said again and added a smile to alleviate Ruben's thickening scowl.

The little bulldog of a man was not convinced.

"He was only venting a little steam," she explained. "It was just a handy coincidence that I happen to be the daughter of the man he was so irritated with." What remained of her stilted smile faded completely. "No doubt he found some satisfaction in that."

"It was nothing personal, Miss Jones."

She appreciated the assurance. It couldn't be personal. The man didn't know her. He'd judged her solely on the basis of her relationship to her father and not for the person she was. The person no one really *bothered* to know.

With a sigh that was more telling than she realized, she grimaced at the weight of the bag that served as purse, attaché and sample carrier and tugged it higher on her shoulder. After twenty-six years as a member of a political family, it shouldn't bother her when something like this happened. Yet no matter how hard she tried to pretend otherwise, it did. Bothering her, too, was what the man had said about her father.

"Wait a minute, Ruben." Instead of preceding him into the crowd as he intended for her to do, Amanda turned to fully face her father's aide. "He was upset about some shelter that's going to be closed because of this project. He said Dad knows about the place but that he isn't going to give it time to relocate. Do you know anything about this?

"Come on," she coaxed when he balked at the question. "You know my father's business as well as he does." He probably knew it even better, but she couldn't say that. Not within earshot of the people around them. She hadn't identified them yet, but she knew there were reporters tucked in among the guests, pencils poised and running shoes polished. Her mother would have her head on her best silver platter if she were to be quoted questioning what her father was doing. Heaven forbid the public should ever see them as anything other than Georgia's perfect first family. "Is there anything to what that man said?"

The washboard lines of Ruben's brow lowered farther. But it was the moment he started mopping at his receding hairline with his handkerchief that she knew he wasn't pleased that the subject had come up.

"Not the way he probably told it. Joe Slaighter doesn't care about the people in that shelter. He's only been using it to further his own interests. It's best you just forget you even met him. You hear?"

Ruben had just called Slaighter by name. Since she hadn't mentioned it herself, it was obvious that Ruben knew of the man. Just as obvious was the ridiculousness of his suggestion. She doubted that anyone ever forgot having met Joe Slaighter. That kind of intensity tended to make an impression, however unfavorable.

"That was exactly what he said about Father. That *he* didn't care."

"I'm sure he did say that. And more." He stuffed the handkerchief into his back pocket, then glanced pointedly at his watch. "I need to remind you that your mother is waiting. She wants to be sure the photographers get a shot of you with the governor by the model of the project. This is a very special day for him.''

That was her mother talking. Not Ruben. He was simply parroting Elizabeth Jones because it was his job to do as he'd been instructed. Because of that, Amanda said nothing to him about how aware she was of what the day meant to her father. She wouldn't have been here if she hadn't known that, especially since she'd had to leave in the middle of an advertising meeting to put in the appearance.

She hadn't left soon enough, though. And since her mother was no doubt already upset with her, another minute or two shouldn't make any difference.

Stalling the change of subject, as well as the aide's attempt to get her moving toward the diaz, Amanda dug in her heels. The group behind Ruben had begun gravitating toward the champagne, and there were fewer people milling around them now. That meant fewer curious ears to overhear. Escaping curious and critical eyes, however, was impossible. Even now, two women at the fringe of one group were engaged in an obviously disapproving critique of either her hemline, her legs, her shoes or all three. At one time or other, Amanda had overheard just about everything about herself picked apart.

She tried to ignore the women, hating the vulnerable feeling that enveloped her every time she stepped into her parents' territory. In it, she was subject to the scrutiny of anyone who bothered to notice her, and fair game for anyone who did.

For anyone, such as Joe Slaighter.

Without realizing she was doing it, she fingered the thin gold necklace she wore. It was an old habit; by now an unconscious one. Yet whenever she felt her security threatened, she inevitably began to toy with the simple gold chain.

''I know my father wouldn't turn children out onto the streets, Ruben. So are you implying that the people running the place are going to be given enough time to relocate? At least time enough to find someplace temporarily?''

It was hard to tell if Ruben was getting annoyed with her persistence or if he was simply trying to weigh how much he should divulge. His forehead pleated in a frown once again. The handkerchief came back out.

Ruben stepped in closer. He'd known her long enough to know she wouldn't give up.

"They were given a month," he said, his voice little more than a low grumble, "which is all the time the city can afford. Your father acted on the recommendations of his committees, and their findings were all sound. I think the best thing for you to do, since you're so concerned about it, is to talk to your father."

"Right," she all but whispered. "As if I can just walk through that crowd around him and ask him what I just asked you." Her question was not the type to be posed in public. Not by her, anyway, and most especially if the answer might reflect badly on her father.

All that, of course, was assuming she'd be granted opportunity for the audience in the first place. Amanda had known since she was six years old that her father's time was not his own. It belonged to the people he served, and it was a fact of political life that family came after public obligations. Why her father chose to shortchange the relationships that should have mattered the most was something Amanda had stopped trying to understand the day she realized she'd grown up without him. Though the public saw them as a model family, they were basically strangers to each other. Still, they were family, and while she and her father didn't see eye to eye on much of anything, she still loved him.

"You have a point," Ruben conceded with understanding. "It's just that there's more going on here than appearances would indicate. The man who told you about the shelter is neither a gentleman nor a defender of the less fortunate. Joe Slaighter isn't a man of principles. If he had principles, he wouldn't betray his own by lobbying for the distilling industry when he refuses to touch a drink himself, and the tobacco growers when he doesn't smoke. He represents those concerns because they'll pay plenty to protect their businesses. He'll take on just about anything anyone pays him to support or decry, as long as it pays enough."

"Maybe he just believes in constitutional rights," she offered.

"The only thing Joe Slaighter believes in is Joe Slaighter. He's an attorney whose loyalty goes to the highest bidder for his services. No one really knows who all he represents because he farms out a lot of work. But he brings in a lot of money and somehow never gets caught in a conflict of interest or ethics breach. At least he hasn't so far," he added with what would have sounded like admiration had he been on Slaighter's side.

"Right now," he continued, his scowl returning to disapproval, "he's representing a developer who wanted the block the shelter was on to put in some kind of fancy farmers' market. Slaighter was only using the shelter to buy time for his client to come up with more money after the city topped the bid for the property. If he was upset, it's because he lost that deal. Slaighter hates to lose."

Genuine apology flashed from behind his thick glasses, his tone becoming sympathetic because Amanda, in a way, had been used by him, too. "It would be quite typical of his type to exploit your feminine concern for the less fortunate, Miss Jones. No doubt he told you whatever best suited his purpose to show your father's actions in the worst possible light. If his objective was to get in a parting shot at your father, I would say he succeeded. But as I told you before, the situation regarding that shelter is under control. You don't need to worry yourself about it."

If Ruben were capable of smiling, Amanda thought he might have just then. Yet, as she finally allowed him to escort her through the crowd—and toward the lecture she would undoubtedly receive from her mother for being so late—Amanda wasn't convinced that "not worrying" about the matter was the right thing to do. To begin with, there was the chance that he was wrong about Joe Slaighter's motives.

It wasn't what Ruben had said about the man's lack of principles that she questioned. It was entirely possible that Slaighter had the ethics of pond scum. But that didn't diminish the anger she'd seen in him. That anger had been too real, too deeply felt. She'd been drawn by its intensity, touched by it in a way she couldn't quite ignore. There had been passion in his hard expression and something akin to pain—something she was sure he wished she hadn't noticed—when he'd spoken of the children. Something she almost wished she hadn't seen because, for a moment, she'd felt connected to his desperation. Until he'd pushed her away.

She wished she could stop thinking about that. But when something mattered to Amanda, she couldn't seem to let it go. That was why the matter of Joe Slaighter's unsettling effect on her became just as troublesome as the other thoughts plaguing her that afternoon. As she'd suspected, she never had the chance to talk privately with her father. The closest she came was when he had his arm around her while they posed with her mother by the architect's model of the new Southend Center complex—with two dozen other people hovering a few feet away.

As her mother had so often warned her, a frown caught by a camera because of a pebble in a shoe could result in heaven only knew what for a headline. So Amanda, calling on years of practice, kept her expression photographically pleasant and her comments strictly social when, still on the diaz, she briefly met the hand-picked members of the project committee—the cream of the state's most prestigious and respected citizens.

Ruben had said it had been that committee's recommendations her father had relied on. There wasn't anything unusual about that. It was impossible for him to look into everything personally, so he depended on others for information all the time. From what Joe Slaighter had said, though, and Ruben confirmed, no one had actually gone to the shelter.

Because of that, the possibility existed that the committee had left something out of its report that might have made a difference in their decisions. Maybe, because of that, her father didn't really know what the situation was with those women and their children.

Chapter Two

Joe's office on Peachtree Boulevard commanded a view of the city that impressed even his wealthiest clients. That was why he'd chosen it. It was also why he'd spent a small fortune appointing the place with the dark woods, burgundy leathers and expensive artwork that subtly proclaimed his success. To attract the kind of client he needed, he had to present the proper image. Corporate leaders, the decision makers, were people with money and power. They expected the same of their legal counsel.

Joe had both.

From his expansive twenty-fourth-story windows, he could see the boulevard leading to the park where he ran nearly every morning—usually scattering ducks and pigeons hanging around the ponds as he passed. Beyond the park, his apartment building, a gleaming Art Deco high-rise, towered above the profusion of maples, poplars, dogwoods and oaks that carpeted the city in emerald. To the south sat Matthew's House, though he couldn't see it from here, and up the street two blocks was a small law firm to

which he referred cases requiring defense work. Three
blocks in the opposite direction was the firm he used for
domestic matters. The corporate and lobbying stuff he kept
himself. That's where the money was.

The only thing not included in the sweeping view was his
tiny cabin on a lake in the Blue Ridge Mountains. Still when
he looked out his office windows, that was usually what he
thought about. The cabin was his escape; the only place he
ever felt any peace.

It had been months since he'd been there. Yet, as he'd
turned from the window a half an hour ago, he'd forgotten
to wonder how long it would be before he'd go back. It was
just as well. Since he was up to the knot of his necktie in
work, the answer would only have frustrated him. He felt
frustrated enough as it was.

The telephone began to ring for the dozenth time that
morning.

Thinking Doris, his secretary, would get it, he stood at his
polished mahogany desk studying the picture in the morning's edition of the *Constitution*. A grainy black and white
likeness of Governor Jones and his family smiled back at
him.

He ignored the campaign-quality smile on Jones's face
and the properly proud expression of his wife's. What held
Joe's interest was the woman who stood between them.
Amanda Jones was a carbon copy of her mother: cool,
blond, aloof. Yet, there was a faint dissimilarity between
them; one Joe wouldn't have suspected had he not met her.
Elizabeth Wadsworth-Jones had a look of aristocracy about
her; a kind of snobbish refinement that came through even
to a camera. Amanda bore herself with that same class, too,
only she looked softer doing it. Or, perhaps, she simply
looked more approachable. Whatever the difference,
something about her spoke of refinement that had somehow rebelled.

The telephone was on its fourth ring. Remembering that
Doris was at the copy machine, he impatiently snatched up
the receiver and turned to his calendar. In less than an hour

he had to meet with the developer who'd wanted the block the Southend project had claimed. Having lost out to the city, his client likely would want his tail on a plate.

"Slaighter," he answered, knowing better than to hope that particular client was calling to cancel.

"Mr. Slaighter," came a soft, decidedly feminine voice. "This is Amanda Jones." A pause followed; a hint of hesitation that said she wasn't sure he remembered her. Or if her call would be welcome if he did. "We met yesterday. At the dedication of the Southend project."

"I remember," he told her and buried his surprise at her call along with the odd sensation creeping along the base of his spine. Something about her voice reminded him of delicate fingers whispering over skin.

She seemed prepared for his less-than-hospitable attitude. Beneath the softness crept an intriguing hint of steel. "In that case, I won't take your time reminding you what we spoke about. I'd like to see that shelter. Would you please tell me where it is? Or at least tell me what it's called so I can look it up in the phone book?"

"Why?"

"I want to go there," she repeated calmly.

"I mean," he returned with equal calm, "why do you want to do that?"

The question was reasonable. Given two seconds to think about it, he decided her reasons didn't matter. Not at the moment, anyway. Joe hadn't made it as far as he had without recognizing opportunity. And this one was as golden as they came. The woman drawing a deep breath on the other end of the line could be the first real break he'd had since Bernie had called asking for his help.

"I'm sorry," he said, because the demand probably had been a little out of line. "Your reasons are your business." For now. "The place is called Matthew's House. If you really want to go, I'll take you."

It was another moment before he heard her say, very politely, "That won't be necessary. If you'll just give me—"

"The address," he cut in, "won't do you much good unless you're already familiar with the area. What do you know about that part of town?"

"I have a map. I'm sure if I have the address, I can find it."

"I'm sure you could. If the street signs were all still standing."

"Excuse me?"

"The street signs. You know, those things on poles that have the name of the street printed on them."

"I know what a street sign is." Exasperation tinged her tone. "Why aren't the signs there?"

"The usual reasons," he told her, wondering if her exasperation showed. He remembered her eyes, how expressive they were. "They get ripped off. Shot up. The same things that happen to everything else in the neighborhood. What you've got, Ms. Jones, is a ghetto next to twenty blocks of either undeveloped property full of abandoned cars and junk, or vacant buildings the city is getting ready to level. Vacant, that is, except for the derelicts and drug dealers and whoever else has staked a claim to a section of sidewalk. It's a rough place. Definitely too rough for someone like you to be wandering around in alone."

Someone like you. Translation, *society type*. That was what he'd meant. Though, for the sake of his purpose, he hoped she'd interpreted something more like *a woman alone*. That was certainly true, too. He never had liked Bernie working down there, but she'd been in worse places, and there was no dissuading a stubborn Irishwoman.

Apparently Amanda, too, possessed a touch of determination. "You're sure you don't mind taking me? I wouldn't want to impose."

Mildly surprised she'd still be interested after his description of the place, he told her he didn't mind at all—then realized that the caution in her tone was more likely due to the company she'd be keeping than to the area she'd be entering. He hadn't exactly been Prince Charming when they'd met yesterday.

"How's tommorrow?" Paper rustled as he flipped the page on his calendar. He had to see Bernie tomorrow, anyway. "How about three o'clock?"

"Where shall I meet you?"

"If you want to keep your hubcaps, leave your car at home and take MARTA to Ducker and Auburn. I'll meet you by the newsstands. Oh, and Miss Jones," he added, doubting she'd ever been on the city's public transportation. "I suggest that you wear pants. And don't bring that big purse you were carrying, either."

He hadn't expected her to thank him. But she did, quite sincerely, and left him staring at the receiver.

Shaking his head, he hung up the phone. He'd actually been given one more shot to help out Bernie. Possibly the best chance he'd had since the woman he'd grown up with had told him that the shelter was going to be torn down. Bernadette McPherson—his self-appointed conscience and, at times, a real pain in the backside—would no doubt believe this chance due to divine intervention or a miracle or some other otherwordly phenomenon, since she believed in that sort of thing. Joe didn't believe in much of anything anymore, but he was willing to chalk the event up to luck, even though he didn't really believe in that, either. Still, the building that was housing Bernie's shelter wasn't scheduled to meet with the wrecking ball for three and a half more weeks. If he worked it right, maybe he could talk Amanda Jones into approaching her father for a delay. The fact that she wanted to see the place told him he was halfway there.

If there was one thing Amanda could do, it was cause a delay. Impediments and hindrances had a way of finding her without any effort at all on her part. The ability had dubious value. No matter how good her intentions, no matter how far ahead she planned, she invariably found herself running twenty minutes behind schedule, thus throwing off the schedule of anyone dealing with her in the process. Today, she swore to herself as she did every morning, would be different. She would make her appointments on time. Especially the one scheduled for three o'clock. Patience, she felt fairly certain, wasn't Joe Slaighter's strong suit.

Sociability wasn't either, but she'd known that before she'd called him—and she'd put that off until it became clear she didn't have any other choice. Ruben hadn't been able to tell her where the shelter was located because he didn't know for sure, and she hadn't been able to talk to her father. Joe had been the only person left to ask, without creating a possible problem. Not that her initial reluctance to call him mattered now. What did, was that with his less-than-amiable attitude toward her, she was not going to keep the man waiting.

That thought pulled Amanda from bed at the first hint of light on the horizon. She rose with the sun every day because mornings were when the light was best in her studio. This morning, especially, she'd wanted to start work early.

By 6:30 a.m. she was at her drafting table. By noon she'd finished sketches of the dress pumps and matching clutch purse she'd brought home from her meeting two days ago; but still had three bras, six pair of panties and a man's bathrobe to do by Friday. Still, so far, she was on schedule and feeling pretty good about it. By 1:15 p.m., she had scrubbed the charcoal from her fingers—most of it, any-way—changed into something more presentable than the old football jersey she worked in and was on her way out the door of her not-quite-remodeled house with a rapid transit schedule in hand. Not sure how long it would take to get to the opposite end of the city by rail and bus, she'd wanted to leave herself plenty of time.

She would have had plenty of time, too, if she hadn't stopped to say hello to the gardener tending the shrubs next door.

"The azaleas look wonderful," she said with an admir-ing glance, and within the minute she realized that her care-fully planned schedule had just been derailed.

She never failed to wave when she saw the gardener and had spoken to him several times before. Now, the white-haired and withered old gentleman said he'd been hoping to see her again. He'd noticed that the azaleas under her front windows weren't looking quite as robust as they could; and mindful of how carefully she tended her own shrubs and gardens, he was sure she'd be interested in how to prod more blooms from the thick foliage. He'd brought some vitamins for her to try and even offered to feed the bushes himself, because he truly appreciated her willingness to listen to a lonely old man. He'd been gardening for over fifty years, he told her, and mentioned how he dreaded the day his arthritis got him so stove-up he couldn't do it any longer. He wanted to be buried with his best pruning shears, he confided, and after that she hadn't had the heart to tell him she really had to go.

She missed the first train she'd intended to take, caught the next one, and only then, after its doors closed behind her and she sat down by the nearest window, did she allow herself to feel the anxiety she'd managed to ignore ever since she'd called Joe Slaighter yesterday. If she hadn't been rushing so, she would no doubt have felt it before now.

Gazing out at the wide, tree-lined boulevards as the train headed out on its elevated track above the suburbs and wound its way into downtown Atlanta, Amanda freely admitted to herself that the man made her nervous. Anyone with a strong, confrontational personality did. Not that she couldn't hold her own in a disagreement. She just didn't enjoy the challenges some people thrived on. She didn't know if Joe Slaighter was that kind of person or not. Since he was an attorney and was paid to be in the middle of problems, she supposed he must be. Yet, despite what she'd been told about him, all she really knew for certain was that he was a very angry man. If there was any truth to what he'd said at the dedication, about the lack of a proper investigation of the shelter, she believed he had a right to be angry. She had the feeling her father would be, too.

The more Amanda had thought about it, the more convinced she'd become that her father didn't have the full picture. She wasn't blaming him for that failing. How could a man who barely had time to put in an appearance on family holidays be expected to know everything going on in his state? The people she blamed were the people he'd trusted to get him facts. She didn't doubt that many of his advisers were good people, but there were always those who looked only for the easy way out—or the easiest way to please her father, which, in turn, gained them favor with him.

Political expediency, she'd heard it called and wondered if somewhere along the line someone had decided it expedient to downplay the shelter's work. Everyone who worked with the governor knew how important the Southend project was to him. Perhaps a well-intentioned adviser had omited a few facts so the project wouldn't be delayed. If that were the case, her father needed to know. He would never sacrifice the welfare of children for a project. No matter how hard he'd worked toward it.

At least, she didn't want to believe he would.

Amanda traded the train for a bus when she reached downtown. Preoccupied as she was, she didn't pay much attention to the passing scenary. It was just the usual assortment of office buildings and parking lots, anyway. Or so it was until, within minutes of town, the bus headed toward an exit to leave the expressway.

Amanda had driven past the exit the bus took more times than she could count, but she'd never before paid any attention to the neighborhoods bisected by the massive throughfare. Traveling along the expressway at scenery-blurring speeds, she'd had only vague impressions of areas slowly crumbling at the feet of the massive and gleaming high-rises that overshadowed them. Not until she was actually on one of those streets, viewing the deterioration up close, did she realize that the decline was actually decay.

Five minutes later, when the bus driver called out "Ducker" and pulled to a stop by a row of chained newsstands, Amanda wasn't so sure she wanted to get off. She'd noticed several people sitting in doorways each time the bus had stopped, but there weren't many people on the street. The only people on it now were two elderly women who'd just left the ethnic market on the corner, a rather rotund and balding man leaning in the doorway of a barbershop with a faded and peeling red-and-white-striped pole, and a biker-type straddling a motorcycle in front of a building with the windows blacked out and the word *Girls!* stenciled on them in neon pink.

Joe Slaighter was nowhere in sight.

"You getting off or what, lady?"

"This is Ducker and Auburn?"

"Sure is. And it's as far as I go before turning around."

Amanda stood at the top of the steps, her hand feeling slightly damp where she clutched the vertical safety bar. Beside her, the driver's glance took in her trim beige slacks, fashionably oversize beige sweater and flat beige shoes. There was nothing remotely flashy or pretentious about her clothing, but they spoke of a quality that clearly hadn't come from this part of town.

The driver cocked his head. "You sure this is where you're going?"

"I guess so," she returned, deciding that the market looked like the safest place to go.

Her feet had barely hit the pavement when the doors closed with a quiet whoosh. She whirled around, taking a step with the bus as it began to move, and hit one of the door's narrow glass panels with her palm. The ungainly vehicle jerked to a stop, and the doors snapped back open.

The driver, watching her curiously, tipped back the brim of his hat. "Change your mind?"

"I just wanted to know when you'll be back."

"This time of day, there'll be another bus by in about twenty minutes. There's a schedule."

He looked pointedly at the folders in the holder by the door, his expression one of extreme forebearance. She was holding him up now.

Amanda already had a schedule. What she'd wanted was someone's word that she had a way out of here. She didn't have to give it another second's thought to decide that she'd be on that next bus if Joe hadn't shown up by the time it arrived.

It was with no small amount of trepidation that she watched the bus pull away in a swirl of paper wrappers, newspapers and acrid exhaust. A moment later, the skin on her nape tingling with the unmistakable feeling of being watched, she backed up to the window by the market door and hoped the owner didn't mind if she blocked part of his ad for chuck roast at $3.79 a pound. She'd have stepped inside if she hadn't been afraid of missing Joe. With the heavy bars on the store's windows, she wasn't sure she'd be able to see him when he pulled up.

She glanced at her watch. The driver had said twenty minutes. It was now 3:07. She had nineteen minutes and ten seconds to go.

Gamely, she looked back up—and saw the man on the huge black motorcycle at the opposite curb swing his leg over the seat. As he stood, he tucked his hands into the pockets of his battered leather jacket and gave a cursory glance down the largely empty two-lane street. A moment later, his boots making dull thuds on the cracked pavement, he started toward the entrance of the market.

That was where Amanda assumed he was headed, anyway, and the unwanted thought that he might have a gun in his pocket materialized from somewhere in her imagination, along with the recollection of a hundred newspaper stories about yet another store being held up in broad daylight.

She didn't watch him. Not directly. The moment she'd seen him move, she'd glanced to the side, finding his size and appearance every bit as threatening as the tumbledown neighborhood. She could see his reflection in the angled window, though. The dark glasses he wore gave him a hard, forbidding look, and his embarrassingly snug jeans accentuated every ripple of his powerful thighs. It didn't help at all that he moved with a loose-limbed stalk that was more like the movements of a panther than something human.

He stopped right in front of her.

"You're late."

The voice was deep, accusing—and blessedly familiar.

Her eyes darted upward. The breath she'd held slowly escaped and, a second later, relief warred with an entirely different sort of tension.

Deliberately Joe removed the dark glasses. His eyes were equally dark, their color reminding her of midnight—dark and dangerous—as they swept her pale features. The same calculated quality she'd noticed in his stride was in his eyes, too, seeming more pronounced now as his gaze moved down her body. Yet, instead of the frankly sexual overtones she'd caught when he'd done the same thing the day they'd met, he seemed interested mainly in seeing that she'd followed his instructions about what to wear.

Amanda straightened her shoulders, willing the tension to ease. Now that his features weren't shadowed by anger, the compelling lines didn't seem so harsh. Even without the shadows, though, it was hard to imagine what he might look like should he ever deign to smile.

Just to show him how it was done, she offered him a tentative one of her own. It wasn't that hard to manage, actually. He could have stared her into the ground for all she cared at the moment. At least he'd shown up.

"Hi," she said feeling a faint chill as he stepped closer and his shadow fell over her.

So much for the object lesson. Her smile faded.

"I know I'm late, and I'm sorry. I ran into the man who takes care of my neighbor's . . . well, it doesn't matter," she concluded, because the reason didn't change the fact, and he didn't seem interested in hearing why she was late, anyway. "I'm sorry. Really."

He didn't seem interested in her apology, either. His glance had moved from her face to the expanse of honeyed skin exposed by the vee of her sweater. With a slight frown, he slipped his index finger under the gold chain around her neck. "Better give this to me." Turning his attention from the pulse beating in the hollow of her throat to the thumb-size, topaz-colored earrings in her ears, he brushed a finger lightly against one studded lobe. "And those."

"They're not real. The stones in the earrings, I mean. They're just costume jewelry."

"No sense inviting trouble."

His hand fell away, though where his knuckle had grazed her skin, a trace of heat still lingered. Trying to ignore the sensation, Amanda removed the earrings and handed them to him. She was a little more reluctant to let go of the necklace her Aunt Helena had given to her.

She touched the delicate chain, the motion protective. "I don't usually take this off."

Joe could see nothing special about the chain. It was simply a gold serpentine with no pendant or jewel or anything else to distinguish it. "If it means something to you, that's all the more reason to give it to me. All it's going to mean to someone else is a bag of whatever's being sold on the street."

"I'll put it in my purse."

"Which will be the first thing they'll go for. If you can trust me to take you where we're going, you can trust me to return your jewelry."

"I didn't mean to imply that I don't trust you." Not that she did trust him. Not looking as he did right now.

She'd thought him intimidating before. Intimidating and formidable. As she worked at the clasp of the chain, she thought him definitely both now, only in entirely different—and more dangerous—ways.

The word *predatory* came to mind.

And *menacing*.

And *male*.

Her Aunt Helena would no doubt have called him *intriguing*.

There was a faint tremor in Amanda's fingers when she handed the chain to him. She wondered if he felt it when, having dropped the chain onto his palm, he caught her hand before she could pull away.

It was her left hand that he held. For a moment, he simply frowned at it, seeming to find something he hadn't expected. No doubt he had. Most grown women didn't run around with permanent dark smudges on their fingers.

He said nothing about the stains, though. Even before she'd curled her short nails into her palm, he'd directed his frown to her third finger.

"No ring?"

She hesitated, as unnerved by his touch as by the reminder in his question. "No ring," she quietly replied.

"I thought you were engaged." And would be wearing a rock the size of a tennis ball to prove it, he might as well have said.

"I was." By now the ring had undoubtedly been earmarked for some other influential man's daughter—or had been hocked to pay for TV air time or whatever else was needed in Jason Cabot's campaign for the Senate. "But I'm not anymore," she added and tugged her hand back from the disturbing warmth of his.

Loath to indulge the litany of self-recrimination that came whenever she considered how gullible she'd been, Amanda determinedly raised her head. Joe was watching her, curiously now, as one might when studying a form of plant life identified eons ago but which has just revealed some unexpected characteristic. Something in his expression softened, if that was even possible. Or maybe what she saw was simply disinterest.

With no ceremony whatsoever, he pushed her chain and her earrings into the pocket of his disturbingly snug jeans. At the same time he inclined his head in the direction of the building with the blacked-out windows across the street.

"Come on. I'll show you what you came to see."

He didn't take her arm when they stepped off the curb. Nor did he touch the small of her back to nudge her forward, though she could feel his eyes resting there and lower. The only direction he offered her was in the terse "Hey!" he called out when he stopped a half-dozen feet behind her.

She turned in time to see him swing his leg over the black beast of a motorcycle parked at the curb.

Confusion swept her features. "Where are we going?"

"What do you mean, where are we going? You said you wanted to see the shelter."

"I thought we were going into one of these." She motioned vaguely toward the semi-boarded up buildings along the block. "We have to ride there?"

Joe almost grinned when he saw her expression. He didn't know which she looked more uncertain about, getting on the motorcycle or the thought of riding behind him. There were about sixteen inches of seat between the sissy bar and his hips. She could use as much or as little of it as she liked.

"You could walk. I don't think you really want to, though. And no," he said, because she'd just looked back toward the bus stop. "You couldn't have taken the bus there. This is as far as the bus line goes. Most of the area beyond this street was all condemned by the city months ago.

"It's probably hard to imagine," he said, seeing her eye the buildings surrounding them. At least these all still had their windows. Most of them, anyway. "But the area's even worse than this."

Straddling the huge machine, the muscles in his thigh bunched as he shoved down the starter. A second later a powerful roar split the silence.

"Just one thing," he said over the engine's rumbling as he handed her a wicked-looking black helmet. "Would you mind telling me why you're doing this?"

He edged the helmet closer. She took it, trying to remember what had ever possessed her to leave the safety of her quiet little neighborhood—of her quiet little *life*—and venture into a place like this with a man who reminded her of James Dean in "Rebel Without a Cause" and had a decided disliking for her father.

Her father.

He was why she was here.

"You said no one from the project committee had gone to the shelter. I want to see the place myself so I can tell my father about it."

"He'll listen to you?"

"He'll hear me out." She didn't think her father would brush her off as he tended to do when he had more important things on his mind. Not that she'd bothered to share anything that mattered to her. Not for a very long time. But this project mattered to *him,* and that guaranteed he'd at least give her his attention.

Joe's glance narrowed, measuring, assessing. "Why didn't you just ask your father where the shelter is? Why did you call me?"

"Would you want your daughter in a place like this?" she returned, refusing to admit that her father hadn't had time to talk to his own daughter. "If I had asked, he'd have been just as vague about the address as you were."

She met his eyes evenly, ignoring the faint tightening in her stomach when a hint of a smile softened his mouth. He remembered baiting her. Apparently he remembered having enjoyed it, too. But as the smile faded, it was impossible to know what other thoughts went through his mind.

For several seconds he did nothing but hold her gaze. Then, with a twist of his right hand on the handle, he gunned the motorcycle.

"Get on. You don't want to be down there after dark."

Amanda had never been on a motorcycle in her life. She had also never encountered a man who so thoroughly unsettled her. Refusing to consider what other dubious "firsts" might await her, she climbed on the reverberating machine. Before she had a chance to wonder where she was supposed to hang on, he told her.

"Put your arms around me."

She was given no time to consider whether or not she wanted to get that personal. Reaching behind him, Joe splayed his palm between the small of her back and where her bottom met the seat and shoved her forward. With her inner thighs pressed tight to his hips and her chest within inches of his broad back, the motorcycle gave a great rumble and took off down the street.

Joe had said they didn't want to be in the neighborhood after dark. Amanda wasn't sure she wanted to be there even in the middle of a bright and nearly cloudless day. They hadn't gone two blocks before she decided that the corner of Ducker and Auburn looked like Eden by comparison.

They'd entered a war zone.

The area was squalid; despair leaking from every bent and broken building. Windows that weren't boarded up were shattered, doors hung askew on rusting hinges, and graffiti was sprayed on anything with a surface large enough to hold a single letter, symbol or shape. The cars on the street were either stripped down to bare metal and looked like the skeletal remains of a nuclear holocaust, or were so new and outrageously expensive that their owners couldn't bear to part with them even now. Or maybe the young men idly lounging against the fenders, watching them roll by with deceptively keen-edged laziness, knew better than to leave them unattended.

Amanda tightened her grip around Joe's waist and pressed against his broad and very solid back. Beneath her arms she felt hard muscle flex, as he adjusted himself to her hold. She told herself she'd worry about what he thought of this small familiarity later. He'd told her to hold on and she would. For now. Shuddering as she watched a grubby and grizzled old man pick a cigarette butt out of the gutter and put it in his mouth, she needed whatever security she could get.

A man gripping a bottle in a brown paper bag lay at the base of what had apparently once been a laundromat. A couple of feet away, a small group of children no more than nine or ten years old bartered with a boy of around thirteen for little plastic bags of something Amanda didn't care to have identified. The young entrepreneur had a silver-handled switchblade stuck boldly in his back pocket.

The only hint of normalcy anywhere—at least normal to Amanda's world—were three little girls playing hopscotch.

Joe must have felt her shudder.

"It's beyond that field over there." They turned a corner as he spoke, the view now one of vacant lots overgrown with weeds and studded with abandoned cars. In the distance rose a span of freeway and an off ramp leading to nowhere. "That's where your father's project starts."

It seemed to Amanda that they had come in something of a wide semicircle; that the fortlike store where he'd met her was the same one she could see at the end of the next block up. Not knowing the area, she thought it could be that everything was just beginning to look the same. Indeed, there was only one noticeable difference between the area they entered now and the one through which they had just passed. The buildings on the far side of the field were all boarded up. The only occupants of the street were those who sat on its curbs waiting to see what passed their way. Or maybe they were only waiting for time to pass, because it didn't seem from their blank faces that much of anything registered.

They were men mostly, though it was hard to tell who or what was buried beneath the layers of clothes each hoarded. These people were homeless. Amanda realized that the moment she saw the bags and the occasional shopping carts so jealously guarded by people who had nowhere else to go. They didn't even have the horrifying, pathetic lodgings of the neighborhood a few blocks behind them.

Turning her face into the back of Joe's jacket to avoid the smell of something rotting, she wondered where these people would go when the bulldozers came.

Joe took her on past another block like the one before it. Then, finally, when Amanda was beginning to wonder just how much farther into this hell-hole they had to go, she saw it. It was the only bit of color anywhere along the spiritless, desolated blocks: a bright blue door on a two-story brick building with iron grates on the windows and a hand-lettered sign, proclaiming it to be Matthew's House, nailed below a wire-caged light bulb by the entrance.

An alley split the block in two. Turning into it, bouncing a little on the uneven surface, Joe slowed to a stop and cut the engine.

Without its droning roar bouncing off the walls, the silence almost echoed in the narrow and deserted space. Listening to that silence, grateful for it, Amanda drew a deep, stabilizing breath.

The motion pushed her chest into his back.

Joe looked down. "You can ease up now." His voice was deep, husky and hinted at a smile. "We're here."

Her hands were clasped at his waist. Low. Near the buckle of his belt. She could feel the edge of that buckle pressed into the side of her hand. Now that she thought about it, she could also feel the hard zipper of his jeans.

Before she could consider what else she felt below the denim, his hand covered hers. The black leather gloves he wore were surprisingly soft. Just as surprising was the gentle brush of his thumb along her knuckles. The movement was slow, almost as if, had his hand been bare, he was testing the texture of her skin. What he was actually doing was trying to find a space to wedge his thumb between so he could pry her fingers apart.

As quickly as she could, with fingers so stiff they felt glued in place, she unfolded her grip and sat back on the narrow seat.

Had she known how to do so gracefully, she would have apologized for holding on so tightly. She would not, however, apologize for being less than comfortable in her present surroundings. Joe was obviously familiar enough with the area to know it wasn't a place where a person wanted to stand out—which explained his attire and mode of transportation. She, on the other hand, couldn't have been expected to know and really hadn't been prepared for what she was seeing. Like the vast majority of people not directly exposed to poverty, hers was only the cursory knowledge picked up from newspapers and television. The media came close at times. But it couldn't touch reality.

Joe pulled the keys from the ignition. "Hang on a minute. I'll be right back."

Amanda had no idea what he was going to do. What she did know was that she didn't want to sit alone in a deserted alley while he did it. "I'm coming with you," she announced and pulled off the helmet.

Hanging the helmet over the top of the chrome bar behind her, since she'd seen Joe take it from there before he'd given it to her, she swung her leg forward over the seat. Had she been astride a horse, she'd have swung her leg the other way, which would no doubt have made her dismount far more graceful. Her legs tingling from having ridden the vibrating machine, she nonetheless managed to avoid tripping as she stood. Being in a hurry, though, she couldn't avoid the extra step it took to get her balance—the one that would have landed her in a pothole had Joe not turned just then.

She wouldn't have thought a man his size could move so fast. One second he was six feet away, scowling at her. The next moment his fingers were curled around her upper arm as her foot slid into the ten-inch depression in the buckled pavement. She felt her ankle begin to turn. Just as suddenly the pressure on her arm increased and she was pulled sideways, her sense of balance totally thrown.

She heard Joe swear. She swore, too, although she didn't think she did it aloud. Not that it mattered. Almost before she realized what had happened, she was standing fully upright against a wall of rock-hard chest and breathing in the scent of leather and spice.

Chapter Three

Amanda didn't move. She scarcely breathed. Joe's left hand gripped her arm. His right curved over the back of her head, pressing her forehead to his chest. When he'd jerked her back from the pothole, he'd stopped her momentum with his body.

"Are you all right?"

His head was bent and his breath feathered the hair at her crown as he spoke. There was concern in his voice. And gentleness. It was the gentleness that threw her. She hadn't expected it. Not from him. Not toward her. That odd gentleness was in his touch, too. Disorienting. Confusing. And far more welcome than she wanted it to be. At that moment, as he held her, she felt almost . . . protected.

He'd wanted to know if she was all right. She most definitely was not. At the feel of his hard body shifting against her, she felt her insides knot. She started to speak, to lie and tell him she was fine. The dryness in her throat made speech impossible.

"I told you to wait."

Joe growled the words against the top of her head. Breathing in, he prepared to tell her why he'd made the request.

The words died in his throat.

Her scent filled his lungs, its soft, clean essence tightening every muscle in his body. Without thinking about what he was doing, his hand slipped down her spine, stilling just below the small of her back. The feel of her soft curves only escalated the tension and made it that much harder to let her go. To keep herself from falling, her fingers had curled around his biceps. Now he could feel her hold easing as she raised her head.

He had no idea what she saw in his expression, but he knew the instant he saw her face that she felt the same distinctly heated sensations he did. That awareness was in the faint darkening of her eyes; in the softening of her mouth. He could even feel it in the way her body seemed to flow toward him. Or maybe it was his own movement that brought them closer. The shift of his hips was entirely involuntary, but the small, slow adjustment aligned them perfectly.

Sweet heaven, he thought, as he watched her eyes widen and felt her draw a shuddering breath, how she would feel beneath him.

In the space of a heartbeat, she pulled back.

The moment she did, Joe's own common sense shifted into gear. His arms slid away.

"You didn't answer me." He sounded annoyed, which he was. At himself for forgetting who she was and why he'd brought her here. At her for feeling as if she'd been tailor-made for him. "You didn't twist your ankle or anything, did you?"

Amanda shook her head, pushing her fingers through her hair as she did. "I'm not hurt."

He didn't look particularly relieved at the news. "It wasn't necessary for you to get off the bike. I just want to see if someone will let us in or if I have to undo all the damn locks. I wasn't going ten feet."

"I didn't know that." Quite unconsciously her fingers touched the base of her throat. The chain wasn't there.

She settled for crossing her arms, the stance decidedly protective. "I just didn't want to be alone out here."

"I wasn't going to leave you alone. You're the governor's daughter. There'd be hell to pay if I let anything happen to you."

Joe turned away. But not before he caught the flash of hurt in Amanda's eyes. She had visibly paled in the instant before she'd jerked her glance from him. He didn't think she'd meant the hurt to show; nor did he know what he'd said to cause it. He did know he wasn't going to ask. When a woman got that kind of look, her usual response was a less than enlightening "Nothing," and a guy was no better off than he'd been before he'd tried to figure out what was going on. The less that went on between the two of them, the better off they'd both be. The way she had felt against him was entirely too provocative, and he had enough on his mind without having to consider why someone like him should keep his hands off of a woman like her.

Silently swearing at himself, he pushed the buzzer beside a huge metal delivery door. No doubt she'd be relieved when this little tour was over, too.

From above them came the sound of a window being raised under protest. The wooden frame creaked and groaned against the sash until, with a precarious rattle when it gave, the window slammed open. Curls of peeling paint slowly drifted down.

A woman with short graying brown hair materialized behind the black security bars. From behind her came the voices of small children singing something slightly off-key about a kangaroo.

"Mr. Slaighter!" she called out. "Hold on. Someone will be right down to let you in."

The window stayed up, but the woman disappeared.

Amanda looked at Joe. "Who was that?"

"One of Bernie's assistants."

"She certainly seemed pleased to see you."

He let the observation pass, which left Amanda with nothing to do but tack another conclusion onto the very short list of what she knew as fact about Joe Slaighter. He definitely wasn't a stranger here.

A dull bang came from behind the metal door. It was followed by what sounded like mice scratching around, and the creak of something heavy being dragged back. A moment later, with a grating of chains and pulleys, the corrugated metal door raised to reveal what had apparently once been a delivery area—the kind trucks backed into to unload their cargo.

The area was now a garage. Inside the dim space resided a ten-year-old white station wagon and a pea green Volkswagen bus with peace symbols painted on its sides and two flat tires under its rear.

A boy of about sixteen, tall, thin as a broomstick and with a shock of curling hair as black as his eyes, sauntered up to Joe. Amanda didn't know how the boy did it, but somehow he measured her up and dismissed her all in one surly glance. That was all the acknowledgment she received from him—which was fine with her. She didn't feel particularly comfortable around someone who wore heavy chains around the ankles of his boots and a black T-shirt with a skull on it.

"You want me to bring it in, man?"

"If you want to roll it. Can't give you the keys."

"Aw, man. I ain't taken it nowhere. I just want to start it up."

"You know what the judge said. You've got six months before you get your license back. Two years if you get caught without it on the street before then." Joe eyed the shirt. "Those colors?"

"This?" The boy pulled at the shirt, just below the grinning teeth. "Nah. SkullBoyz don't do Grateful Dead. This is cool."

Joe seemed satisfied. Amanda, on the other hand, didn't have a clue what they were talking about. She simply stood there, feeling as if she'd stepped onto another planet, and watched the boy look back at the motorcycle.

"I wouldn't take it on the street."

Joe hesitated for about three seconds, just long enough to make it appear that he had reservations before he tossed out his keys.

His eyes narrowed as the youth caught them. "Just into the garage."

The boy punching the air, loped off toward the bike. Seeming to have dismissed the youth, Joe directed Amanda toward an open door off what had once been a loading platform. "We can go in through here," he told her, while behind them a mighty roar ricocheted off the brick walls lining the alley.

When the engine was gunned a second time, Joe turned around, his voice carrying through the cavernous space. "That's enough, Rocky. Bring it in and park it."

Whether Rocky actually heard Joe, which Amanda doubted considering the deafening noise, or if he knew better than to push the man—which seemed more likely considering Joe's implacable expression—he shifted the motorcycle into gear.

Tires squealing, he streaked forward, shooting into the garage and leaving behind a black stripe of rubber on the cracked cement.

Certain the kid was about to drive himself and anything in his way straight through the wall, Amanda scooted up the short flight of steps and stood with her hand flattened over the pulse in her throat. Joe never so much as blinked. He simply stood with his hands on his hips and watched the kid screech to a stop next to the station wagon.

Dust swirled in behind him while Rocky grinned. "Great machine."

"I know." Joe held out his hand for the keys. "Let's go in now."

It was with some reluctance that Rocky turned over the keys, but instead of going in with them, he backed away. He was supposed to sweep the alley while he was down here, he told Joe, and headed into a dark corner of the garage.

Since that particular alley was already cleaner than any of the other areas she'd seen in the last fifteen minutes, Amanda thought his task odd. But it was none of her business if he wanted to sweep it again. Provided that was what he was going to do. He wasn't someone she would be inclined to trust.

He did pick up a broom, though.

"Did you know he was going to ride it like that?"

"I thought he might."

"Why did you give him your keys then? He could have hurt someone."

"He wasn't going to hurt anyone. He was just testing."

"Testing? The motorcycle?"

Joe's expression grew as indulgent as his tone. "He was testing me. To see if I'd trust him." The indulgence faded. "He needs to know someone does."

Amanda wasn't sure why she felt so certain of it, but as Joe moved past her, she had the feeling that she'd just heard the voice of experience speaking—the hard-earned kind of experience that tends to mark a person and maybe gives him a little insight into someone else in that same position. Yet when she caught up with Joe to ask how he knew so much about the boy, she could discern nothing that would make him particularly sympathetic. As he led her through the doorway and into a long, unlit hall that smelled vaguely of mildew but mostly like disinfectant, he said little to indicate any particular interest in the boy at all. According to him, Rocky was just someone Bernie was trying to help.

"The kid was convicted of car theft a few months ago," he told her, when she asked why Rocky's license had been suspended. "He lives somewhere around here with his grandmother, but while he's on probation, he has to do community service work and stay in school. Bernie knew the grandmother, so she's got him working for her and making sure his homework gets done." He shoved open another door. Voices came from deeper within the building. "She's trying to help him, like she'll try to help anyone who comes to her. She never has learned how to say no."

"She must be a very special person."

"She is."

There was no chance to say anything else. From a narrow hall, they had stepped into a room that, at first, reminded Amanda of a gymnasium. The place was filled with row after row of beds and cots and folding chairs upon which sat cardboard boxes. The voices Amanda had heard hadn't come from here, though. Except for a woman looking through some boxes near the front door, there was no one in it. The voices came from behind a partition at the opposite end of the room.

At the sound of their footsteps, the woman near the door pushed her fingers through her copper-colored curls and turned around. Blue eyes smiling at Amanda, she brushed her hands off on her jeans and crossed her arms over the tie-dyed swirls of color on her mostly hot pink and purple T-shirt.

"Why do you have to do that?" she asked, looking straight at Joe. "Every window in this place rattles when you rev your engine like that. As rotten as the wood is, it's a wonder they don't all fall out."

Standing a few feet behind Joe, Amanda didn't see him smile. She had the feeling he did though. She could hear it in his voice. "Wasn't me this time. It was your delinquent de jour."

"You let Rocky ride your bike?"

"Don't look at me like that. He didn't take it on the street."

Joe ignored her exasperation. Leaning forward, he brushed a kiss across her cheek, then frowned at the stack of boxes behind her.

"You want me to move those into the back?"

"Absolutely. But how about introducing me to your friend first?"

The woman smiled at Amanda, the little lines crinkling the corners of her eyes speaking of both humor and maturity. She looked to be in her mid-to-late thirties; somewhere around Joe's age, Amanda guessed, or a year or two younger.

Stuffing his hands into his pockets, Joe looked first to Amanda then to Bernie. "This is Amanda Jones. She's the governor's daughter," he added, pointedly. "Ms. Jones, this is Sister Bernadette McPherson."

"Of the Little Sisters of Mercy," the woman added, and held out her hand. "Hi."

Amanda's glance shot toward Joe. She'd never suspected that the woman he was going to so much trouble to help was a nun. A nun he seemed to know quite well, too. Now, however, was not the time to consider how odd the association seemed—especially considering his reputation. She didn't want to be rude.

Quashing her surprise, she reached for the woman's outstretched hand. "I'm pleased to meet you. You're the director?"

"That's my official title, but it's really just a fancy way of saying I get to keep all the keys." She lifted a leather thong attached to the loop of her jeans. A small wooden cross dangled from the end, along with a collection of keys thick enough to choke a goat. "I also get to do all the paperwork."

Sister stepped back, still smiling, but she made no pretense of her interest in her vistor. "So, your father is Governor Jones. I'm sure you must be very proud of him."

Amanda knew her smile faltered. She felt it, though she tried desperately to keep it in place. Even after years of practice, she couldn't always mask her reaction when people, by implication or accusation, held her responsible for what her father did. That was how she'd heard the woman's comment—as a thinly veiled reference to her father's failure to give her the time she needed to relocate the shelter.

At least that was what Amanda thought, until she saw Sister Bernie's puzzled expression. Seeing it, she realized that there hadn't been the faintest trace of such sarcasm in the woman's comment. She looked as sincere as she apparently was, and her observation had been an honest one. It therefore deserved an honest reply.

She'd never thought about being proud of her father. "I suppose I am," she returned, wondering, as she'd often done, if he had ever felt proud of her. "He's accomplished a lot."

"I'm sure he has. And I know as busy as he must be, he can't possibly be everywhere he's needed. Joe tried to get him down here, but I'm sure he's already told you that. I'm just delighted that you came. So," she continued, graciously dismissing Amanda's earlier hesitation, "Joe said you wanted to see what we do here. Ready for the tour?"

Amanda wasn't sure why she looked to Joe. It wasn't necessary to seek his permission to go with his friend, and it seemed pretentious to ask if he was coming with them since he was so much more familiar with the place than she. Still, she sought his eyes anyway—and immediately wished she hadn't.

His glance was hard on her face, his eyes searching hers as if he'd seen something there he either didn't understand or didn't like. Or maybe he just didn't like the way he reacted to her. That being the case, she could certainly sympathize. Even without him touching her, she could recall the heady quickening she'd felt in his arms less than five minutes ago. She felt it now, just looking at him.

It seemed he was considering those same disconcerting moments, too. His jaw was locked tight enough to shatter teeth as his scrutiny moved from her mouth to where her fingers covered the hollow at the base of her throat.

A person would have to be as dense as the building's concrete floor to miss the tension snaking between the two of them. They stood there, Joe looking vaguely accusatory and Amanda trying not to look as shaken as she felt, while she waited for someone to make a move.

More enlightened than most people would expect a nun to be, Sister Bernie calmly looked in Joe's direction. Curiosity danced in her eyes. "Are you coming with us?"

Not liking the what-are-you-up-to-now? arch of her eyebrow, Joe pinned her with a look of his own. "I'll move the boxes."

"That would be nice," she returned mildly. "Would you mind checking the pipe under the sink in the kitchen while you're at it? It's leaking."

"Do I look like a plumber?"

"You look like the closest we're going to get to one. We take what we can get around here." Teasing marked her tone, encouraging him to smile. It didn't work. "Oh, and check with Sister Rose Ann, too, please? She's upstairs with the children. The chalkboard is coming off of the wall."

"Again?"

"I'm afraid so."

The creases in his forehead deepened. "What do you do when I'm not around?"

"We do what we always do. We try to fix it ourselves and when that doesn't work, we pray someone will show up who can." She shrugged. "It obviously works."

The overhead lights picked out hints of silver in Joe's dark hair as he turned away. Muttering something under his breath—something Sister Bernie would no doubt chide him for had she heard—he headed back in the direction they'd come to get the tool kit.

"He's the one who insisted on buying full-size classroom chalkboards," Sister said, shaking her head as he disappeared. "Smaller one's would have been just as good, and they wouldn't have been so heavy that they'd keep pulling out of the plasterboard. But it was his decision. He funds our school, you know.

"I guess, you didn't," she concluded when Amanda's eyebrows rose at the comment.

Suddenly looking as if she'd just said more than she should, looking, too, as if she hoped she'd be forgiven for it, she quickly motioned toward the sounds of conversation coming from behind the partition.

"Let's start with the kitchen. Some of our residents are working back there now, preparing the meal we'll have this evening." She drew Amanda forward. "We share what we have with the men on the streets, if we're able. The mission over on Sutter gets most of them, but we usually have thirty or forty who show up here every evening, too."

"You serve them in here?" Amanda asked, looking around. An area at the far end of the space had a couple of sofas and some overstuffed chairs neatly arranged around a throw rug, a coffee table covered with magazines and a television set. The rest of the space was filled to the walls with beds and cots.

"We serve them in the alley from the garage. We don't usually allow males in here. Unless they're dependent children of our residents, of course."

"I take it Joe is an exception?"

Sister Bernie smiled. "Joe is an exception to just about everything. Have you known him very long?"

"I just met him. I really don't know him at all."

The good sister looked remarkably sympathetic. She also looked concerned, as if she had been for a very long time. "No one really does, Amanda." She shook her head, the lively bounce of her coppery curls seeming suddenly restrained. "But he's a lot better than he thinks he is."

The odd comment lingered in Amanda's mind even as the shelter's director began to explain the program at Matthew's House. But since Amanda wanted to comprehend what the woman had to say, she made a concerted effort to ignore her growing curiosity about the man who'd brought her here and concentrated on what were known as "The Rules."

They were simple and straightforward. No drugs, no alcohol, no weapons. If a woman wanted to stay longer than a week and was physically capable of it, she would look for work, or attend high school equivalency or vocational training classes. Many of the residents held part-time, minimum-wage jobs, hoping to save up enough to put their own roof over their heads, and attended classes, too. Something they were able to do because there was always someone around to keep an eye on their children. All the residents

earned their keep, one way or another. Even those too
pregnant to be out pounding the pavement—such as the
women Sister Bernie called "Ida" and "Mary" as she
greeted them in the brightly lit kitchen.

There were other women in the room also—one mixing up
powdered fruit drink, others preparing sandwiches—and
Sister introduced them all, including Amanda, only by their
first names. It was the two pregnant women who drew
Amanda's attention, though. Looking distinctly uncomfortable with their respective girths, they sat on stools at a
long counter sorting through boxes of semiwilted vegeta-
bles. A local produce broker had dropped the food off a
while ago, Sister Bernie explained, adding that what was still
fresh enough for salad would be used for supper. Anything
else that was edible would go into the huge pot of vegetable
soup simmering on the stove.

The women didn't return Amanda's reserved smile. The
woman named Mary changed her expression from specu-
lation to hostility as she looked from Amanda's unscuffed
shoes to her understated, but fashionable, attire. Ida, a tiny
scrap of a girl with bruises on her upper arms, turned away
before making eye contact, her cheeks seeming flushed with
embarrassment.

The two reactions shook Amanda. But, then, so had just
about everything she'd seen in the past half hour.

They had just started out the kitchen doorway when a
young girl who'd been stacking donated canned goods on
the shelves in the pantry motioned to Sister Bernie. Someone had come to the door and the girl now drew the new-
comer, a woman with hair as gray as her tattered clothing,
toward her.

In a small, quiet voice the girl said, "She needs something to eat."

Sister Bernie didn't hesitate. Excusing herself, she left
Amanda standing in the doorway. Her eyes kind but keen as
she studied the woman's weathered face, she led her to one
of the two kitchen tables. Within the minute, Ida had slid
from her stool to get the woman a glass of juice, and one of

the women who'd been making sandwiches had approached with one of her creations and a bowl of broth from the steaming pot on the stove.

Amanda stood back, feeling terribly out of place. What struck her wasn't the poverty, though it fairly leaked from every building on these streets. What affected her far more deeply was the unquestioning ease with which these women welcomed the pitiful soul huddled at the table. These people had little themselves, yet they hadn't hesitated to share what they did have. Except for the girl who'd announced the woman's need, no one had said a word. They'd simply done what was needed to be done without thinking much about it.

A few moments later, as Sister Bernie left the women in the kitchen in charge of their latest guest, Amanda followed closely behind, feeling certain that her father hadn't been told about the work going on here.

She was even more positive of that when she saw the day school. Sister Bernie had told her that, at last count, there were fifteen children under the age of fourteen living here with their mothers. As they approached a door leading to a stairway at the back of the building, it sounded to Amanda as if every one of those children were doing a rain dance on the ceiling.

She glanced up at the thundering sound. The bare light bulbs overhead were swinging on their cords with the commotion. "What is that?"

"Pent-up energy," Sister replied. "The children need to go outside and run some of it off, but there really isn't anyplace for them to play except the alley. I hope Rocky's finished sweeping it up so there aren't any needles out there," she said to herself. "It sounds like Sister Rose Ann just let class out for the day."

The words were no sooner spoken than she stepped aside. Calmly reaching for Amanda's arm, she pulled her back, too. A second later the door at the foot of the stairs was flung open, bounced back, then wobbled on its abused hinges as children went tearing down the center aisle of beds and headed straight for the kitchen.

Amanda glanced back at the stairway.

"It should be safe now." Sister Bernie, her tennis shoes making soft squeaks on the steps, started up. When she heard no one behind her, she glanced back over her shouder. "Really," she added, totally nonplussed, and continued the steep-pitched climb.

Not all of the children had joined in the stampede. When Amanda entered the long, surprisingly cheerful room at the top of the stairs, she found several more. Some sat at low tables working on drawings to add to those already on the soft yellow walls. Others, the bigger kids, draped themselves over brightly colored vinyl beanbags or sprawled out on a big square of royal-blue carpet to flip through old magazines and books. One child—a little girl of five or six— sat alone in the far corner, doing nothing but hugging her knees and watching everyone else with the biggest brown eyes Amanda had ever seen.

Sister Bernie headed up a row of old-fashioned wooden desks, apparently thinking Amanda would follow. "Well, I see you got the chalkboard back up," she said, not noticing that her visitor had stayed back near the children.

Joe, minus his leather jacket, stood by the teacher's desk with his hands on his hips and his back to Amanda. Sister Bernie stopped on his right side. On his left stood an older woman with short gray hair, a baby on her hip and a small wooden crucifix around her neck. The baby, teething and not too happy about it, had the crucifix in his mouth.

"It's up," the woman Amanda assumed to be Sister Rose Ann confirmed as she rubbed the fretful child's back. Two more children sat at her feet; one trying to color while the other tried to take the crayons away. "But I'm wondering for how long."

Well-honed muscle bunched beneath Joe's polo shirt when he crossed his arms. Like the two sisters, he continued to scrutinize the long green chalkboard.

"Why does it keep coming down?" he wanted to know. "And why only on the one side?"

The baby was now gumming the collar of the older woman's white blouse. She didn't seem to mind or even to notice. Her attention was on the man who apparently came to their rescue with some regularity.

It was she who responded. She called him Mr. Slaighter instead of Joe, her formality a decided contrast to Sister Bernie's casual, almost irreverent manner with him. According to her, the reason the chalkboard kept coming off the wall was because some of the older children used the chalk tray as a step to reach the shelf above it. That's where the good books were, the ones that had all their pages.

"Perhaps the solution would be to move the shelf. You could do that, couldn't you, Mr. Slaighter? It shouldn't take too long if we help."

Sister Bernie didn't seem to think it should take too long, either, and, since Joe pulled the hammer out of his back pocket, Amanda assumed he must have agreed. To the estimated time, anyway. Since Sister Rose Ann already had her hands full, he told the older nun that he and Bernie could handle it themselves.

Amanda, seeing nothing for her to do, moved farther back in the room.

The little girl she'd noticed when she'd first entered the room was still hugging her knees. She looked rather sad back there all alone. And more than a little lonely. Amanda understood all too well how awful that feeling could be. Yet there probably wasn't a person who knew her—with the possible exception of her Aunt Helena—who would believe she definitely understood how it felt to be isolated, separate.

"Hi," she began, crouching down beside the child. Her skin was the color of rich coffee, and she wasn't much bigger than the huge Raggedy Ann doll laying a few feet away. She even had the same kind of yarn bows tied on the ends of her numerous pigtails. "Anything interesting going on over here?"

The little girl's expression didn't change. She just continued to look at Amanda with those huge brown eyes. "Can you read?" she suddenly asked.

The question seemed odd, but then Amanda hadn't had many conversations with young children to know just how off-the-wall their questions could be.

"Yes. I can. Can you?"

The little girl shook her head, her pigtails bouncing. "Not yet. My mama says I'm gunna go to a real school when we get a 'partment and then I'm gonna learn." Her little mouth twisted. "Mama's at work 'n' I have to stay here. I don't know nobody."

It was no wonder the child looked so lost. Amanda's voice grew quieter. "Don't they teach you how to read here?"

"I dunno." She gave a disheartened shrug and rubbed her nose with the back of her hand. A moment later, after a very deep sigh, she looked up at Amanda. "Will you read to me?"

It wasn't the question that threw Amanda this time. It was the hope in it. That same hope was in the little girl's eyes as she all but held her breath waiting for a response.

"Amanda. Come on. We've got to go."

From her position on the floor, Amanda glanced over to see Joe's boots planted about eighteen inches apart. The stance was as firm as his command. As her eyes traveled upward, she decided that he looked very big from this angle. Intimidating, too. He also appeared more than a little annoyed.

"I thought you were going to move a shelf."

"It wasn't worth the trouble. They've got to be out of here in a few weeks, anyway, so they're just going to put the books in a box for now. It's almost five-thirty. We need to be going."

You don't want to be down there after dark. He'd mentioned that a couple of times.

Looking from gray eyes that she found remarkably unsettling, she turned to meet brown ones that nearly broke her heart.

Huddled in the corner, the little girl stared at a spot on the wooden floor just beyond her bare toes. "It's okay," the child said in a voice so quiet Amanda barely heard her. "Nobody else has time, either."

More affected by the child's dejection than anything else she'd seen, and considering only that she needed to make that dejection go away, Amanda covered the child's clasped hands with her own. "Do you know what a rain check is?"

Without looking up, the child shook her head.

"Usually it's a ticket or something that gets you into a performance when the one you wanted to see was rained out. Sometimes it's just an expression that means that you can have the same thing later if what you want isn't available right not. I can't read to you today, but if you'll take a rain check, I'll read to you tomorrow."

Slowly the little head came up. Unshed tears made her brown eyes bright. "Really?"

Amanda smiled. "Really."

"Tomorrow?"

"Tomorrow."

"Amanda."

She ignored Joe, along with the warning in the way he'd said her name. "Do you want a rain check?"

"Yeah," the little girl returned with a smile that revealed two missing front teeth.

"I'll see you tomorrow then." She started to rise. Halfway up, she dropped back down on her haunches. "I forgot to ask your name."

Her name was Lucy and she was six. Amanda was able to learn that much before Joe, looking at her as if she'd just committed some unpardonable sin, reached down, took her by her upper arm and pulled her to her feet.

When he had her facing him, he pulled her closer. Close enough that she could see the individual hairs in the beard shadowing his jaw when he bent his head toward her.

His voice was low. "Don't go making promises to the kids. That's not why I brought you here."

"I only said I was going to read to her."

"I heard what you said. Did you hear *me?*"

"Yes." The word was little more than a whisper. "I heard you. But I don't understand what your problem is. Would you please let go of my arm?"

His grip eased, though as it did, she realized that he hadn't been holding her as firmly as she'd thought. It was almost as if his touch had been enough to keep her in place.

As confused as she was by his sudden vehemence, she found her own unwitting deference even more unnerving.

Her consternation must have been evident. Sister Bernie had come up behind them. She had a picture of a house—or maybe it was a flower—in one hand, and the hand of a pouting little boy in the other.

"It looks like little boys aren't the only ones who get testy around dinnertime." The sister's glance bounced between the child and Joe, fixing more firmly on the latter before easing its way to Amanda. "I have to get back to the kitchen," she told her. "We'll start serving in about a half an hour. You're welcome to join us if you'd like."

Joe saw Amanda hesitate.

"We've got to go," he reminded her, just in case she was actually thinking about staying.

She didn't seem to appreciate the reminder. But at least she agreed with him in the moments before he went off in search of his jacket. The last thing Joe wanted was for her to do more damage than her father had already done. It seemed to him that the whole purpose of bringing her to the shelter was somehow being circumvented, and the sooner he got her out of here, the better.

He found the jacket downstairs where he'd taken it off before rewrapping the leaking water pipe. If he had to look on the bright side—which Bernie told him he rarely did—the one positive to come out of the impending demolition would be that he wouldn't have to worry about the overworked and ancient plumbing much longer.

Amanda was waiting by the door to the garage. She looked a little wary of him, which he supposed she had a right to do, given that he was acting like some kind of Neanderthal. Or maybe it was the ride back she was thinking about. The look on her face definitely wasn't anticipation. Whatever was causing her hesitation, he needed to take her mind off it. He needed to get a time extension for Bernie. Having Amanda upset with him wouldn't exactly help that cause.

Telling himself to mind his manners, he nudged her into the hallway and out into the open garage. From the loading platform, he could see Rocky and a few of the older boys in the alley, tossing a ball into a basketless hoop anchored to the brick wall.

Not wanting an audience, Joe stopped Amanda before they came within earshot of the kids. There, in the back of the garage, in its dusky light and relative privacy, he did something he found very hard to do. He apologized for something he should actually have jumped down her throat for doing.

"Amanda," he began, feeling oddly ambivalent about the way she'd stiffened at the touch of his hand to her arm when he'd stopped her. "I'm sorry I came down on you the way I did. Up in the classroom," he added in case she was thinking of some other transgression he'd undoubtedly committed somewhere along the way. "I'm sure you meant well, but that little girl actually believes you're coming back. Life's tough enough for these kids without adding more disappointments."

The soft shadows somehow magnified the fragilty of her features. Those same shadows also hid much of her frown. "I don't understand."

"Which part? The apology, or how hard it is for these kids?"

"The part where you don't think I meant what I said. I have every intention of coming back here."

"Yeah," he muttered dryly. "And you know what they say about the road to hell."

"This is your idea of an apology?"

The question was mild, surprisingly so, for the offense she could have taken at his implication that she would forget all about her good intentions. If anything, her expression seemed quite calm—and very practiced.

He didn't know why that irritated him.

"It's about as close as I get," he told her and decided to drop the matter before his apology made the situation any worse. "Let's get out of here."

Amanda watched him head toward his motorcycle, then hurried to follow him when it occurred to her that he'd looked annoyed enough to leave her there. She knew he wouldn't, though. After all, she was the governor's daughter.

Not particularly impressed with her own sarcasm, she abandoned it in favor of more productive thought. As she avoided a puddle of oil on the concrete, it occurred to her that "getting out of here" wasn't going to be as straightforward as it had sounded when Joe had said it. She'd assumed she'd get home by taking the bus, since that was the way she'd arrived. Now, with the approach of dusk and not nearly as naive about the neighborhood as she'd been when she'd left, she knew she did not want to plaster herself to the sign for beef at $3.79 a pound, while she waited for the bus to arrive.

The motorcycle started with a satanic roar. Taking a tentative step toward it, she stopped near Joe's denim-clad knee. He was pulling on leather gloves, his attention fixed on the dials and gauges of the thundering machine.

Deliberately she dragged her gaze from his spread thighs. "Would you mind taking me downtown?" There would be plenty of people in town, commuters on their way home from work. "I'll catch a cab from there."

For an instant his hands stilled. Then slowly, as if considering her question, he finished pulling on his right glove.

"I'll take you home."

"That's not necessary."

"I want to talk to you."

"So talk now."

"Your old lady giving you heat, man?"

Joe glanced back over his shoulder. Rocky stood at the threshold of the garage, spinning a basketball on the tip of his finger and grinning for all he was worth.

Ignoring the remark, refusing to look at Amanda to see what she thought of being referred to as his "old lady," Joe swept back the kickstand on the bike.

"Lock up the garage when we leave, Rocky. And get the other boys inside. Sister Bernie wants you in for dinner." The same slightly exasperated tone was turned on her. "Will you please get on?"

Amanda was happy to comply. If for no other reason that to put an end to a conversation that had been on a downhill slide ever since it started. The part she wasn't happy about came when she had to find a place to hang on once she'd positioned herself behind Joe.

She tried not holding on to anything as he backed them around and turned into the alley. But not holding on felt awfully precarious, so she tried gripping the edge of the seat the way she'd seen men do when they rode double. Had she had more experience being a passenger on a motorcycle, that might have worked. The first bump though—which they hit turning from the alley onto the street—resigned her to the inevitable.

She put her arms around his waist and actually felt relieved when he didn't stiffen or comment. It was as if he expected her to hold on to him.

Joe had started down the street at what she considered a reasonable speed. Somewhere around ten miles an hour or so. He wasn't going any faster because, almost immediately, they turned the corner.

Amanda's natural inclination was to stay vertical to the pavement. Apparently, staying upright wasn't what she was supposed to do.

"Don't fight it," she heard him call back. "Lean when I lean. It's easier for me to steer when you move with me."

"But if feels like we'll tip over."

"We won't. When I turn, don't pull the other way. Relax and work with me."

He hit the accelerator, jolting them forward just in time to make a light as it changed. Clinging to his hard torso, Amanda didn't bother to wonder if two cops handcuffing a streetwalker at the end of the block noticed the maneuver. As they rumbled down the grim, depressing streets, she even forgot to be nervous about the gangs that had defaced the crumbling buildings with their territorial signs, and the derelicts digging through the trash. Her only thoughts as they shot toward the freeway were about what Joe had just asked her to do. Relaxing was impossible. As for working with him, as edgy as they seemed to make each other, that seemed pretty impossible, too.

Chapter Four

The tension slowly seeped from Joe as the squalor of the southside gave way to the tree-lined boulevards and drives north of the city. He never realized how uptight that part of town made him until he felt the cords in his neck and shoulders unknot with every mile he put between himself and those godforsaken streets. He didn't go there often. Certainly, no more often than he had to. The place was worse than Kettletown had ever been. But the proud little borough where he'd grown up had been closed in on all sides by that same kind of encroaching decay, and the sights and the stench of the southend were close enough to trigger a whole host of unwanted memories. It had taken him years— years of fighting, running, denying—but he'd finally settled into a kind of armed truce with those memories; that past. Or so he'd thought until Bernie had called about the Southend Center. The similarities between that project and the one that had destroyed his family twenty years ago had brought him face-to-face with all he'd tried to forget.

"It's two blocks up." Amanda pointed off to the side. "On the right."

With a tight nod to acknowledge her directions, Joe felt her shift against his back as she reclasped her hands at his waist. His inner tension hadn't dissipated all that much. It lingered even now, taunting him in ways he knew better than to consider. His mood wasn't helped by the fact that the woman whose help he needed represented just about everything he'd spent those last twenty years resenting. It was also a little irritating to find the feel of her so damned tantalizing.

Chalking his physical reaction up to the Fates' twisted idea of a joke, he pulled his motorcycle into the driveway she indicated and pulled the key from the ignition.

He had his helmet in his hand, his glance taking in the recently renovated houses in the quiet neighborhood, when she slid from behind him and handed him the helmet she'd been wearing. He took it without looking at her, vaguely aware of her motions as she ran her fingers through her boyishly short hair while he checked out her house.

The place was not what he'd expected. Not that there was anything wrong with it. The charming white bungalow had neat gray shutters framing its paned windows, yellow tulips and some kind of feathery purple stuff in long windowboxes and two white wicker chairs on the pillared porch. It was nice. Comfortable looking. And not the least bit ostentatious. He'd been prepared for rolling lawns and antebellum gentility.

"You live here? I thought you lived in Buckhead."

"Why would you think that?"

The sun was setting, the dimming light seeming to magnify the peaceful sounds of birds settling into budded trees. That same pale light made her skin look like alabaster: smooth, cool, almost too perfect to touch. But then his eyes were drawn to the soft pout of her mouth, and its sensual warmth would have ruined the ice-princess image had it not been for the polite arch of her eyebrow.

He wondered if they gave lessons on mastering that look in finishing school. "It just seemed like the kind of place that would appeal to you."

Her eyebrow curved a little higher. Buckhead was where her parents lived, or, more accurately, where the governor's mansion had been built. The area fairly reeked *society, money* and *class*. The most palatial homes were there, along with the best stores and the trendiest restaurants. It was a place where people went to see and be seen, and Joe hadn't meant his observation as a compliment.

"You said you wanted to talk to me," she reminded him, not caring to discuss why she lived where she did.

"How about we go inside?"

Amanda hesitated. She didn't want him in her house. He had already invaded too much of her space. "Will it take that long?"

"It'll only take longer if we stay out here talking about where to talk."

He had a point, though it goaded her to concede it. Amanda tended to keep to herself, but she knew her neighbors well enough to know they'd be curious about her company. The quiet, revitalized-and-renovated neighborhood was populated with young, professional families who tended to be fairly conservative in their choice of transportation and dress. Joe would have attracted attention no matter how he'd been attired. He was simply the kind of man people noticed. But his beat-up jacket and worn jeans gave him a disreputable look that fit him all too well, and the way he straddled that wicked-looking motorcycle was sure to raise an eyebrow or two. Especially this time of day with everyone arriving home from work.

A Volvo station wagon drove by, its driver's neck cranked around so far that he nearly missed his house. Her conclusion confirmed, Amanda turned on her heel.

Joe, his boots making determined thuds on the alyssum-lined walkway, followed.

The door had barely closed behind him when she saw him frown.

He looked so very big standing there. His large frame completely hid the oval lead-glass window in the door, but the light coming from behind him made him look almost surreal. Or maybe it was demonic, she thought, dragging her gaze from his powerful stance.

"It's paint stripper," she said, assuming his frown was for the odd smell filling the foyer. "I guess I should have left the upstairs windows open so the fumes wouldn't be so strong."

Joe's hands were on his hips as he glanced up the gleaming mahogany staircase. The spindles were so highly polished that the light slanting through the gun-slot windows at the landing made the wood seem to glow. "You're having some remodeling done?"

"It's not remodeling really. I'm just refinishing the banisters."

He touched the ornate cap atop the newel post. "You did this?"

The way his long fingers traced the carving was almost sensual. He moved slowly, deliberately, as if testing texture and grain. She knew how gentle his hands could be, and how strong. She also knew that to feel his hands moving over her in such a way was not something she should be standing there considering.

Fearing the heat in her midsection might have made its way to her cheeks, she turned away. Still she managed to keep her tone dry as she picked up the mail the postman had delivered through the slot in the door. "Yes, I did. Amazing isn't it?"

Extreme forbearance marked his expression. "I didn't mean to insult you. But, yeah. It is amazing. I'd never thought someone like you would be interested in doing this sort of thing."

Goaded by what to him was no doubt a rational deduction, her expression now matched her tone. "Interested in the restoration? Or the actual work?"

She knew what he thought of her; what preconceived ideas he had about who Amanda Jones was. He thought her a spoiled little socialite, a woman who enjoyed her status and her family wealth and who seldom dirtied her hands, either literally or figuratively if it could possibly be helped. He'd confirmed that in one way or another a half dozen times since she'd met him. A childish part of her—a part she didn't feel very proud of—would have taken a certain pleasure in punching holes in his assessment; of proving how little he knew. A very adult part—the part that had learned self-preservation—told her to let him think what he wanted. Letting him know her, even allowing him in enough to admit the sense of accomplishment she felt when she would pull the beauty out of something old and venerable, could make her vulnerable.

She felt far too vulnerable around him as it was. Especially when he looked at her as he was now, as if he needed to figure her out, though he didn't necessarily want to.

He came to stand in front of her, his gaze direct and assessing. "The work. It's hard to picture you sanding down newel posts. You surprise me, Amanda."

His smile was unexpected. It transformed his features, taking away the harder edges. Or maybe it only made them more compelling. Whatever it was, the effect of that smile would have devastated any woman who didn't have the brains to be wary.

"It does explain something I've been wondering about, though."

Before she could begin to guess what he was talking about, he'd circled her wrist to raise her hand.

"I couldn't figure out why your hands looked like this."

It was her left hand that he had cupped in his, a dull gray cast clearly visible on the sides of her ring and little fingers. Her middle finger had a bump near the first knuckle. The smudge there was even darker.

Amanda didn't polish her short nails. Color made them more noticeable and she avoided calling attention to her hands whenever possible. Though they were small, soft and slender, they didn't look terribly feminine to her. They definitely didn't look feminine to her mother. In the past five years, there hadn't been a birthday go by that her mother's gift hadn't been yet another pair of gloves. Although, held in Joe's strong hand, hers looked terribly fragile; almost childlike.

There was nothing the least bit childlike about the warm liquid sensation in her stomach when she felt his thumb brush the delicate veins in her wrist.

"That's not from the refinishing. I usually wear gloves when I'm staining." She gave her hand a slight tug, but he didn't let go. "That's charcoal."

"Charcoal?"

"From a sketching pencil" was all she would say.

She pulled her hand back again. This time, his eyes still steady on hers, he let her go.

She knew she should move. But as he had once before held her only by his touch, he held her now, it seemed, by the disturbing intensity in his eyes. No expression betrayed his thoughts. There was only the penetrating quality of his gaze telling her, as surely as she stood there, that he was seeing far more than she'd wanted him to know.

She suddenly felt like prey; as if he were looking for weak spots to home in on later. No doubt he was a formidable opponent in the courtroom.

Feeling far less sure of herself than her manner would indicate, she motioned to the room beyond the double French doors. "We can talk in here."

Joe swore at himself. It had been stupid to touch her. But he'd needed to do something to make her stop looking at him with the cool hauteur that he found so irritating. It didn't suit her, anyway. And he had been curious about her hands.

Now that he thought about it, though, only her left hand had the curious dark smudges on it. What was it she sketched? he wondered, and as he entered her living room, he found himself glancing at the paintings on the pale blue-and cream-striped wallpaper for some evidence of how she spent her spare time.

The paintings gave no hint of her talent. The pictures on her walls were all prints of French Impressionists' work. All

Joe could discern about her from them was that she favored soft, tranquil scenes, and that she had a definite
preference for blue. The deep blue in a copy of Monet's
Water Lilies was the exact shade of blue in the delft print
sofa over which it hung; the shades of blues and pinks in the
print of that artist's garden were reflected in a vase on the
glass table.

Whatever it was she sketched definitely wasn't displayed
in this room, he decided, and passed up a delicate antique
chair in favor of a sturdier, overstuffed one near the arched
windows.

He didn't sit down, though. Instead he watched Amanda,
her hands clasped between the low pockets of her oversize
beige sweater, when she stopped in the middle of the cream-
colored carpet about four feet away. She wasn't comfortable with him in here. That was obvious in the way her eyes
had darted toward everything his own had touched upon—
as if checking to see what he had noted. She also didn't quite
seem to know what to do with him. That suited him just
fine. It was easier to get what he wanted when the opposi-
tion was off balance.

"Tell me what you thought of Matthew's House."

Her brow furrowed, either at the question or his abrupt-
ness. He couldn't tell. Nor did he really care.

"I think it's awful," she said, then shook her head when
she saw he hadn't understood. "I don't mean what your
friend is doing. What Sister Bernie has done with that old
warehouse is wonderful. What's awful is that a place like
that is so necessary." Wishing he'd stop watching her so
closely, knowing he'd keep right on doing as he damn well
pleased, she sank to the edge of the sofa. "I've never seen
such..."

Poverty was the first word that came to mind. Yet, it
hadn't been the poverty that disturbed her so. Heaven knew
she'd never seen anything like it before, but it had been
something deeper than that. Something less tangible.

"Injustice," she finally decided.

For a moment Joe, considering, said nothing. Then, as if he wanted to refrain from influencing her, he simply said, "Go on."

So Amanda did, thinking of the bleakness she'd seen in little Lucy's eyes; a sadness no child should ever have to know. It had been difficult enough to meet adults so down on their luck that they had to rely on charity to put a roof over their head; harder still to see the ragged bundles of humanity living on the streets. To her, the drug dealers and the pimps in their flashy cars simply gave new meaning to the word disgust. But it was thoughts of the children that would undoubtedly haunt her for a very long time.

"That little girl. The one I was talking with." Even now Amanda could picture the child's eyes; the hope in them that didn't want to die but which was slowly being eaten away by a lifetime of disappointment—just as Joe had said. "She wants to learn. She's eager for it," she stressed, though her voice was subdued. "But she can't be enrolled in school if she's not living anywhere in particular, and without some kind of structure and stability in her life—"

Amanda shook her head, cutting herself off before she began voicing all the complications in such a child's circumstances. The enumeration wasn't necessary. Joe was obviously already more than aware of the problems. "I'm not blaming her mother for the situation," she had to say, however. Despite what Amanda had told herself about not caring what this man thought of her, she needed for him to know that. She wouldn't judge the woman. She didn't even know her, much less the circumstances that had led her to Matthew's House. "I just wonder how children like Lucy stand a chance of escaping the cycle without education."

"She has the school at the shelter. It might not be the most ideal program, but it's more than she has otherwise."

More than she'll have if it has to be shut down.

He hadn't said the words, but Amanda heard them, anyway. They were in his eyes, the unspoken reality of her father's decisions echoing between them.

Don't accuse me, she wanted to insist. *Don't blame me for something I had nothing to do with.*

She said none of that, though. She never did. "I wasn't questioning its value." It was the root of the need for it that bothered her so much. "The day school is a wonderful idea, and I can see how hard it will be to keep it intact if it has to be closed down until a new location can be found." As unstable as their situations were, she couldn't help but wonder what would happen to the residents in the meantime. "Do you have anyplace at all in mind?"

"Nothing that will work," he told her. "We've checked out an old factory, but the plumbing and electrical are shot, and someone at Bernie's motherhouse got a lead on some modular classrooms. The problem with using them is that there's no available property to put them on. The kind of housing we really need is in residential areas. But like I told you the other day, nobody wants a homeless shelter in their backyard."

We. He kept talking in the plural.

Amanda tipped her head, studying him as he turned toward the window. She didn't want to be intrigued by him. Yet she couldn't deny that she was. "Would you mind telling me how you got involved in all this?"

"Bernie asked for my help."

That was not the response she'd been looking for. Hoping for something more illuminating, she tried again. "How do you know her?"

He stood by the window, where the light filtering through wasn't nearly as reliable as it had been a couple of minutes ago. Dusk was settling, the shifting shadows of the early evening making his features seem more brooding. "She's an old friend."

"I see," she said, when all she really understood from his terse response was that she'd met her match when it came to reticence. It was a dubious trait to have in common.

"Do you always go to so much trouble for your old friends?"

He turned to face her, the look on his face remarkably tolerant. "Whether or not I do has nothing to do with what we're discussing."

He didn't want to elaborate on his involvement. In fact, to Amanda, it seemed he wanted it ignored altogether.

She couldn't do that. "She told me that there wouldn't be a school program if it weren't for you. As I understand it, the program was even your idea. I think what you've done for her and those women . . . what you're trying to do for them now," she added, because he hadn't given up yet, "is very nice."

Amanda hadn't realized until just then that she wanted some kind of middle ground with this man; a truce, if necessary, so they could carry on a conversation without one of them putting the other on the defensive. She'd intended the compliment as conciliation. She'd truly meant what she'd said, because she admired what he was doing even if she didn't care for the way he made her feel while he was doing it.

Instead of a white flag, she seemed to have waved a red one.

His tone grew deceptively mild. Yet something cold and decidedly forbidding swept his strong Celtic features. "Don't go getting the wrong idea about me, Amanda. I'm not a *nice* person. I do what I do for very selfish reasons, so don't go mixing me up with someone who actually gives a damn. My only interest in this is to see that Bernie gets the time she needs. I'm sure that's not what you heard. Or even what you might believe. But it's the truth."

So much for détente.

"You're right. It's not what I heard." She stood then, facing him because he'd invited the challenge. "What I heard was that you were interested in the shelter only because you represent a developer who wanted that property. I also heard that you'll use just about any means available to get what you want. That may or may not be true, but I don't appreciate you deciding what I believe."

What was it about this man, she wondered, that made it impossible for her to maintain the quietly dignified presence she sought to present to her father's public? Why did she allow him to bother her, rather than letting his comments go as she would have with anyone else who saw her only as a means to an end?

She turned away. He really didn't have to explain anything to her, and his reasons for wanting to help really made no difference. Despite what Ruben had told her—and despite Joe's own curious and terribly transparent denial—Amanda knew his concern for the shelter was real. What did matter to her was why this man refused to admit his concern when it was so obvious that he cared very much about his friend and the work she was doing. He even cared about Rocky, though he'd tried to make it look as if his interest in the boy meant nothing.

The light in the room was fading rapidly. Not wanting to stand there in the dark, which was how she felt, anyway, she switched on the lamp on the end table. A pool of soft light lifted the encroaching shadows.

She stood in that light, her back to Joe, and took a deep breath.

Frustrated, Joe raked his fingers through his hair and watched her regain her composure. This conversation wasn't going at all the way he'd intended. When he'd said he wanted to talk to her, his agenda had been quite clear. He'd planned to find out what she thought of the shelter, to beef up her perceptions about it if necessary, then get her on the phone to her father. After wanting to shake her for promising that little girl that she would come back tomorrow, he also needed her to understand that he didn't want her getting involved beyond that. Amanda, however, was not being all that cooperative with his plan. What she *was* doing was confusing the hell out of him.

He hadn't expected her to give him the benefit of the doubt. But she had, and seemingly without question. Unless his analytical abilities had just taken a hike, she'd ignored the rumors about him using the shelter problem to further his client's interests and chosen, instead, to believe in his cause. For some reason he couldn't begin to define, he felt oddly grateful to her for that.

He wasn't comfortable with that feeling. Still, her refusal to judge him by his reputation somehow made it necessary for him to be as honest with her as he could. "The only way my client will benefit at this point is if it decides to sue the city, the state, the architects and whoever else we can think to name and the defense decides to fold instead of fight. I don't think that's going to happen. Personally, I don't give a damn who puts what on that block. All I care about is that Bernie gets the time she needs to relocate."

"I believe you."

"I meant what I said before," he told her, not wanting to care about how her words made him feel. It was as if she expected his intentions to be honorable; that it hadn't occurred to her to consider otherwise. "I didn't take you down there to get you to do volunteer work for Bernie. If you're smart, you'll stay away from that place. It's dangerous for a woman in that area." He paused, wanting her to remember what she'd seen, what she'd felt as they'd traveled those forbidding streets. When he saw her draw in another deep breath, he knew she had the picture. "The only reason I took you down there was for you to see what the sisters were doing so you can have your father delay the demolition. That's all I want from you, Amanda."

His honesty was commendable, she supposed. He wanted nothing more from her than whatever concession she could get from her father. That knowledge shouldn't have bothered her. Not this time. Her purpose in going to the shelter to begin with had been to tell her father what it was all about. That was still her purpose. For the most part.

Amanda had long ago learned that when she didn't agree with someone, it was simpler to remain silent on the subject—then quietly go about doing whatever needed to be done. That was why she made no comment about returning to the shelter tomorrow and simply said, "I'll talk to him."

"I'd appreciate it."

The deep bong of the grandfather clock in the foyer cut through the sudden silence. It sounded again, the silence between the mellow reverberations growing more pronounced as Joe stood there telling himself it was time to leave. He had accomplished what he'd set out to do in having her agree to speak with the governor. There was no reason to stick around any longer.

He found that thought strangely disappointing. There was more to Amanda Jones than he'd first suspected; more he would like to discover. Under other circumstances. Certainly she was gutsier than he'd thought she'd be. Definitely more independent.

As he crossed the carpet, heading for the French doors and the foyer beyond, he knew she had no intention of staying away from the shelter tomorrow. The stubbornness he'd glimpsed in her had told him that. Or maybe it was more the rebellion he thought he'd recognized. Whatever it was, that same headstrong quality had kept her from admitting that she'd been scared to death of his motorcycle when she'd first climbed onto it. And that same stubbornness had prevented her from admitting, once she'd gotten used to it, that riding it hadn't been so bad after all.

He almost smiled. She'd ridden that motorcycle considerably farther than she'd had to—since he'd deliberately taken the long route to the shelter.

He stopped in the hall, silent now that the clock had struck its last note, and waited for her to open the door. He had the feeling she'd actually found riding his motorcycle exciting; that she'd even be tempted to try it again, if he were to ask. She was too much of a lady to admit it was a turn-on, though. Which was a pity, he thought, because she certainly turned him on. Under other circumstances, he'd be sorely tempted to pursue the temptations of her lovely body. The way she'd fit herself to his back, crushing her breasts against him and hugging him low around the belly had him hardening just thinking about it.

He reached into his pocket as her hand curled over the knob. Her cooperation was far more important than a leisurely tumble in bed. Not, he was inclined to admit, that she'd be likely to invite him up her stairs.

"You'll call me after you've spoken with your father?"

She nodded, turning to face him as she started to open the door. She would, she started to say, but his hand closed over hers on the knob.

A moment later he pulled her hand away. Holding it in his, he turned it palm up.

"I almost forgot," he said, and folded her earrings into her palm.

His face was a study in stone as he reached back into the pocket on his snug jeans.

He pulled out her necklace, but he didn't give it to her. Instead, the thin gold chain looking incredibly delicate in his large fingers, he stepped forward.

Before she realized what he intended to do, she felt the feather-light touch of the chain around her neck and the weight of his wrists on her shoulders. There were calluses on his fingers. She felt their roughness against her smooth skin as he fastened the clasp.

A whisper of sensation skittered through her as she raised her eyes to his face. Or maybe it was the way he slowly trailed one finger along the delicate chain that altered her breathing. His face had lost all expression, his concentration seeming focused only on the mesmerizing movement as he followed the gold serpentine over her collarbone to where his finger came to rest just below the hollow of her throat.

From somewhere beyond the door came the honk of a car horn. Behind them, the grandfather clock quietly echoed her syncopated heartbeats. Amanda didn't move. She wasn't sure she even breathed. His glance moved to her mouth, his own parting as he raised his eyes to hers. It was then that she saw the heat; a kind of primitive heat that made her ache deep inside.

His hand fell. "Let me know what your father says."

A moment later he'd let himself out.

* * *

Amanda couldn't reach her father that night. Her parents were out to dinner when she called, so she told their housekeeper she'd try him in the morning at his office. She did reach him the next morning, but his secretary warned her that he was on his way to a meeting.

Talking to her father when he was rushed was pointless. That was why she asked him to call her later, when he had time, only to learn that "later" he'd be in Kentucky because he and her mother and some of their friends were going to the horse races. They wouldn't return until Monday. So, even though the circumstances weren't optimum, she swallowed her misgivings at the timing and quickly told him what she'd been up to when he asked.

"I've been to a place called Matthew's House," she told him, looking up from her drawing table to the mannequin wearing the man's plaid flannel robe she was sketching. Then, absently blending in lines on the large drawing with the side of her little finger to form shadows in the robe's folds, she told him about Sister Bernadette and the work the nuns were doing, and asked if there wasn't a way for the demolition of the old warehouse to be delayed so the women and their children could stay together. Assuming his silence meant he was listening, she hurried on to tell him how many of the women were in GED and vocational education programs that would be disrupted if the shelter had to close and, remembering Lucy, about the children who attended the day school. Because he still hadn't said anything, she asked if he'd known any of this.

He had, he assured her and yes he was aware that no one on the fact-finding committee had visited it. His only concern was who else knew about what she'd seen.

Joe Slaighter's name hadn't yet come up, and her father hadn't asked how she'd found out about the shelter, which could only mean that Ruben had already briefed him about her encounter with Joe at the dedication. No doubt he'd also mentioned her subsequent questions about the situation that had been brought up that day. Yet, when she mentioned Joe as being the only person she'd talked with about it, other than Ruben, her father didn't say anything that Ruben hadn't said already. All he did was expand on it by telling her that the man was a thorn in the side of progress. Slaighter had a remarkable talent for tying up legislation or projects. However, whether or not Slaighter's concern over the shelter was genuine was beside the point, even though he seriously doubted the depth of such concern from a man who chose his clients by the size of their pocketbooks.

While he questioned the sincerity of Slaighter's position, the governor didn't discount his daughter's.

"I appreciate your concern about this, honey," he told her, sounding hurried but willing to give her what time he had. "But you know as well as I do that it's impossible to please everyone. The committee looked long and hard at the advantages and disadvantages of topping the bid on that property, and it just came down to a matter of more good being done in the long run by acquiring it. The property won't do us any good if we can't use it. And to use it, we have to tear everything down."

It was a matter of jobs and progress he went on to tell her. And economics, which Amanda had long ago learned was always the bottom line. What he said even made sense, because she truly understood that there never was any one solution to every single problem. But her father hadn't been to the shelter. He hadn't seen the children. In her mind these were people with faces. In her father's, they were only statistics.

"The people in that shelter will be absorbed into existing facilities," she heard him say. "The census counts on the homeless are actually starting to drop in some places, and there are beds available. They'll be taken care of, honey. I promise you that. But I need for you to promise me that you'll just leave the matter rest now. Your involvement with that particular place could be used to generate unfavorable publicity about the whole Southend project and that publicity could cause delays the city and the state can't afford. A lot of people have worked hard to see that project put together," he reminded her. "And a project of this size and scope can seldom be put together without stepping on toes."

"But no one went to Matthew's House," she had to say. "So how could anyone on your committee know how important the work is there?"

"It wasn't necessary for anyone to see it." His displeasure was now evident. Not with her. Not really. To his credit he wasn't annoyed with the questions she posed. Not like her mother would have been. The impatience in his voice had more to do with the necessity of the answers. "I've seen plenty of reports on that type of facility. Now," he said, and by his clipped tone she could almost see him frowning at his watch, "I want you to promise me you'll stay away from that shelter. And that Slaighter character, too. You hear?"

She heard. But she didn't promise. She simply offered an obedient-sounding "Yes, Daddy," when he said he had to go and added that she hoped he and her mother enjoyed the horse races this weekend, before flipping the Off button on her cordless phone.

For a moment she sat at her drafting table, toying with the chain at her neck, while the soft strains of a Mozart concerto filtered in from the stereo in the living room. Yesterday country ballads had kept her company while she'd worked. The day before it had been an ear-splitting collection of retro stuff from the seventies. Her music depended on her mood. Today she felt in need of something tranquil to calm the odd agitation with which she'd awakened.

Scarcely aware of the soothing sounds at the moment, she put the phone near her coffee cup, avoided looking out the huge window of the plant-filled solarium studio because the birds and the flowers and trees would only distract her, and picked up a charcoal pencil.

Her motions were automatic as she finished the robe and detailed the head and body of the illustration for Murdock Department Store's men's loungewear sale ad. It was the last piece she had to do for this campaign. If she hurried, she could drop the work off at the store, pick up the photographs her art gallery account wanted incorporated into their new brochures—which reminded her that she'd promised Joanie, the gallery's wonderfully outspoken owner, that she'd have lunch with her—and be at Matthew's House by one o'clock. Or thereabouts.

Her father was wrong. A person did have to see to understand the impact a particular shelter made on the lives of the people who lived in it. Now, having seen this one, she understood some of Joe's frustration with a system that tied its own hands when it came to helping the little guy. Maybe, too, she felt a little of what he'd felt when he'd tried to get someone—anyone—from her father's office to come to the shelter.

Not that her appreciation of Joe's feelings made any difference in the overall scheme of things. He was far too complicated a man to be truly understood. And far too angry to let anyone close enough to try. Not that she wanted to understand him, she assured herself, then wondered if, in some ways, she didn't understand him already. He was a very compelling man—in a dangerous and defiant sort of way. And something about that rather rebellious side of him appealed to a part of herself she usually preferred to ignore. The part of her that needed to be accepted for who and what she was inside, and not merely as the image her family had created for her.

Joe had an image, too, and not a very desirable one. Yet, where she would have given just about anything for the freedom to shake hers off, he seemed almost content with his less-than-honorable reputation. Still, she had the nagging feeling that they might be more alike than either of them would have thought, which would explain why they seemed to rub each other the wrong way. As most children learn in grade school science, as opposite poles attract, like poles actually pushed each other away.

The illustration finished, she wiped her hands on the hem of Jason's old football jersey—the only useful thing left of that relationship—and stood back to check her work. She'd added a pipe to the model's hand to add interest to the picture and drawn him in profile because the store's marketing department wanted a mysterious, macho image in this campaign. It was a good profile, too. Strong. Virile. Compelling.

Amanda tossed her gum eraser onto her supply table. The drawing looked just like Joe.

Chapter Five

"Do my shoes come from a clobber?"

"A cobbler?" Smiling at Lucy's mispronunciation of the unfamiliar word, Amanda set aside the book they had just finished. The child had an insatiable appetite for stories. This was the fourth one Amanda had read to her and, as had butchers, bakers and candlestick makers, cobblers required a certain amount of explanation. Especially for a child who knew little of the world beyond tenements.

"I'm pretty sure a cobbler didn't make your shoes. There isn't much need for them anymore. Cobblers, I mean. Your shoes came from a factory." By way of whoever had donated them to the shelter, Amanda thought with a glance at the shiny Mary Janes some other child had outgrown. Lucy had said she hadn't had shoes when they'd arrived at Matthew's House. Apparently they'd been left behind along with her toys and clothes when they'd "runned away" from her mother's boyfriend a few nights ago.

"That's what my mommy wants to do. Work in a factory."

"Where does she work now?"

"She makes hamburgers," Lucy replied, though she didn't know exactly where. "Do you have a work, too?"

Amanda sat cross-legged on the patch of blue carpet in the back of the classroom. Lucy, her black hair neatly corn-rowed and the braided ends sporting little pink beads that made faint clicking sounds when she moved her head, sat across from her, their knees almost touching.

"I have work," Amanda told her, reminding herself to be grateful for it. "I'm what's called a commercial illustrator. And I do something called graphic design, but mostly I draw pictures of what people want to sell."

"You draw pictures for work?"

A smile came with Amanda's nod.

"Of what?"

"Oh, lots of things," she said, amazed at the number of questions the child asked, and went on to tell the wide-eyed little girl how she sometimes did illustrations of hairstyles for salon ads and occasionally drew pieces of furniture. She didn't enjoy doing furniture very much because she had to sit in a store or a warehouse to do her sketching, unless she could take a photograph and sketch it from that. Mostly though, she illustrated items for a department store, she explained, and found Lucy as caught up in what she was saying as she'd been in the books now lying forgotten on the floor beside them.

Joe found himself rather interested in what Amanda was saying, too.

He stood in the doorway at the top of the stairs, well back from where she and the child sat facing each other in the corner of the room. It was nearing four o'clock and the rest of the children were either in the alley playing basketball, gathering around the television in the "living room" or hanging around the kitchen, where Sister Rose Ann had last been seen handing out carrot sticks. Only the little girl and Amanda were in the unusually quiet space. And both were oblivious to his presence.

Joe and a mover he'd brought over to talk to Bernie had arrived about ten minutes ago. But Bernie hadn't mentioned that Amanda was here until after the mover had started wandering around with his measuring tape and calculator. Depending on what happened in the next few weeks, the beds and boxes of donated clothing and food would either be moved to a new location or stored until a new location could be found. The man who owned the company was an old client of Joe's, a man who hadn't been able to pay for the kind of representation he'd needed to fight a zoning change that would have put him out of business a few years back. Tony Carlucco, of Carlucco Moving & Storage, was now paying Joe back by donating his services to Bernie.

Crossing his arms over the Atlanta Braves logo on his T-shirt, Joe leaned his shoulder against the door frame. It wasn't very polite to stand there blatantly eavesdropping, but he didn't want to interrupt the conversation. Not just yet, anyway. He wanted to hear whatever else Amanda had to say to the solemn little girl listening to her so intently.

It seemed that Amanda Jones led a far quieter life than he'd suspected. As he'd heard her tell the mesmerized child about the sunny room where she worked and, then, because the little girl wanted to know if she had a yard, about the flowers she liked to tend in her garden, it sounded to him as if she spent a lot of her time alone; as if she even preferred it that way.

The revelation surprised him. So had what she'd said about her career.

He hadn't considered that she might work for a living. He'd figured her to be part of the garden party, charitable event, ladies-who-lunch crowd and really hadn't given the source of her income any thought. He'd simply assumed she had money available to her. From her parents, possibly; or, a trust. Whatever it was rich people arranged for their children. Certainly, he'd never thought the sketching she'd alluded to as being of any consequence. When she'd explained the smudges on her hand, he'd assumed any artwork she did to be a hobby; nothing more than a way of passing time. She hadn't bothered to disabuse him of that conclusion, either. In fact, she'd offered nothing about herself that might have shed any light on the subject. What she had done—much as she had when he'd noted the absence of her engagement ring—was pull away from him. Literally and figuratively. It was as if he'd threatened to intrude upon a part of herself she didn't trust him to know. The part of herself that, in Joe's mind, was the only part of her worth knowing.

A frown creased his brow as he pushed himself from the door frame. It wasn't like him to lose his focus. Yet with this woman he found his thoughts straying from his purpose with disturbing regularity. He didn't need to know anything else about her. Certainly he didn't need to stand there wondering what had happened between her and her fiancé. It was none of his business. His only concern was whether or not she'd talked to her father. That was why he'd come up to see her.

The squeak of tennis shoes sounded on the stairs behind him. Turning, he saw a petite young African-American woman in a pink waitress's uniform coming up the steps. She couldn't have been more than twenty, but when she glanced up and met Joe's eyes, he had the impression of someone who felt as old as Methuselah. A lot of women he'd seen here looked like that.

She didn't smile when he stepped aside to let her pass. She did offer a quiet "Thank you," though, as, almost flattening herself to the wall to avoid brushing against him, she scooted by. It was only when she spotted the little girl in the corner of the room that the smile she hadn't had the energy to produce finally eased the worry from her face.

"There you are, girl." It wasn't accusation in her voice. It was relief, as if the woman had panicked when the child hadn't been where she'd thought she would be when she'd come in moments ago. "Why weren't you waiting for me?"

Lucy scrambled to her feet, the braided ends of her hair swinging against her tiny shoulders. "It's okay, mama. Me and 'Manda are reading stories. See?"

With the quickness of the very young, Lucy snatched up one of the books on her way over to where she attached herself to her mother's leg. Since Amanda's back was to the door, she turned as she rose, her easy smile meeting the caution in the mother's expression.

Amanda's smile faltered. Not because of the way Lucy's mom eyed her expensive haircut and neatly tailored slacks and jacket. Her own expression became wary because, over the woman's shoulder, she could see Joe standing near the door at the end of the room.

"You a real teacher?"

The question drew Amanda's glance back to the young woman. A curved waitress cap, the kind held on by bobby pins at the sides, straddled the center part of her heavy hair. The uniform she wore was easily two sizes too big and nearly swallowed her waiflike frame. It was from her that Lucy had inherited her sweet, heart-shaped face and lovely dark eyes. But Lucy's eyes didn't reveal the distrust so evident in her mother's. Not yet, anyway.

"No," Amanda said, as conscious of Joe moving toward them as she was the woman's odd displeasure. "I just came to read to Lucy."

"You from some church, then?"

Already at a loss over the woman's suspicious attitude, Amanda barely had time to say she wasn't before the woman took a step backward, addressing her daughter as she did.

"Thank the lady for reading to you, child. We're going downstairs now."

"But mama, 'Manda was telling me—"

"Lucy. I said thank the lady."

"Yes, mama," Lucy said with a greatly exaggerated sigh. Then, drawing out all the vowels the way children can when they need to let adults know how truly annoying it was to have to patronize them, she added, "Thank you, 'Manda."

"You're welcome, Lucy."

The child's eyes brightened. "Will you read to me tomorrow?"

"That won't be necessary," her mother cut in. "We aren't taking up this lady's time. You bring your books and show 'em to me."

She didn't look at Amanda again, but her pride came through her weariness as she straightened her shoulders. With her head high, she led her daughter, who was chatting away about cobblers, out of the room.

Amanda's confusion was evident as she watched her go. "What did I do?" She turned to Joe, a few feet away. "I was only reading to her daughter. The way she acted you'd have thought I was going to steal her."

Joe shrugged, the motion deceptively nonchalant. Deceptive because there was really nothing casual about Joe Slaighter.

His answer was simple. "You embarrassed her."

"Embarrassed her?" She held out her hands, clearly uncomprehending. "How?"

He moved closer, thinking it rather interesting to see Amanda as she was now: unguarded and so obviously bewildered. She really didn't have a clue where that woman had been coming from. To be fair, he supposed he shouldn't fault her for that. It was a place Amanda certainly had never been.

His glance moved from her neck to her feet; his assessment, for once, focused more on what she wore, than on how she might look not wearing it.

"Other than the obvious economic differences," he began, finding his last thought provocative despite his intentions to stick to the business at hand. "You were horning in on the only thing she really has. If she's living here, she has no home, damn few possessions, and probably next to no self-esteem. All she has is her daughter, and she comes in to find that daughter all wrapped up in you. To top it off, you were doing something she probably either can't do, or doesn't have the energy for, after working for peanuts all day."

"Reading to her little girl," came Amanda's uncomfortable conclusion.

"You're very quick."

Amanda let his sarcasm go. Her concern, at the moment, was with the mother. "I never meant to take anything from her. I'm certainly no threat."

"That's not the way she sees it."

The certainty in his voice drew her. She found his conviction odd, considering what Sister Bernie had said about him. According to the nun, until she'd called him about the business with the Southend Center a couple of weeks ago, Joe hadn't been here in months. He contributed money for whatever was necessary, and if Sister Bernie sought his intervention, he would see that a resident's legal problems were handled. But he never became personally involved with any one individual's difficulties. He preferred to keep a certain distance between Matthew's House and himself. He always had.

For a man who sought distance, he surely seemed close to this particular subject. "How do you know so much about this kind of thing? About what she's feeling?"

He hesitated, the bleakness that would have entered his eyes overshadowed with a defensiveness that was becoming awfully familiar.

"Let's just say I've been there. If I've learned anything at all, it's that not measuring up to society's idea of success can put a real chip on a person's shoulder. It can also make them awfully suspicious of anyone who wants to help. Especially someone who's obviously never needed help themselves."

It was with the vague feeling that she'd just been put in her place that Amanda watched him pick up the books she and Lucy and been reading. He might well be right about how Lucy's mother felt toward her. That Joe felt that same hostility was equally apparent. He was just a little better at masking it when his purposes demanded deference. At least, he usually was.

Glancing at the book's covers, he made a sound halfway between derision and disgust. "Fairy tales," he muttered, snapping her attention to the books he held out to her. "Just what these kids need."

Amanda looked down at the books, wanting to ask what was wrong with putting a little fantasy into lives that were all but drowning in reality. She also wanted to know where he'd come from; what place or experience had given birth to his anger and created his empathy with the women here. But she knew from his closed expression that she wouldn't get an answer to the latter. Pursuing the former would only result in a disagreement.

She took the thin volumes from him and turned to the shelf.

"How did you get here?" she heard him ask, his frown following her movements. "You didn't walk from the bus stop, did you?"

"I took a cab."

"You got a driver to bring you here?"

She almost smiled at his tone. "My street-smarts are improving, Mr. Slaighter." She knew why Joe sounded so surprised. Cabbies were favored targets of certain gangs. She'd learned that little tidbit from the two drivers who'd passed on her fare. She'd also learned that everyone had a price. "I tip generously."

Joe didn't want to be impressed. But he was. She'd been determined to keep her promise to the child, so she'd come—completely disregarding what he'd said about staying away from the neighborhood and the shelter. If the stubborn tilt to her chin was any indication, she expected him to mention that next.

Since she wasn't being all that cooperative with his idea of how she could best help the situation here, the least he could do was be unpredictable.

"Did you have a chance to talk to your father?"

She *had* expected a challenge. He wasn't sure why he was so pleased with himself for having anticipated her, but a moment later her chin came down and she turned her glance to the floor.

A set of building blocks lay scattered on the wood beyond the carpet. Feeling oddly restless with him watching er, she set to picking them up. "Yes," she said quietly, her back to him.

"And?"

"He said a delay isn't possible. It would cost the city too much money."

Remembering how incensed Joe had been at the dedication, she braced herself for his anger. Her tone subdued, because she wasn't happy with the news, either, she added a few other points her father had made—such as how the people at Matthew's House would be absorbed into other facilities and how it was impossible to please everyone. She kept straightening things as she spoke, moving on to pick up the cars scattered around the toy box after the blocks and coloring books were put away.

When there were no toys left out of place to provide a distraction, no more reasons to offer, she turned to face him. "I'm sorry."

"You're sorry," he repeated, his tone as flat as the tire on the old Volkswagen bus in the garage. "That helps."

She met his cool glare; matched it, actually. "I don't appreciate your sarcasm. I don't care if you believe me or not. But I am truly sorry I wasn't able to help."

He wasn't interested in her apology. Accusation darkened his expression. Heat entered his tone.

"I thought you said your father would listen to you."

"I said I hoped he would. I can't *make* him change his mind. It was miracle enough that he heard me out to begin with."

She wished she hadn't said that. Immediately she made her voice quieter, though she really hadn't raised it. "I did what I could, and I told you what he said." Except for the part about staying away from you, she thought, but repeating that was unnecessary. "It should make you feel better to know that he doesn't want me down here, either. And in case you're thinking of telling me to stay away again, save your breath. If I choose to come here, that's my decision. Neither you nor my father have any right to tell me how to spend my own time."

To make that statement completely honest, she should have added *unless whatever I'm doing results in unfavorable publicity for my family,* but she didn't feel like exposing any more of herself to a man who was totally capable of using any knowledge he could glean about her for his own purposes. She also didn't feel like dealing with the sudden surge of anger at being forced to defy her father's wishes to do something she felt was right.

She wasn't the only one curbing displeasure. Joe's voice was deadly quiet. "Ask him again."

"Didn't you hear me?"

"You said you wanted to help."

"I do..."

"Then ask if he's got a facility Bernie can use. If the government can't afford to delay the demolition, it can at least come up with a place for these people to go."

"I already told you," Amanda began in restrained exasperation. "He said the people here will be sent to other shelters. If I ask again, he'll say the same thing."

Joe knew what she'd said. But it wasn't good enough. It was a cop-out solution. One he wasn't going to accept. No way would he roll over and play dead the way some people did when faced with bureaucratic decisions.

The image in Joe's mind was disturbingly real. So were the feelings of helplessness and anger knotting his stomach. He could almost hear his father meekly accepting the decision other people—other officials—had made for him. *There's nothing a little guy like me can do, son,* he said, staring at a bottle of cheap whisky on the table. *Nothing I can do,* he'd repeated, and lacking the nerve to look his son in the eye, he'd taken yet another drink.

The image was shoved back, leaving only the bitterness. Years of suppression kept the rage from surfacing. "Ask him again," he repeated.

He watched in frustration as Amanda swallowed whatever she'd been about to say. The sound of feet hurrying up the stairs made her turn from him, but he didn't bother

ooking toward the door himself. He knew who it was by the
energy and quickness in her step.

Bernie's timing stunk. It seemed every time she found him
with Amanda, the two of them were engaged in some sort
of stand-off.

"Hi," he heard Amanda say, sounding relieved. "I was
just coming down."

"I can see I'm interrupting." Ignoring Amanda's relieved smile, she met Joe's glare. "I'm sorry. But Joe, Mr.
Carlucco is ready to leave now. And Amanda," she went on,
her expression lacking its usual good humor. "As soon as
you're through here, I'd like to speak with you. About
Lucy."

"I was only reading to her, Sister. Honestly, I never intended to cause a problem."

"I'm sure you didn't." Sister Bernie, sitting behind the
metal desk in her closet-sized office behind the kitchen, offered a sympathetic smile. "When LaVonne asked that I
keep 'that blond lady away from her daughter' I had to
know what had happened. You understand, don't you?"

Of course she did. Partly. "She found me reading to
Lucy. That's all that happened. You already know I'd
promised Lucy yesterday that I'd come to read to her today. I told you that, when I called to see if it was all right for
me to come down."

The nun only nodded; the motion an acknowledgment as
much as an indication to proceed.

Wanting to cooperate, Amanda offered the only explanation she had. "Joe said she saw me as a threat to her relationship with her daughter. He thought she might not have
the energy to read to Lucy after working all day. Or maybe
that she didn't know how to read herself, and that embarrassed her. Or something like that." Her heart sank as she
watched Sister frown. "It never occurred to me that she'd
see it that way."

"LaVonne can read," Sister Bernie replied, flicking the
edge of a thick, official-looking form someone had started

to fill out. "Which is more than I can say for some of these ladies." Her frown deepened thoughtfully. "The rest of the analysis makes sense. You say Joe said all that?"

"He seemed to relate to her suspicion of me. He didn't think she'd trust my motives because I'd never needed help myself." Those weren't his exact words, but they were close enough to convey the point. "It seems there was a time when he didn't have much, either. I think what he said was that 'he'd been there.'"

Amanda kept her hands folded tightly on her lap while she watched her words being weighed. Sister wasn't being unkind. She was being protective, and Amanda could appreciate her concern—even if she wasn't to pleased with having caused it.

Yet it didn't appear to be her encounter with this La-Vonne that had Sister so curious now. It was Joe's behavior that seemed more questionable.

"I'm surprised he told you that," came the woman's thoughful reply. "Do you mind if I ask what else he's told you about himself?"

"Not at all," Amanda returned, curious herself at this woman's interest. "Except he hasn't said anything. I don't think he'd have said that much if he hadn't been so angry with me for being here."

"That sounds like Joe."

"You know him quite well, don't you?"

Blue eyes, wise and perceptive, settled on Amanda's open and frank expression. She seemed to appreciate the lack of pretense. "I'm just one of his causes, Amanda. That's all Joe Slaighter lets himself care about. Hold on a minute. I'll go get LaVonne. I'm sure we can straighten this out."

As Amanda watched the slim, T-shirt and jean-clad figure hurry out the door, she didn't feel quite so confident about the situation. Sister hadn't seen the distrust in La-Vonne's eyes—the distrust that was still plainly evident minutes later when Amanda tried to apologize for causing her any worry. It wasn't until after Amanda said she would be protective, too, if she'd had a child as sweet and well-mannered as Lucy, that the woman softened enough to stop scowling. It wasn't much in the way of progress, but at least LaVonne heard the compliment Amanda intended and stopped looking as if she expected Amanda to abscond with her daughter. It almost broke Amanda's heart to think she'd caused the woman any more worries than she already had.

LaVonne seemed to sense that. "I guess it's okay if you read to her," she finally conceded, and only then did Amanda feel she'd been forgiven.

It was never a question after that as to whether or not Amanda would return to the shelter. It was just something she did, since she had to go downtown anyway to drop off and pick up work. Each time, she brought flowers from her garden, which the women put in jars near their beds to brighten up the place, and after Lucy showed the picture Amanda had drawn of her to a couple of the other children, she was kept busy doing caricatures of the rest of the kids, which they taped to the walls or the chairs by their beds. She even did a sketch of LaVonne holding Lucy in her lap; the Madonnalike pose finally earning Amanda the woman's tentative smile.

Amanda wasn't quite sure what LaVonne's difficulties were. Not wanting to pry, she didn't ask, but it became evident from some of the woman's comments as they'd spoken later, that she'd escaped an abusive relationship when the abuse had been turned on Lucy. That was all Amanda had to hear to admire what the woman was trying to do. LaVonne was determined to make a life for her and her little girl, independent of anyone. The way LaVonne looked at it, having wound up here, she had no place to go but up.

As unfortunate as it was, LaVonne's story wasn't so very different from many of the other women at Matthew's House. And like all those other women, she would have to start over all over again if Matthew's House had to close.

It was that prospect that Sister Bernie wrestled with as she pulled a pair of ratty polyester pants from a bag of donations and tossed them into a box marked Rags. "If our prayers aren't answered and we do have to close," she told

Amanda, who was helping her sort through the boxes now that the children had made the afternoon stampede to the kitchen. "We'll still keep looking for a new location. The longer it takes, though, the harder it will be to get everyone back together. Being forced to close is already putting a strain on everyone."

"I really hope you find something," Amanda said.

"We always have hope." The nun's smile was gentle, if not just a little sardonic. She was a woman who held her beliefs fiercely, finding a spiritual peace within them, or within herself, that Amanda would have envied had she not admired it so much. Yet there was a wry practicality about the nun, too, and a subtle irreverence that made her very human.

"What we *don't* have is a building. Joe said he has another lead. An old school, I think he said." She shook her head and added a blouse to the size fourteen box. "I know we'll find something eventually. It's just a question of when. My problem is that I wish *eventually* was right now. I've never had patience," she confided. "And I stopped praying for it ages ago. All God did when I asked for it was send me little tests to strengthen whatever patience I had. I'm absolutely convinced that was why he sent me Joe Slaighter."

"I heard that."

At the sound of Joe's voice, Amanda's heart gave a funny jerk in her chest. Looking up from her task of taping the box of mens' clothing that had been sorted out from the other donations, she felt it jerk again.

"Speak of the devil," Sister Bernie muttered and turned her grin to the man striding toward them.

Joe's frown lacked any hint of sincerity. At least it did as long as it remained on the woman with the rebellious red curls. When his glance slid to Amanda, that frown faded to something less discernible.

"Reading to the kids again?"

"I was," Amanda admitted, a little surprised by his effect on her.

"Until I borrowed her from Sister Rose to help me," Bernie added when Amanda said nothing else. She had been doing a lot more than reading to them, but Bernie had the feeling Amanda wasn't the type to expound on her own generosity. "She's spoiling them rotten."

Amanda smiled. "They can use a little spoiling."

She had wanted to see him again. As she felt her heart settle down, she didn't bother denying that to herself. She did fudge a bit as to the reason, though. Now that he was here, she had a little bone to pick with him.

He looked tired. Seeing him glance at his watch, he also appeared to be in a hurry.

She set the roll of tape atop the stack of boxes. "You're here for Rocky. I'll go get him."

"How'd you know why I was here?"

"Rocky told me you were coming for him, when he met me at the bus stop this afternoon."

"When he met you?"

"At the bus stop," Sister Bernie repeated, since seconds had passed and all Amanda and Joe had done was frown at each other. Keys jangling, she rose from the box where she'd been sitting. "He walks her from the stop when she gets here, then walks her back when it's time to leave. He does it with the other ladies, too, if they have to take the bus alone."

"It's really not that far, you know. Only a couple of blocks." Amanda's tone was pure honey. "Not nearly as far as you made it seem the day you brought me here."

The hint of discomfort in his eyes disappeared as quickly as it registered. "I wanted you to get the full flavor of the neighborhood."

"The grand tour?"

"Something like that."

"Is that why you made me ride that motorcycle, too? To get the full flavor?"

His glance narrowed. It was either a trick of the lousy lighting, or there was a definite smile in her eyes.

"I don't like bringing my car down here. I'm kind of attached to all its parts. In case you didn't notice, there's no room for another car in the garage."

"Tell you what," Sister Bernie cut in. "You two argue with each other, and I'll go get Rocky. If his hearing is at three o'clock, you're going to have to hurry. It's nearly quarter after two now. I know the hearing's just routine but he doesn't need to be late."

Sister didn't have to go far. Rocky showed up within seconds, and seconds later Joe and the boy were headed for the very car he truly didn't bring to this part of town any more often than he had to. The modest American sedan wasn't terribly expensive, certainly not what he could have afforded, but it was new, and Joe had no desire to hassle with a rental while an insurance company tried to track down either the whole vehicle or any of its respective parts. The car, however, wasn't what occupied Joe's thoughts as he escorted Rocky to meet the attorney Joe had hired for him when he first got into trouble. His thoughts were pretty much on the same subject that had sabotaged his work for the past several days—the woman he'd actually hated to walk away from just a short while ago. For a moment there, seeing Amanda's teasing smile, he'd almost felt good. But then, as Bernie said that evening when he took her out for dinner, Amanda made a lot of people feel that way.

If wasn't often that Joe could get Bernie away from Matthew's House. There were occasions, however, when he could talk her into a plate of ribs at a greasy little barbecue joint that served good food cheap. The ribs were hot, the coffee hotter, and he could talk to her here without trying to ignore where he was.

Trying to ignore the clatter of plates, cutlery and conversations in the diner was something else. People didn't come here for the service or the decor. There wasn't any. Plain white walls, dented chrome and mother-of-pearl green plastic chairs and oilcloth-covered tables didn't exactly earn the place four stars in the restaurant review guide, but the food coming out of the noisy, open kitchen kept the place crowded even mid-week.

Joe considered them lucky to have found a table by the back, farthest from the shouted orders coming from the kitchen. If he'd been alone, he'd have sat at the counter. Wanting to talk, the wall offered the best opportunity to be heard.

Elbows on either side of his heaped plate, he glanced across the table at the woman he'd practically grown up with. He still found it hard to believe that she'd actually made it through to her final vows. Especially after having been kicked out of the novitiate. Twice.

"As much as I hate to see them close you down, I'll be glad when you're out of that neighborhood," he told her. "It's the worst in the city."

"That's why I needed to be there." Sleeves pushed to her elbows, the lady, who one mother superior had called "incorrigible" just because she'd had a little trouble kicking her smoking habit, lifted a rib dripping pungent red sauce. "But it won't hurt my feelings if we find someplace a little safer for the children. That old schoolhouse you told me about sounds perfect."

Joe eyed his own meal, deciding to start with the thickest rib first. "Well, don't get your hopes up. It sat vacant for the last twenty years, but since I started asking about it, so have other people. It's not just that historical society..."

"Will you please stop worrying about it," she said. He'd already mentioned the potential problems. There was no point reiterating them. "You can't do anything right now, so eat that thing before it attacks back. It's a wonder you don't have an ulcer."

There were times when he swore he was working on one. "That reminds me." He made his tone as nonchalant as possible. Bernie had an annoying habit of reading more into something than truly existed, so keeping his tone and expression neutral was his safest bet. "Why is Amanda hanging around the shelter so much? She's been there the last two times I have."

"Why do you want to know?"

"Because I'm curious," he said flatly.

Sopping up sauce with a piece of bread, Bernie smiled. To her credit she didn't push, but to Joe's annoyance she did seem to think he would ask about the lady in question.

"She's been there more than that. And she comes to read to Lucy. You know that."

"Isn't it some kind of sin or something to be deliberately obtuse?"

"Heavens, I hope not."

Dressed in a black Harley Davidson T-shirt and jeans, Bernie did not look like a nun. She looked much as she had when she'd been fourteen years old and teasing him just as mercilessly.

"Bernadette," Joe said slowly, the only way he ever said her whole name. "Are you going to answer me or not? I don't want to know what she's doing there, I want to know why you think she's doing it. She said something about her father not wanting her to go to the shelter," he added, omitting that he'd done the same thing. "Do you think she's doing it because he told her not to?"

The teasing faded, but he knew Bernie had already guessed that his interest was more than cursory. She knew him well enough to have understood exactly why he'd brought Amanda to the shelter. He suspected now that she knew this really had nothing to do with how much—or how little—influence Amanda had with her father.

"No, Joe," she said gently. "I don't think she's that kind of person. I expect the reason she's hanging around, as you put it, is because she's found something there that she hasn't found anywhere else."

Joe frowned. Bernie was usually better with her psychology than that. "Come on," he muttered. "She's got everything. What could she possible want?"

"Acceptance," came the unhesitating reply. "Contrary to what you might think, Joe, we all need it. When Amanda is at the shelter, she's just a woman helping out. No one other than Sister Rose and I know who she is, so no one has any preconceived ideas about her. The way you do,'' she added with a significant little pause.

''She has talents we can use and she's very generous with them. In fact,'' she went on, while Joe digested her little dig about his reverse snobbery, ''she's going to help us with our discussion groups. We're working with the ladies on how to handle job interviews, filling out employment applications, that sort of thing.''

''I thought she came to read to the kids.''

''She does. She helps wherever she can. But I think she'll be a big help to our ladies in the discussion groups. She's been through the process of interviewing for jobs, so she can offer first-hand advice. Besides, she's very stylish. Heaven knows we can use help with poise and proper dress and makeup.''

''Heaven knows,'' he muttered.

''You know, Joe,'' she went on, in a way that made him think she knew she'd given him enough to consider. ''These ribs are really very good tonight. I'm going to take mine back for anyone who wants them. Before we go, let's see if the manager has anything he'd like to donate to the homeless. The last time we were here he sent us out with thirty pounds of coleslaw and several bags of rolls, remember?''

''I'm not asking him for a donation. You want to take something back for the ladies tonight, I'll buy it.''

''You don't have to ask. I will. Besides, if you pay you're denying the manager the chance to feel good about helping the less fortunate. We shouldn't be that selfish.''

Joe didn't even bother trying to figure out her logic. Getting Bernie to take something for herself was next to impossible. But when it came to getting donations for others, the woman simply didn't understand the word no.

Two days later he was beginning to think Amanda didn't understand it, either.

Chapter Six

Friday was one of those late-April days that made Amanda want to forget about work and responsibilities and spend the day in the park. It was simply too nice to be indoors. That was why she worked on her illustrations for Mother's Day ads in her garden that morning—and why she took all the children outside to play that afternoon, instead of reading to them on the stuffy second floor of the old warehouse. Even with the windows open, there hadn't been so much as a breath of a breeze coming through the bars to cool off the space. The pleasant seventy-five-degree air outside, when concentrated under a corrugated metal roof, rose to a stifling ninety-plus degrees inside. It was no wonder Sister Bernie had begun an extra novena for air-conditioning in whatever place her first novena helped them find.

"Jamal's not giving me the ball!"

"That's because you have to take it from him, you dweeb."

With a look that told Rocky it wasn't necessary for him to call the younger kids names, Amanda balanced on the balls of her feet and stuck her hand palm down between ten-year-old Jamal's hand and the ball he was dribbling. A quick flick of her wrist and she had the ball in her possession. A dribble later, she was behind Wayland, the chubby little boy whining about Jamal's lack of sportsmanship.

"Take it from me the way I took it from Jamal," she said to him. "Slip your hand under mine as soon as the ball starts back down. Come on," she coaxed over the sound of the ball echoing off the brick walls every time it hit the cracked concrete. "Try it."

"Told you he was a dweeb."

The insult, delivered by Rocky with an innocent smile, was apparently all the provocation Wayland needed. His bottom lip tucked between his teeth, he reached out with both hands to grab the ball. He caught it, too, along with more flack from a couple of nine-year-olds, but managed to make it far enough down the chalked-off court to shoot at the basketless hoop. He didn't make the basket, but as he walked off, brushing his hands together, he shot Amanda a grin. When a kid was as uncoordinated as Wayland, even close counted.

"Hey, 'Manda," one of the girls on her team hollered. "Block Travis!"

Busy watching Wayland, who looked pretty pleased with himself, Amanda had forgotten to pay attention as the other team tossed the ball back in. Within seconds, she was back in the game that included most of the boys over the age of nine and any girl who could put up with their roughness. The rest of the girls were inside watching television—except for the preteens who'd designated themselves cheerleaders and were bouncing around on the sidelines. Every one of them seemed oblivious to the fact that they were being ignored by everyone else. Most of the attention was centered on the real action in the alley.

Joe's attention certainly was.

A couple of weeks ago he wouldn't have believed what he saw as he turned off the street and idled his motorcycle to a stop. The court was toward the center of the block-deep alley, and the kids were going nuts as Amanda snatched the ball midair and spun around to sink a basket.

Within seconds the decible level of enthusiastic shouts faded enough for the low rumble of his motorcycle to be heard. Several heads swung his way, but only Amanda had his attention. In his mind's eye he could still see her as she'd looked jumping for that ball; her arms raised above her head and her waist-length pink T-shirt riding up to expose her midriff and outline her firm breasts. The pale blue jeans she wore fit the way jeans were supposed to fit a woman: snug enough to show the flatness of her belly, the curves of her hips and the length of her legs.

She couldn't have been in that suspended position for more than a second. Yet, the impression of long, lithe limbs and graceful curves seemed indelibly burned into his brain.

Feeling a distinctly carnal pull below his midsection, Joe approached the makeshift court. As he did, the boys affected various slouching postures in an attempt to look cool, and the girls moved off to giggle with their counterparts on the sidelines. It was Amanda who had Joe's attention, though. Surrounded by the kids, she stood with the ball tucked under her arm, her weight shifted to one hip. From the rapid rise and fall of her chest, he could tell she was trying to catch her breath. As she pushed her fingers through her short and shining hair, he could also see her protective mask slip into place.

Her smile had vanished the moment she'd seen him. Now the coolness he'd once mistaken for hauteur settled over her features. The more he'd thought about it, the more he'd had to consider that she might very well be protecting herself with that coolness. From people like him.

For reasons he didn't care to question, he wanted to restore her smile. Bernie had alluded to her talents at dinner the other night. It seemed those talents were more varied than he'd suspected.

"Where'd you learn to play like that?"

The impish light entering her eyes had nothing to do with him, he was sure. Still, her coolness couldn't survive the warmth that looked far more natural, and removing that chill was all he'd wanted.

"My aunt taught me."

"Your aunt?"

"My mother's sister," she expanded, seeming to enjoy his amazement. "She's a very unusual woman."

He'd just bet she was, but Joe was given no time to consider how a blue-blood would come to teach her niece such an unrefined sport. Rocky stepped into the group, parting two of the boys staring up at Joe and Amanda as he did.

"What's up, man? Like we're playing a game here. With the little kids. Know what I mean?"

"Yeah, I know what you mean," Joe returned, meeting Rocky's high-five. "We'll get out of your way. I just want to talk to Amanda."

Amanda and Rocky both spoke at once.

"She can't leave—"

"I can't—"

Joe frowned at them both.

"I'm on this team," she said to explain why she wasn't moving.

"Yeah," Rocky concurred. "And they need her. Their playing sucks.

"Well, it does," he said when Amanda glared at him. "Okay. So they play lousy," he amended, realizing it wasn't his attack on her team's ability that had earned him the frown, so much as his description of it. "But it still wouldn't be fair to them if you stopped playing now."

If Joe remembered correctly, Rocky didn't like playing with the smaller kids. In fact, Bernie had said he grumbled about it so much that she'd finally stopped asking him to play with them and simply told him to keep an eye on them while they were outside so no one wandered off or got hurt.

"I thought you didn't like baby-sitting," Joe said mildly.

A sheepish look stole across the young man's face. Beneath his olive skin rose the hint of a blush.

"'Manda sorta asked me to help her play with them. It's too nice out here to keep them all cooped up, you know."

Rocky stood a little straighter, meeting Joe eye to eye. There was a new depth in his voice, along with what Joe could have sworn was a hint of protectiveness. Unless he missed his guess, that protectiveness leaned in Amanda's direction.

Despite his stance, this was not the defiant youth Joe had met six months ago. The changes, Joe felt certain, were due mostly to Bernie's patient but firm guidance. But there was a difference about the boy now that Joe suspected had little to do with Bernie's influence.

The two males stared at each other, the younger seeming more grown up by the second.

"Can we play, please, 'Manda?"

The kids were getting restless. Joe turned to see a child tugging on Amanda's shirtsleeve and heard her quiet assurance that they'd get back to the game in just a minute. What bothered him, though, was the way her glance skittered from his the moment she looked back up to see him watching her.

Amanda knew exactly what Joe wanted to talk to her about. She knew, too, that he wasn't going to like her response. Avoiding the inevitable, wasn't possible, but it could be postponed for a while. "It's almost time for them to go in," she told him, since snack time was coming up shortly. "We can talk after they do."

Her tennis shoe squeaking as she turned, she passed the ball off to one of her teammates. She'd thought Joe would go inside to wait. That's what she hoped he'd do, anyway. Instead, seeming in no hurry at all, he propped himself against the brick wall and crossed his arms to watch the action.

His presence proved rather interesting. Some of the kids were actually pretty good at the game. Better than Amanda had first expected them to be. With Joe watching them play, even those with minimal talent were suddenly putting out more effort. They were either trying to impress him or be noticed, she supposed, then wondered if Joe was even aware of how hard they tried to get his attention.

Joe wouldn't regard himself as either a father figure or a role model. In fact, he'd probably laugh at the very idea. But every kid here looked up to him. Including Rocky. Especially Rocky. The young man suddenly seemed bent on stuffing the basket with even the most impossible shots.

The way Joe saw it, Rocky was only trying to impress Amanda. He couldn't blame the kid. She was the kind of woman most males would want to impress. Especially when she moved the way she did. All that grace and energy was mighty provocative. She was also the kind of woman a man wanted to protect, though Joe was sure he didn't feel that need himself. From what he'd seen, she was quite capable of taking care of herself. He could see, though, where other men might be affected by the little traces of vulnerability she sometimes couldn't quite hide. But, for the most part, he was sure the instincts she aroused in him had far more to do with possession than protectiveness.

By the time Amanda called the game a tie and sent the children racing through the garage, Joe was feeling a little tense. Thinking about her tended to make him edgy, anyway. Thinking in terms of possessing her made him downright restless.

"Later, man," he heard Rocky call over the echo of high-pitched voices and stomping feet.

"Yeah. Later," Joe returned and finally let himself head to where Amanda stood in a shaft of sunlight by the gaping door. He stopped behind her, listening as the door on the loading platform slammed a second time.

Quiet suddenly filtered out into the alley as the dust settled in the garage.

He saw Amanda shake her head, her hair gleaming silver and gold in the sun. She didn't turn, though. Her attention was fixed on the one child taking his dear sweet time about going in. "It's amazing how much noise they can make, isn't it?"

"Yeah. The quiet sounds good."

"I think I prefer the chaos." Watching the lone straggler slip inside the building, Amanda smiled. Until she'd been exposed to it, she'd had no idea how utterly, boringly *quiet* her own life had been. "At least they were having a good time."

"They seemed to be."

"They like being outside. It's too bad they don't have a park or a yard to play in."

"Yeah. Bernie's mentioned that."

Small talk. Amanda was a pro at the art, but with Joe it didn't feel comfortable at all. Not much about him did, she admitted, then heard him change the subject.

"Did you do it?"

It wasn't only the subject that changed; so had the quality of Joe's voice. It had become quiet, its deep, seductive tones even more disturbing. There wasn't much of anything about him that didn't affect her, she realized, and she found that thought disturbing, too.

Turning, she faced the alley—and the broad expanse of his chest. He had a white dress shirt tucked into his jeans. The combination stuck her as being right somehow. Joe was part of two very different worlds. She couldn't help but wonder, though, which he felt more comfortable in. Or if, like her, he didn't feel he really belonged at all.

She really wished he wouldn't make her consider such things.

"If you want to know if I've asked my father about a delay again, the answer is no. I didn't ask about the city finding a building, either. I told you already, it won't do any good." She mentally braced herself. "There's nothing else I can do."

His voice grew quieter still. "I understand that."

Prepared for the attack that hadn't come, Amanda hesitated. A moment later, not convinced enough to relax, she sought to confirm what she'd heard. "You understand?"

"Yeah. I think I do." Joe had actually understood the situation two days ago, but he'd been too busy being angry to admit it. "You don't get along with your father, do you?"

It wasn't really a question. His words were more a statement that required no answer because the truth was so obvious. That he had seen what she so carefully concealed, made Amanda that much more wary.

"I didn't say that."

"You didn't have to."

It was miracle enough that he heard me out to begin with.

She remembered saying those words to Joe. It was clear enough that he remembered them, too.

The scream of a siren drifted through the warm air. Mingled with that too-frequent sound was the chatter of children and the faint drone of the television drifting through the open windows around the corner. But what Amanda noticed most, in the silence that fell between her and Joe, was that the edge had vanished from his tone.

There was no harshness in his features, either. What she saw in his expression was totally unexpected, and far more difficult for her to deal with than the veiled animosity she'd come to expect from him anytime mention of her father entered the conversation. Joe actually looked as if he was sorry he'd made her say what she had. Or maybe what he was sorry about was that her relationship with her father wasn't what he'd thought it to be—not for his purposes this time, but because he felt bad for her.

A strangely sympathetic look entered the dark intensity in his eyes. It was almost as if he understood the sense of alienation she sometimes felt; as if he'd even been there himself.

She turned her glance to the cracks in the pavement, her focus drawn to a single blade of grass struggling to survive its hostile home. She didn't want to think that Joe might understand. It was too tempting and far too easy to believe empathy was there simply because she needed it to be.

What she'd needed had never been there for her. Not from her parents and not from the man she'd almost married.

"It's complicated," was all she would say.

"According to Bernie, relationships usually are."

If he'd tried to sound sympathetic, he didn't succeed. His familiar cynicism was back. In a way, Amanda was relieved to hear it. Any rapport they shared was coincidental; any common ground irrelevant. "You speak as a man who avoids them."

"Probably," he conceded too easily. "I have a feeling we're a lot like each other in that respect."

Lord, she hoped not. "I don't avoid relationships."

"No?" For a moment he said nothing more. He simply stood there, his features expressionless as his dark eyes held hers. It was as if he somehow knew she no longer risked making herself vulnerable, and that if he pressed the point, she'd be unable to deny it. "Then why do you make it so hard for people to know you? Whether you avoid relationships or prevent them, it's the same thing."

She didn't know if it was the accuracy of his insights or his lack of compunction about sharing them that punched the hole in her cautious reserve. That reserve inevitably failed around him, anyway. She'd already let it down enough for him to guess that her father listened more readily to the groomer of his polo ponies than his own daughter. But he was way off target on this one.

She started to tell him so, too. Only to find a nagging hint of truth in his words stopping her.

Not wanting to consider how complicated Joe was making her life, wondering if he found some perverse sort of pleasure in it, she matched his patient stare. "I'm sure I'm keeping you from something."

"Actually, you're not. Bernie doesn't expect me for another ten minutes."

"I'm sure she knows you're here by now. Even if she didn't hear that thing," she added with a nod toward the monster of a motorcycle she'd once had to ride, "the kids would have mentioned seeing you."

"Are you trying to get rid of me?"

The light in his eyes was definitely a smile. Prompted, no doubt, by the same memory of that first ride on his bike.

That she'd found the darn thing kind of fun—thrilling, actually—was something she'd just as soon keep to herself.

"I'm trying to end this conversation without us getting into an argument. In case you haven't noticed, that's something we don't manage very often." With an innocent smile of her own, she watched him reach down to pick up the basketball none of the kids had bothered to take in.

He handed it to her. "No sense tempting fate, huh?"

"Something like that. Are you here to hang the chalkboard?"

"Is it down again?"

From his expression and his expletive when she said it was, it became obvious that the matter of the dangling chalkboard hadn't been mentioned by Sister Bernie. It also became apparent that Joe wasn't going to challenge Amanda's abrupt and obvious change of subject. He had other things on his mind.

He turned from her, sweeping back the kickstand on his heavy bike to push it into the garage. "I didn't come to hang the chalkboard. I came to tell Bernie to forget the old schoolhouse I was checking into. We have to keep looking."

Hugging the basketball, Amanda followed. "What happened?"

"For starters, within three days of the neighbors getting wind of what we wanted to do with the building, they'd petitioned the City Council to prohibit its occupation. They also joined an historical society to have the school declared an historical landmark." Inside the garage now, he knocked the kickstand back into place and reached for the pulley to lower the door. "I have no idea what they're basing their application on. The damn thing's only sixty years old. Not to mention an architectural nightmare."

The frustration in Joe's tone deserved to be there. Bernie had told Amanda about the building. Even though she'd tried not to be excited about it, because there'd been so many other disappointments, Amanda knew she'd thought it their best hope.

"It doesn't sound like they were taking any chances, does it?"

"It sure doesn't." Over the groan and squeak of the hinges, the corrugated metal descended. Shadows fell where sunlight had been. "They didn't know what our deadline was, but two and a half weeks isn't near enough time to fight them on the legal issues."

"Maybe it's not such a bad thing. She wouldn't want her ladies and the kids in a neighborhood where they obviously weren't wanted."

Joe had to agree, even if he didn't buy into the every-cloud-has-a-silver-lining attitude. He didn't say anything, though. Fed up with running into brick walls, he simply watched the way Amanda moved as she preceded him into the building. He wondered how a woman could make the ordinary act of hurrying up a short flight of stairs look so incredibly seductive.

Joe could have called Bernie with his news. Until a week ago, that was exactly what he would have done. But as they entered the main room of the shelter and he saw the animation in Amanda's face when little Lucy abandoned her cartoons to get one of the hugs Amanda so generously lavished on the children, he knew he'd come because of her. He'd wanted to see her again. It was the reason he'd wanted to see her that he didn't entirely trust.

Joe was usually pretty good at dissecting motives—those of others as well as his own. However, his motives where Amanda was concerned weren't quite as clear as they'd once been. He wasn't at all happy about her inability to get the demolition delayed. But he understood her powerlessness all too well, and he wasn't so closed minded that he'd blame her for something she couldn't control. She'd risked a lot by coming to the shelter. Not only her safety, though Bernie said she always came midday when the risk was the least. But she'd gone against the express wishes of her father to help people she didn't even know. Bernie had said she thought part of reason Amanda had done that was because working here fulfilled some kind of need in her. He didn't know about needs and fulfillment. As far as he was concerned, that kind of talk was so much psychological gibberish. All it did was confuse people.

He left her with the children, certain that what he felt had nothing to do with "need." Want maybe. But then he'd gone a long time already without satisfying that particular craving.

What he needed was a little distance, a little perspective. She was the governor's daughter, after all, and his life was complicated enough as it was.

To Amanda it felt almost as if she and Joe had reached some kind of an understanding that afternoon; a sort of cease-fire now that there wasn't anything he wanted from her. It was because there wasn't anything she could do for him that she was a little surprised by his offer of a ride, when he prepared to leave a short while later.

Since she'd left her car in a parking structure near the MARTA station downtown, she accepted. Amanda still wasn't particularly fond of the bus, even though the trip wasn't nearly as threatening as it had once seemed. Had there been any room to park her little convertible in the garage at Matthew's House, she might have considered driving to the shelter. With the broken-down van, the station wagon and a couple of battered bicycles in there, though, there wasn't room to park anything bigger than Joe's bike. She wasn't about to leave her car on the street. She'd experienced no trouble at all walking the couple of blocks from the bus stop, but if she were to leave her car out unattended, she might as well put a sign on it that said Take Me, I'm Yours.

Her growing comfort with the area was relative—much as was her comfort with Joe, when they left the shelter that afternoon on his motorcycle.

Riding was easy this time. It felt almost... natural. But it wasn't the feel of the wind against her skin or the freedom of speed as they raced down the road that occupied her thoughts. It was the tautness of his body and the way he sucked in his breath when she shifted against him. His tension was unmistakable. She could feel it as she leaned against him, and with him—as he'd once instructed her to do.

"You didn't forget," she heard him shout back to her and wondered if he was pleased or amazed with the knowledge.

There wasn't anything she could forget about him. With her arms tight around his waist, the feel of him brought reminders of other times when she'd been as close; other times when she'd found herself holding her breath in anticipation of what he might do, if only he would forget who she was.

Such thoughts were dangerous. But then, so was he, and that was definitely part of his appeal. He was a mystery, too. Nothing at all like the "safe" people she tended to associate with. People who posed no threat to her, because she didn't let them get close enough.

Why do you make it hard for people to know you? he had asked.

As Joe gave a quick glance over his shoulder to ask which lot she'd parked in, she had the uncanny feeling that he might be the one person who would understand how difficult it was to let people get close. What she didn't know was if he'd understand that what she really wanted was the very closeness she avoided—if she could only get behind the barriers *he'd* created.

Thinking it might be easier to scale Everest, she nonetheless tried to imagine how she might do that as they snaked through the heavy downtown traffic. She wanted him to know that maybe it was as he'd said—that maybe they were more alike than she'd thought. But when he pulled up to the curb marked No Parking, there wasn't time for anything but the most basic pleasantries. Ignoring the cabbie leaning on his horn, Joe said nothing more than that he'd probably see her around and waited long enough for her to thank him for the ride before jockeying back out into the flow.

For several seconds Amanda stood at the curb while people intent on getting home for the evening hurried past. Joe's message couldn't have been any clearer had he plastered it on the billboard above the office building across the street. She hadn't gotten him what he'd wanted, so there was nothing else to say. The companionable attitude and the offer of the ride had just been his way of saying he didn't hold a grudge.

A vaguely hollow feeling settled in the pit of her stomach as she turned away.

The hollow feeling was still there the next morning, as she sat toying with her necklace while attempting to look interested in Murdock's regular Thursday ad meeting. For the most part she managed to ignore the uncomfortable sensation by concentrating on other, equally uncomfortable ones. Thanks to Joe Slaighter she had a whole raft of them to contemplate.

Until she'd met him, she'd always managed to contain her restlessness. If she couldn't work off excess energy in her garden, she'd strip a wall or paper a room or sand something down to a pile of sawdust. Last evening nothing had worked. She still felt edgy and tense, and she was not at all pleased with the combination.

Neither was she pleased with the other little matter she'd never had to deal with before: his assertion that she prevented relationships from forming. Until last night, when she'd lain in her bed watching the stars disappear into daylight, she'd thought of herself simply as "selective;" choosing to associate with people who had nothing to gain through her relationship to a politically powerful man. If she shut people out, it was only to protect herself.

Despite appearances, it seemed she still wasn't very good at that.

It didn't matter that Amanda wasn't paying a whole lot of attention to what was going on at the conference table. When the marketing department started arguing with the purchasing department over the availabiltiy of sale items, everyone's eyes tended to glaze over until the current crisis resolved itself. Today's crisis revolved around a potential shortage of studded coats for an August winter kickoff sale because the manufacturer they were supposed to push was having production problems. Since it was only the end of April, coats weren't big on Amanda's mind. She understood the retailing business, though. Stores stocked a full season ahead, so if the coats weren't arriving as the summer stuff was being pushed in the spring, then the whole system stood in danger of collapse.

That was precisely how the marketing director analyzed the situation as he tugged at the knot in his eye-popping print tie while pacing the length of the sample-strewn conference table. Amanda hadn't heard who he blamed for this particular crisis. But when something went wrong, it was always some other department's fault and somewhere a head would roll. Being an independent contractor whose sole function was to illustrate whatever the advertising department handed her, she felt confident that her head would remain securely on her shoulders. What finally brought her attention back to the meeting, though, was the purchasing director's rebuttal to marketing's accusations of shortsightedness.

The director, a woman who looked like a black and white photograph except for her blood-red lips, was the polar opposite of the flamboyant and passionate guy from marketing. With her arms crossed, she all but backed him up to the wall—ignoring the yawns of the half dozen other store employees in attendance who'd been subjected to versions of this performance before.

"Look, Blakely," the woman said in a voice as harsh as her makeup "Since my buyers weren't gifted with a crystal ball, it wasn't possible for them to foresee the flu epidemic that has over half of that manufacturer's employees flat on their respective backs. They're in the process of hiring additional help, but they've got five times the orders they expected on those coats, so it may take them a while. Instead of substituting something we don't even have yet, why don't we give the company a week, then see where the order stands?"

It was a reasonable suggestion. Too reasonable for marketing to accept immediately. What Amanda heard, though, was that the company—a local clothing manufacturer—was hiring.

Knowing her presence wouldn't be missed, Amanda shrugged in apology at the jealous looks of those who had to stay and quietly slipped out of the room.

"May I use your telephone, Kathy? And a phone book?"

The executive offices' receptionist, an extraordinarily tall and slender young woman with the bluest eyes Amanda had ever seen, motioned a perfectly manicured hand toward the receiver. "They still at it in there?"

"Afraid so."

"You know, you don't have to sit through all that, Amanda. I could call you when Bill's decided on the next promotion and you could just come in and pick up the stuff." Slipping a message she'd just taken into one of the slots near her typewriter, she frowned as if trying to remember something. A second later she reached under the desk for the phone book. "I could even send it to you, if you want. It's the white sale, right?"

"Fourth of July," Amanda corrected. "I overheard Esther say they're going with a photographer on the white sale."

Amanda appreciated Kathy's offer to mail the samples, but she'd long ago learned that some corners weren't worth cutting. Her presence was necessary only for advertising's portion of the meeting. Even then, it wasn't mandatory. "It's easier for me to ask about how they want an item presented when everyone's together. That way everybody agrees on what I'm supposed to be doing and I don't have to do it over again. If I come in to pick things up after a meeting, then I have to track down someone who can answer questions if I have any. You know how hard it can be to find Bill sometimes."

"Do I ever," the girl muttered as, straightening, she held up the two heavy volumes of Yellow Pages. "Which do you want?"

Amanda took the one listing garment manufacturers, thinking as she did that she probably could just have asked Kathy for the phone number she wanted. She was just so accustomed to doing things for herself that it hadn't occurred to her.

As it was, within minutes, she had all the information she wanted. Trying not to grin as she hung up from that call, she then dialed the number for the shelter and asked for La-Vonne. Unless LaVonne could finagle extra hours by covering for someone else, she didn't work on Thursdays. Today she hadn't been lucky enough to get the extra hours—which turned out to be a blessing in its own way.

When LaVonne came on the line, Amanda told her about the jobs at the factory. The best part was that if they kept her on after ninety days, she'd be eligible for benefits: an employee bonus program and medical insurance for both herself and Lucy. LaVonne had no garment manufacturing experience, but she could certainly move racks between machines and stack and box coats if she had to.

It was as Amanda mentioned the part about stacking and boxing that Kathy looked up from the mail. Since Amanda was on the other side of her desk, it was impossible for her not to overhear what was being said. Waving her hand at Amanda to get her attention, she cut in to say she knew that the department store was hiring receiving clerks, if her friend didn't mind loading and unloading boxes.

Amanda, smiling her thanks as Kathy went back to her sorting, passed that information on, too.

The thought of having *two* interviews excited LaVonne so much she didn't know which questions to ask first; where the factory was, how to get to the department store, or what time she should be where first. Then, as suddenly as it had entered her voice, the excitement faded.

"They won't want me."

"Of course they will," Amanda returned, not sure which "they" she'd referred to. "They probably both will. You've got a good head on your shoulders and you're a hard worker. Just because you don't have any actual experience at this type of work doesn't mean you won't pick it up in a hurry." Amanda's voice gentled. "Believe in yourself, remember?"

That was the primary message at Matthew's House. LaVonne didn't sound too receptive to it at the moment, though.

"The more you look like you need a job, the harder it is to get one."

There was an ironic truth to that adage.

It wasn't fair. But fair or not it was a fact, and Amanda knew that how a person presented herself was terribly important. The point was stressed over and over in the classes Sister Bernie held for the women. A person didn't need to look like a fashion plate by any means. Nor was such a look even desirable. A neat, clean and reasonably well-fitted outfit was necessary, however. Unfortunately LaVonne's wardrobe was limited pretty much to what she'd acquired from the boxes of used clothing donated to Matthew's House. None of it fit particularly well—except for the pair of black jeans and pink sweater she'd arrived at the shelter wearing. Those would probably work all right for her application at the factory. They wouldn't do at all for a downtown department store. Not for the interview, anyway.

Amanda barely had time to reassure the painfully silent woman. The meeting having progressed past the routine crisis, one of the advertising assistants motioned for her return. Amanda only had time to offer a quick, "Don't worry," before telling LaVonne she'd see her later this afternoon. She would take care of the situation. A nice, simple dress could make a world of difference in a woman's confidence. Since she and LaVonne were about the same size, as soon as she got home, she would grab a couple of outfits for LaVonne to try and head for the shelter.

She was back in the meeting before she remembered she was supposed to meet Joanie from the art gallery for lunch. Having already cancelled the date once before to meet a deadline she'd almost missed because she'd spent the previous day at Matthew's House, she couldn't very well cancel again. Watching Bill Applewhite bring out the truly horrid floral duster she was supposed to make everyone want to buy for their mother, she gave in to the fact that it was just going to be one of those days.

Amanda's resignation was actually more bravado than acceptance. The hollow feeling in her stomach had returned with a vengeance at the thought of returning to Matthew's House. Not because of the shelter itself or the people in it. She was beginning to care a great deal about certain people there. The feeling had to do with the man who had introduced her to them. Joe's dismissal had hurt. It still did, and this time it was harder to pretend the slight didn't matter. Her usual argument about how he didn't know her, so it wasn't really her he was rejecting, wouldn't work this time. It didn't help, either, to know she had no one but herself to blame for letting him get to her. He'd told her from the beginning exactly what he'd wanted—and she had now served her purpose.

She only hoped that she wouldn't run into him when she got to the shelter.

The meeting lasted just shy of forever. Because of that, Amanda was late meeting Joanie who, after a relatively quick bite at a trendy eatery in Buckhead, insisted that Amanda come back to the gallery with her to see the "utterly enchanting" work she had on exhibit for a young artist she planned to promote. She'd also just acquired exclusive rights to a very popular wildlife artist, which meant new brochures for Amanda to design. Yet, as pleased as she was to get the job, the layouts for those brochures were the last thing on her mind when, two hours later, the bus she'd just barely caught groaned to a stop at Ducker and Auburn.

Amanda had tried to get a cab. But it had been right at five o'clock by the time she'd made it back downtown from her home, and there hadn't been an available taxi in sight. In a hurry to get to the shelter before it got much later, she'd completely forgotten to call ahead and ask Rocky to meet her. If she remembered correctly, his stint at the shelter was over somewhere around six. Since it was a quarter of, he should still be there.

She wasn't really concerned by her oversight. There was a pay phone outside the little ethnic grocery store on the corner. She could call the shelter from there. Her greatest concern at the moment was that she'd forgotten to add a slip to the two dresses and accessories she'd packed for La-Vonne in the small beige overnight bag she carried. She'd been in such a hurry that she hadn't even had time to change from her straight-skirted navy suit and heels. The outfit was not exactly ideal for walking.

The bus was more crowded than usual, typical for the time of day, and several passengers got off with her. The woman who'd sat next to Amanda with a bag of cleaning supplies between her knees, and who'd seemed asleep for the whole trip, was one of those to disembark, along with a maintenance man and three rather menacing-looking teenagers with stripes razor cut into their hair. One of the youths shouted something distinctly offensive at Amanda, then sauntered into the market punching at his friends.

Trying not to think about the boy's rudeness or the stares aimed at her back, Amanda hurried past the newsstands chained to the curb. A half dozen steps later, she slowed to a halt. Two young girls were using the pay phone. One was gabbing away between the bubbles of gum she blew. Her friend had draped herself over her shoulder trying to talk into the receiver, too. A guy shouldering a boom box with the volume in the stratospheric range slouched against the wall next to them. Since the tap of his foot looked more like impatience than an attempt to match the beat of the noise, she assumed he was waiting his turn at the phone.

The woman with the bag of cleaning stuff shuffled past. Amanda started after her. The lady was headed in the same direction she needed to go. Having no idea how long it would be before she could use the telephone herself, Amanda figured she and the woman could unofficially accompany each other as far as their respective paths took them. It was nearing dusk, but there was still enough light to forestall fears about Joe's warning that she didn't want to be here after dark. Most of those fears, anyway.

Since it *would* be dark by the time she'd finished at the shelter, she would just ask Sister Bernie if she could use one of the empty beds. No way was she going to attempt this little trek back until morning.

A block and a half later, her companion, who'd given her a dirty look for following too closely, turned into a run-down building with crumbling steps and the sounds of a heated argument emanating from one of the upstairs rooms. Since Amanda only had a couple more blocks to go, she picked up her pace and crossed the street to head toward the alley that split the block where Matthew's House was located.

She felt a touch of trepidation now that she was alone. Or maybe the surge of insecurity was because the buildings here blocked the fading sun. Her heels tapping on the cracked and buckled sidewalk, she glanced out across the overgrown vacant field with its skeletons of cars and tried to picture the gleaming new center her father had so long envisioned there. She couldn't manage the distraction. The row of buildings facing the lot was deserted and there wasn't another soul in sight. Yet she had the horrible feeling there was someone behind her.

She wasn't quite running, but she was moving as quickly as she could in her slim skirt and heels when she turned into the alley. She'd been listening for the voices of the children, even though she'd had a feeling they wouldn't be out this late. As she expected, the children weren't there. The narrow passage wasn't empty, though. Twenty-some-odd ragged and dirty men were lined up by the closed garage door at the far end of the alley, waiting for the ladies of the shelter to feed them.

The thought of passing through that miserable lot should have unsettled her even more. Instead she found their presence easing the heavy beat of her heart. No doubt it was only her active imagination that had her inventing bogey men to follow her in the fading light. It was amazing how much different her perceptions of the area could be from midday to evening.

She hadn't taken two steps into the alley, when she felt her overnight bag being jerked backward. The next thing she felt was the sting of her purse strap as it snapped against her neck and the downward pull brought her to her knees. But it was the knee in her back and the hand shoving her face into the pavement that hurt the most.

Chapter Seven

Mrs. Doris Pomeroy was the only woman, other than Bernie, who had a relationship with Joe that had lasted longer than a weekend. She'd been his secretary for six years. During that time she had lost her husband, married off her daughter and become a grandmother to triplets. Yet she swore to Joe that every one of her gray hairs had been caused by him. She worried about him as if he were her own son. He seemed to work eighteen hours a day, often beating her to the office in the morning and returning there to finish up something or other after a dinner meeting in the evening. From the stack of dictation she inevitably found waiting for her on Monday morning, she concluded he spent most of his weekends in the office, too. Joe knew it had become a point of pride with her that she stayed on top of his output.

"If you'll sign these, I'll drop them in the mailbox on my way out," she said as she walked into Joe's office with letters in one hand and a stack of phone messages for him in the other. "It's almost seven o'clock. Your dinner reservation with Mr. Hewlett is for seven forty-five at the Brasserie. Here's the check for his fees. You'll have to sign it."

As Doris tucked her silver-framed glasses into her pewter gray hair, Joe glanced up from the yellow pad on which he'd been making notes. He hadn't realized it was so late. Doris should have gone home by now.

"Which cases are these for?" he asked, reaching for the checks she held out across his cluttered desk.

"Jasmine Washington and Edward Lubick. Those are the only cases the Hewlett firm is handling for you right now. They didn't charge for Rocky Delacorte's last hearing. Are you coming back here tonight?"

"Plan to."

"I'll put fresh coffee in the filter. All you have to do when you come in is flip the switch."

Doris no longer questioned his long hours and late nights. Nor did she succumb to her maternal instincts and subtly suggest that he take a vacation or get a girlfriend, a hobby or a life. Joe wasn't a man to be dissuaded from either his convictions or his habits, and it had quickly become apparent that he had no intention of slowing down. He needed to bill the hours he did to cover checks like the one she had just handed him.

Those particular cases were for a woman trying to get child support from a deadbeat father, and for a man whose civil rights had been violated by a greedy landlord. There had been others like them over the years as well as cases that involved child and spousal abuse, and disputes between ordinary citizens and bureaucratic government agencies. The clients in those cases invariably had no money, so Joe paid for their representation himself out of the fees he charged his own, much wealthier, clients. In a way he took from the rich to give to the poor, but any comparison Doris might have made to the legendary folk hero known for that same sort of deed remained unspoken. Joe didn't take anything from his clients that he didn't earn, nor did he invite comment about his causes.

He didn't invite small talk, either. His was the sort of efficiency that tended to border on abrupt.

The phone rang as he signed the letters.

Joe didn't look up. "Get that, would you? Whoever it is, I'm not here."

Doris dutifully answered the telephone, picking up his extension instead of removing herself to her own desk. As he heard her crisply efficient "Law Office," he was well aware of the frown she aimed at the top of his head. She didn't believe in saying he wasn't there when he was. She would do as he asked, though. But she would change the phrasing to "He's unavailable."

That wasn't what she said at all. After what couldn't have been more than five seconds of silence, she told the caller to hold a moment and punched the red Hold button.

"It's Sister Bernadette. Do you want me to tell her you'll call her back?"

Even as she posed the question, she held out the receiver. Doris knew he would always take Bernie's calls. It was the good sister who referred the Jasmine Washingtons and Rocky Delacortes to her boss. It had taken Joe a long time to trust Doris with the reason he was so accessible to the nun. That he had done so inspired her undying loyalty, and her silence.

Tossing his pen aside, Joe reached for the phone.

"Do you need anything else?" Doris asked, quickly gathering up the letters he'd signed.

"That's it. Thanks," he added. With a distracted "Good night," he was on the line before she was out of his office.

"Joe, I'm so glad I caught you." Bernie's voice was urgent, her tone muffled as if she didn't want to be overheard. "Amanda's been mugged. She won't let me call the police or an ambulance, and I don't have a car. Can you come down here?"

Her hurried words jerked him from his preoccupation. Not questioning his own reaction, he aimed for the practical. "Where's your station wagon?"

"Sister Mary Rose went to the motherhouse for a meeting. She won't be back until tomorrow."

"How badly is Amanda hurt?"

"More than she'll let on. She's awfully shaken. I think her arm might be broken, and she's pretty scratched up."

"I'm on my way," he told her and grabbed his suit jacket from the back of his chair.

His next words were to Doris. Stuffing his arms into his jacket sleeves, he flew past her desk where she stood folding the letters he'd just signed. He didn't slow down at all when he asked her to call Hewlett and cancel dinner.

"What happened? Why was she leaving so late? Why wasn't Rocky with her?"

Joe followed Bernie through the narrow hallway from the garage, where he'd parked his car in the station wagon's space. She'd been waiting for him. Now she was waiting for him to stop with the questions so she could answer them.

"First of all, she wasn't leaving. She was on her way here with some clothes for one of the ladies." Her tone was calm, a direct contrast to the agitation she found so revealing in Joe's. "As for Rocky, he didn't know she was coming, or I'm sure he'd have met her before he went home. This isn't his fault. It isn't hers, either."

From the sound of the terse expletive Joe muttered, he didn't agree. "She could have donated clothes anytime."

"That's not what she was doing." The nun rounded on him, stopping him in his tracks and planting her hands on her hips as she used to do when they were kids and he was being obtuse. Even in the corridor's dim lighting he could see the spark of Irish temper she'd never been able to suppress.

"She arranged job interviews for LaVonne and was bringing her something to wear that might bolster her confidence. The interviews are tomorrow and, because of her other obligations, she couldn't get here before she did. For her efforts, she was jumped by three young men who made off with the clothes and her purse. She's lucky they didn't pull a knife on her.''

The chastisement rankled. She intended it to.

''She's hurt, Joe. And she's not handling it near as well as she wants us to believe. She's a strong person, but you're not going to do her any good at all if you go in there telling her that you told her to stay away from here and that this wouldn't have happened if she'd listened to you. Don't you dare tell me you weren't going to,'' she hurried to add when he opened his mouth to deny that very thing. ''It's bad form to lie to a nun.''

Ordinarily Joe wouldn't have let her off for pulling rank. Bernie hadn't always been a nun, and he had enough on her to curl the pope's miter. But concern over something she had just said overrode any need to defend what he couldn't defend, anyway.

''*Three* kids jumped her?''

''She thinks they were on the bus with her.''

''They jumped her when she got off?''

''No. That happened right outside. She'd just come into the east end of the alley. Several of the men we feed saw the whole thing, but the kids were gone before anyone could do anything.'' Not that they would have, was the sad, unspoken comment. On the streets it was rare for anyone to get involved in someone else's crisis. ''We were just starting to open the garage to serve supper when one of the men came up and told us there was a lady hurt in the alley.''

They had moved on as they talked and now entered the main room of the shelter. Several of the women with smaller children sat with them in front of the television set, while, from the sounds of clanking pots and pans, others had pulled clean-up duty in the kitchen.

Joe paid little notice. Amanda, looking like a small and vulnerable child, was curled up on a spare cot along the far wall. A young black woman he recognized as Lucy's mother sat with her.

He and Bernie had made their way down the rows of beds when he saw LaVonne patting Amanda's shoulder.

"Hey, girl," he heard her say. "You're not going to sleep, are you?"

The question brought a shaky smile from near the bottom of the blue washcloth covering Amanda's forehead and eyes. Amanda held the cloth in place with her left hand. An angry red abrasion marred the delicate skin along her right jaw and flecks of rock and dirt were clearly visible. Her right arm was wrapped in a thin towel and had an ice bag perched on it.

"No, LaVonne. I'm awake. My head just hurts."

"Well, don't you dare go falling asleep on me. Sister Bernie says I'm to keep you awake, and that's what I'm going to do. You want me to get you something to drink? Water or juice?"

"How about a straight Scotch?"

"I hear you, girl, but we got no booze here. Rules, you know?"

"I was only kidding."

"Well, if I could get you some, and it'd make you feel better, I'd do it. Rules or no. It was on account of me that you were coming here." Disbelief softened LaVonne's tone. "Nobody's ever done something like that for me before. Brought me their own good clothes to borrow, I mean."

Feeling as if she were moving in slow motion, Amanda pulled the soothing cloth from her forehead. She didn't want LaVonne blaming herself for what had happened. She was glad to do what little she could to help the woman get back on her feet—even if she wasn't crazy about the aches making themselves felt in various parts of her body at the moment.

Supporting her throbbing arm as she sat up, she was prepared to tell her that, too. At least she was until she saw Joe standing five feet away.

His presence explained why the conversations taking place around the television set at the end of the room had suddenly reduced to whispers. It also explained the quick deference in LaVonne when she rose from where she'd been sitting on the cot's thin mattress. He reminded Amanda of some great medieval overlord as he stood there; a man people either feared or respected. His stance was deceptively casual, quite unlike his expression, as his glance swept from her disheveled hair to her torn nylons and the dirt clinging to her skinned-up knees.

Something dark and forbidding tightened his expression, along with an indistinct quality she didn't recognize in her present state. Still struggling with the effects of the attack, the senses of helplessness, violation and her own anger at the gall of the three little creeps who'd taken her belongings, she didn't know what to make of the quiet anger Joe attempted to suppress. Dressed in an impeccably cut suit and crisp white shirt, it was clear enough a trip to the shelter hadn't been on his agenda tonight. It was entirely possible his irritation was due to being called away from whatever he'd been doing.

Wincing at the pain in her arm when she moved, trying to ignore it, she turned accusingly to the woman with the untamable cinnamon-colored curls. "I asked you not to call him."

Sister Bernie appeared quite nonplussed with the reminder. "You didn't leave me any choice, Amanda. You were so adamant about my not calling the authorities that I had no other option. I appreciate that you don't want the police involved, but you need medical attention."

"He's not a doctor."

"No," she returned mildly. "But he's big enough to carry you to one, if need be. Your arm is swollen and you've got a bump on your head. What if you have a concussion?"

"I don't have a concussion." Her head actually hurt less now than it had at first. More than having it shoved into the cement, she felt certain the pounding had been caused from the sheer stress of the incident. As for her arm, since she could wiggle all of her fingers, she didn't think that was too serious, either. "I'm all right. Really."

"You haven't looked in a mirror."

The nun was ruthless. She was also concerned. Amanda appreciated that. A lot. But there was more at stake here than was immediately apparent.

"I can't risk being recognized," she said to Bernie, preferring the nun's perplexed expression to Joe's implacable one. "I've already told you that. Governor's Daughter Mugged in Back Alley isn't a headline my father will appreciate. He didn't want me getting involved with the shelter in the first place. But my disregarding his wishes wouldn't be nearly as bad as his finding out about it in the papers."

Gingerly she touched one of the aching spots on her forehead, careful to avoid the large abrasion she hoped her bangs would cover. Her last thought had prompted another, even more uncomfortable one. "He specifically warned me about causing any publicity connected with this shelter. The only way I could explain my presence in this neighborhood would be by mentioning it. I don't know what the media would do, but I can't risk finding out." Weariness robbed her voice of strength. "I can't do that to him."

For several seconds silence fell over the small group gathered around the cot. LaVonne stood twisting her hands, wanting badly to help but not knowing how. Bernie, no stranger to personal dilemma, absently reached for the small cross at the end of her key chain for assistance in contemplating the less-than-straightforward circumstances. Only Joe seemed unappreciative of the situation. At least it seemed that way to Amanda.

Two steps put him squarely in front of where she now sat on the edge of the cot. He reached down, his eyes hard on her pale features, and took the washcloth from her hand.

It was with a sudden sense of dread that she watched him turn to LaVonne. "Rinse that out for me, would you? And soap it up."

"What are you doing?" Bernie wanted to know.

So did Amanda, but she didn't have a chance to echo the question.

"I'm taking her to the hospital."

"No." Amanda's voice shook. Partly because she hadn't yet stopped shaking inside. Mostly because the situation actually seemed to be getting worse. "I told you that I can't."

There was no earthly reason Amanda should have felt the sense of betrayal that suddenly overwhelmed her. But that was exactly what she did feel when she saw Joe's absolute determination. He'd heard every word she'd said. He even knew how tenuous her relationship was with her father. Yet, none of that mattered to him.

Joe Slaighter hates to lose.

Ruben had said those very words to her the day she had met the man silently daring her to challenge him. Those words came back to her now as she realized the opportunity Joe had no doubt just seen. She hadn't been able to delay the demolition by talking to her father, but the publicity Joe could generate about her involvement could easily tie up her father's project for weeks.

It was almost as if he'd read her very thoughts. The look in his eyes was forbidding; the tone of his low voice just short of curt. "Don't, Amanda," he warned and took the cloth LaVonne had wrung over the bowl beside the cot.

He crouched in front of her, bringing her to eye level with his impatience. "You're hurt and you're going. No one's going to know who you are."

He took her chin in his hand to keep her from turning away. Stopped in her mental tracks by his last statement, Amanda thought he simply meant to check out the various scrapes and scratches decorating her face. What he did nearly stole her breath.

His fingers slipped to her throat, the harshness suddenly fading from his eyes. A thin band of raised and red skin arched along the side of her neck. Without seeming to think about what he was doing, he traced his fingertips just below the angry welt. "They got your necklace."

There was a grim set to his jaw when he moved his hand around to the back of her neck. With gentleness all the more amazing for the lack of it in his expression, he wiped the cloth over Amanda's cheek. The unblemished one. As he did, he frowned at the two-inch-wide abrasion above her right eyebrow. With her bangs pushed back, the nasty scrape was clearly visible, but he didn't go anywhere near it with the cloth. Nor did he attempt to cleanse the scrape along her jaw or at the side of her face. He wasn't washing her up to make her more presentable. Quite the contrary. It took her a moment, but as he worked at the area under her eyebrow, she realized that he was taking off her makeup.

"We need to get you some other clothes. Bernie?" he called, not looking away when he drew a clean edge of the cloth over the fullness of Amanda's bottom lip. His glance darted to hers at the intimacy. Just as quickly he looked back to his task. "Suppose you could find something to make her look a little less affluent? And maybe a scarf or hat for her head?"

Bernie was right behind him. "They'll just take a scarf off at the hospital."

"That's okay. By the time we get there, maybe it'll have smashed her hair down. I want her to look like she hasn't had a place to stay for a while."

He hesitated for a moment. It seemed to him that Amanda should have said something by now. At the very least, she should have objected to the way they were talking about her as if she weren't even there.

She did nothing but draw a deep breath.

Telling himself to be grateful for the acquiescence, not sure he really cared for it, he turned his attention to the smudge near her nose.

"I don't know any other way to do this," he told her, deciding to leave the little streak of dirt. "If you don't want anyone to recognize you, then maybe we can make you look like you came from here. You can make up a name, but let me do the talking when we get to the hospital. You can't show up wearing that, though."

He watched her glance down at her navy skirt. Except for a few dusty spots, which should brush out easily enough, it had escaped the experience remarkably unscathed. Likewise for the matching jacket folded at the foot of the bed and the white and yellow pinstripe blouse she wore.

"I'll leave what I'm wearing here for you," she said to LaVonne. "If you don't mind having to clean it up."

LaVonne's skeptical glance bounced from Amanda to the smartly tailored jacket. "You mean, I can wear it to the interviews tomorrow?" Her face brightened. "Hell no, I don't mind. I mean, *heck*, Sister," she said in a chagrined verbal shuffle. "I mean, *heck* no."

Having heard far more inventive profanities over the course of her life, Sister Bernie passed that one off without so much as the twitch of an eyebrow. She knew exactly what LaVonne meant. Amanda was literally giving the woman the shirt off her back. For her to ask if it would trouble her to clean it had hardly been necessary.

Even Joe seemed to realize that.

Telling him she was sure she could find appropriate clothing, Bernie hurried off, leaving him to finish what he'd started.

With the makeup gone, Joe no longer had any reason to touch Amanda, so he balled the cloth into his fist and tossed it into the bowl with a splash. Touching her was dangerous. He had felt her trembling. The kind of trembling that comes from so deep inside that nothing on the outside can stop it. She'd been frightened; no doubt scared half to death by a trio of punks who respected no one's rights but their own. Joe wasn't sure what he wanted most at that moment. To rearrange three faces or to pull Amanda into his arms until the awful shaking stopped. The one thing he did know was that he didn't want to sit there with LaVonne watching him while he thought about it.

Seeing a way to make herself useful, and to avoid Joe's perplexed glare, LaVonne bent down to set the bowl aside before he got more water on the floor. "I'll help her change," she said in a tone that made it clear his presence was neither desired or necessary for the upcoming task. "Instead of her having to walk into the bathroom, it might be easier if you waited in Sister's office."

Joe's intentions were far from prurient. But he supposed there were certain proprieties to be maintained. Especially in a place inhabited mostly by women. The woman hovering over Amanda now wanted to make sure he got that message, too. She had that mother-hen look that Bernie got sometimes. He wasn't concerned about clucking females at the moment, though. His concern was for Amanda.

That he didn't attempt to justify that concern should have troubled him. He simply accepted it as unavoidable and pushed himself to his feet. In a voice as tight as his fists when he shoved them into his pockets, he let Amanda know he'd be ready whenever she was.

Her response was little more than a nod.

That bothered him. Other than to lend LaVonne her clothes, Amanda hadn't said a word in the past several minutes. Nor had she made any attempt to protest the way he'd taken over. Not that he wanted to argue with her, though heaven knew they certainly knew how. She needed to see a doctor, and the last thing he wanted to do was get into an argument about that. It just wasn't like her to be so docile. This wasn't her usual clamming up when she felt her space was being invaded. It was more like the spirit had suddenly been drained from her.

As quiet as Amanda had been, she became even more so during the ride to the County General. Bernie and La-Vonne had helped her change into a baggy shirt and a pair of polyester bell-bottom pants that had hung in the back of someone's closet for the last twenty years. They'd also given her some thongs and a flower print scarf, which she'd tied babushka-style over her hair. He didn't ask if they'd thought to give her different underwear. Dead certain that Amanda's tastes ran toward the kind of lacy underthings he would love to spend a long time removing from her, he decided not to consider the issue. Nurses usually made people strip down and wear those ridiculous hospital gowns, anyway, so it was possible no one would see her undoubtedly expensive undergarments. Amanda stripped naked was also a thought he didn't feel like entertaining. What he felt toward her right now had nothing to do with sex.

Bernie and LaVonne had done an excellent job of achieving the look he'd wanted. Too good, actually. Huddled as she was against the door and cradling her injured arm as she stared at the window, Amanda reminded him very much of the people he'd seen on the streets. People who'd stopped feeling because they simply couldn't bear what was happening to them.

He wondered if she was in shock. After what had happened to her, he supposed it was entirely possible. Or maybe, since she'd hit her head, something else was wrong.

"Amanda?" He glanced from the traffic and saw her turn toward him. "Are you all right?"

Amanda didn't know how to answer him. The strange foreboding she felt made no sense. She wasn't in any danger. Not now. Not with Joe. Yet, she couldn't seem to stop the shaking. From the moment she'd finally let go and let him take over, that was all she had felt. The cold. The trembling and the nagging sense of dread.

"I don't know."

She didn't hear what Joe muttered, but the car picked up speed. A moment later she felt his hand fold over hers.

Thank you, she thought. Or maybe she said it. She wasn't sure. She knew only that she was grateful for the contact. His hand felt warm, his hold firm, and she could almost feel the strength in him flowing to her. She needed that strength very badly right now. There seemed such a sense of unreality to everything that had happened—to everything that was still happening. This morning she had awakened in her own bed, had coffee in her familiar kitchen, then dressed in her own clothes before going about a day that had run familiarly behind schedule. Then she'd stepped off a bus at Drucker and Auburn and, from that moment on, her sense of control had been shot. Now, with no identification and no money, she was costumed in strange clothes in an unfamiliar car and driving through a dark and even more unfamiliar part of town. When Joe led her into a bustling emergency room ten minutes later, even her name wasn't her own.

It was her choice of name that, a few hours later, finally allowed Joe's smile.

"Couldn't you have come up with something more imaginative than Jane Smith?"

"It was all I could think of."

Joe shook his head at the pitiful waif beside him. He shouldn't laugh at Amanda, but he could feel the smile forming as—at a little after midnight—they left the emergency room by way of a set of large sliding doors. With a white gauze patch on her forehead, an elastic bandage supporting her sprained right wrist and the truly awful fashion rejects she'd put back on, the defensive tilt of her chin was almost comical. The small show of spirit was also a fair indicator of her resilience. She'd been through the mill tonight, but she was showing signs of life again.

Still, she didn't look like she was up to running any marathons.

Looking from the bright lights behind them to the darker parking lot, she pushed her fingers through her distinctly disheveled hair. He didn't ask what she'd done with the scarf.

"Come on." Palm in the middle of her back, he nudged her forward. "Let's get you out of here."

Amanda let him lead her to his car, much as she had let him take over nearly every other aspect of her existence during the past several hours. She didn't care to question her uncharacteristic passiveness. Nor was she inclined to make too much of it. For now, she was simply grateful that he'd been willing to handle the thornier aspects of the evening. And grateful, too, that no one had pressed the issue of bringing in the police. One of the nurses had filled out an incident report that went into some sort of file, but no one could ever connect the governor's daughter with an indigent by the name of Jane Smith and three unidentified muggers. Joe had been remarkably adept at covering his own tracks, too.

She knew now why he had brought her to the emergency room of the huge teaching hospital. As busy as it had been, the harried staff had been too preoccupied with meeting medical needs to pay any particular attention to yet another mugging victim. Especially one from a charity shelter. Only Joe's involvement had been questioned, and that because his urbane appearance so obviously contrasted with hers. He had explained his presence to the admitting clerk with nothing more elaborate than the truth. He'd brought in Ms. Smith because the director of a shelter, a friend of his, asked for his help after a woman who'd come to spend the night had been mugged. He would take care of the expenses himself, he said, and write them off as a donation.

That had suited the admitting clerk just fine. If Mr. Slaighter paid, she wouldn't have to fill out all the paperwork required for an indigent, so the hospital could be reimbursed by government agencies.

Amanda hadn't even thought about making arrangements to pay.

"Thank you for taking care of the bill for me," she said, remembering the admitting clerk's faint distaste when she'd first noticed her. "I'll pay you back when I get home."

Preoccupied, she didn't notice Joe's slight hesitation. "No rush," he told her and shifted his car into gear.

"Thanks for putting up with the doctor, too." Picking at one of the many loose threads on the garish pants she wore, she frowned. "He really could have said all of that to me. It wasn't necessary for him to bore you with it."

"I think he just wanted to make sure someone else understood what you were supposed to do."

There had been more to the doctor's attitude than that. Thinking about how competently Joe had handled everything as they left the huge medical center complex and wound through the late nighttime traffic, Amanda wanted him to know it, too.

"There isn't anything too complicated about resting for a couple of days and keeping my wrist wrapped until the swelling goes down. The doctor treated me the same way the admitting clerk did. Either as if I weren't even there, or like I couldn't possibly understand what they wanted to explain." The way she'd been treated had been very disturbing. It had also been very revealing. "I was labeled incompetent the moment we walked in there."

Her voice, already thoughtful, became quieter. "They saw me as destitute—therefore, I was something less than everyone else."

Amanda wasn't complaining. Far from it. The experience had been uncomfortable and embarrassing and she wouldn't wish it on anyone. But she had gained from it, too. Having tasted the indifference and disrespect with which some people were treated, she could now appreciate in some small way how easy it would be for someone who was already down and out to completely lose faith in herself. Many of the people in the waiting room had looked at her as if she were nothing more than refuse. Others had seemed to look right through her, as if by pretending they didn't notice her, she didn't exist.

No one, however, had ignored Joe.

She caught the discrete flash of his unembellished gold cuff link as his hand slipped to the top of the steering wheel of his modest sedan. There was nothing overstated about him. Nothing he did or wore or seemed to possess was designed to draw attention. Yet the man epitomized success.

He must have felt her watching him. He glanced toward her, his features illuminated by the glow of the dashboard lights. "How did it make you feel?"

The question lacked the veiled scorn it once might have carried. He sounded genuinely curious, and not at all interested in pointing out the irony in what had transpired between them. Because of that, and because she had the feeling he would understand, she found herself voicing what she wasn't sure she would care to share with anyone else.

"Insulted, at first. Then a little angry."

"Only a little?"

"I was playing a role, so being upset was a waste of energy. That's what I told myself, anyway. I think what I felt most, though, was just sort of invisible."

His response was the slight tightening of his jaw.

Had he ever felt that way, she wondered, studying his strong profile. He'd alluded to once having had very little. Had he been treated with that awful indifference? Was that why he seemed so driven now?

"Some people count, Amanda. Some people don't. It's been that way for forever. It's unfortunate that the measure of whether or not a person matters is in what he possesses." He hesitated, seeming to weigh his next words. "Or in what he's perceived to possess."

There seemed to be an import to his words that she wanted very much to question. She would have, too, had they not just passed the street they needed to take to get to the expressway. She turned, motioning behind her. "That was our turn."

He kept his glance straight ahead. "I'm not taking you to your house."

"Why not?"

Amanda didn't sound pleased. He hadn't thought she would.

"First of all, the doctor said you need to be watched for the next day or so. That means someone has to wake you up every couple of hours. Just because your X rays came back negative doesn't mean you couldn't have a problem." There was also the possibility of post-trauma reactions, but he didn't think it necessary to mention that. He didn't want to remind her of the mugging if she wasn't already thinking about it. "Then there's the small matter of your keys. Since your purse is gone, I assume you don't have your house key. It's almost one in the morning, and I have no intention of hanging around your porch waiting for a locksmith . . . who probably wouldn't let you in looking the way you do, anyway. Especially without ID. You can have my bed. I'll take the couch."

Chapter Eight

Amanda had long ago accepted that some decisions were beyond her control. Some choices—such as who one had for parents—simply weren't open to options. Those circumstances she accepted with resignation and simply determined to make the best of them. The decision Joe had just made for her, however, didn't seem quite as unavoidable as he'd made it sound.

"I can't stay with you. I mean, it's not necessary for me to...to put you out like that. You've done so much already."

His capitulation came far too easily. "Fine," he said, sounding like a man with an ace up his sleeve. Or perhaps it was a whole deck. "Tell me where to take you, then. Who do you want to wake up and explain all of this to?"

Amanda opened her mouth, then closed it again. His smugness didn't deserve comment, but the matter itself required a little more consideration than she'd have thought. Going to her parents' house was obviously out of the question, as was turning to any friends of the family. There were the people she knew through her work, of course. But as she went through that dishearteningly short list, she had to admit she wasn't close enough to any of them either to impose at this hour or to trust them with the knowledge of what had happened tonight. The only person she could trust was Bernie.

"You could take me back to the shelter."

"Not at this time of night."

So much for that idea, she told herself, though, in a way, she was relieved with his refusal. Even though the shelter itself was safe—bolted and barred as it was—driving through that dark and deserted part of town after midnight was not. Given what had happened to her only a few hours ago, it was truly her last choice.

It was that thought that made her realize she had no other. As sobering as it was to admit, her last choice had been her one and only option.

Ornate brass lamps, supporting large round globes, lit the long blocks ahead of them. Watching the flash of light and shadow as they passed one pole after another, a kind of dull disappointment settled over Amanda. If her energy had not been so depleted, the truth she so unexpectedly faced might not have shaken her quite so badly. But a little low on reserves, and her usual optimism having taken a temporary leave of absence, she wasn't prepared for its impact.

For years she had understood the need for discretion in her public actions. It had been hard when she was younger, but over those years she had learned to channel her spirit; to curb the individual inside her who wanted to rebel against conformity because conforming to the role her parents wanted her to play was so limiting. Still, she'd managed to find her own creative outlets, her own style, and to make her own life while being the dutiful daughter. Only, until this very moment, she hadn't realized that the private life she'd been so proud of building for herself had become just as limiting as the one of her parents' creation. The life she'd made for herself was little more than a neat little glass box with no one in it but herself.

"You didn't answer me."

"I'm sorry." She hadn't realized he'd spoken. "What did you say?"

The circular drive of a gleaming Art Deco style high-rise apartment building came into view. Joe took the drive just past it, turning into the underground parking. "I asked if you'd come up with anyone else you'd rather stay with. If you haven't, we're here."

"No." Fatigue stole the energy from her voice. "There's no one."

She saw him glance toward her, then quickly away to cut wheel. She didn't want it to matter that he now knew she had no one else to ask for help. From the way he'd taken over, she figured he'd suspected as much anyway. It *did* matter, though. The more she exposed of herself, the more vulnerable she became.

"Guess you're stuck with me, then. Don't worry about it," he added, as if he were sorry he'd pushed the matter as far as he had. "I told Bernie I'd take care of you."

Just like I take care of all her hopeless causes, he might as well have added. But Amanda was too busy being grateful that he didn't say it to notice the worry that had settled in his face.

Amanda didn't ask what the night watchman said to Joe when, a minute later, they entered the garage lobby of the building. She didn't want to know. The uniformed man greeted Joe with familiarity and deference, but his expression changed to curiosity coated with distaste at the sight of her. She could well imagine the man's thoughts as her rubber thongs slapped on the polished entry tiles on the way to the elevator.

"I don't suppose you have a sister or someone who might have left some clothes in your apartment?"

Joe's glance slid down her slender frame, hidden beneath her baggy ensemble. "Only child," he replied as the door opened and they stepped inside. The doors slid closed with a refined whoosh. "Sorry."

Since he didn't volunteer anything about the possibility of an unrelated female having had occasion to disrobe at his place, Amanda decided not to press the issue. Impressed with his discretion, thankful for it, she wearily watched the numbers on the panel by the door race from one to twenty-two before the doors opened to a spacious foyer.

Four sets of double doors lined the area. Joe headed to the set straight ahead. He didn't move ahead of her, though. As he had when they'd left the hospital and downstairs in the garage, he stayed at her side, surreptitiously watching to make sure she was all right. He didn't touch her, not even to offer the implied support of a hand at her elbow or at the small of her back. Yet Amanda found his nearness supportive in its own way.

As he opened the door to his apartment and let her step in ahead of him, she became aware of something she should have found equally reassuring. By not touching her, by deliberately keeping a discreet distance between them, he seemed to be telling her that she was safe with him.

Amanda kept her back to him as he flipped on the light to reveal a stark, gray marble entry. She supposed she should have appreciated his silent assurance. But right now, tired, battered and feeling more alone than she ever had, she didn't want to think about whether or not she felt safe in his presence. She wasn't even sure what she was supposed to feel safe from.

She'd give just about anything to have him hold her.

The thought was jarring. Not because it was unwise or unexpected. The thought of being in those strong arms was startling, simply because she had no inclination to fight the need.

"The bedroom's this way." From behind her she heard keys jangle, then go silent as he pushed them into his pocket. His footfalls heavy on the marble tiles, he moved ahead of her, flipping on another light as they moved down a short hallway covered with pearl-gray grass cloth. They passed a large room, dark except for a view of a million lights be-

yond a wall of windows, and turned into a room that
stopped her in her tracks.

The thick carpet was pale gray, and the same gray grass
cloth of the hall covered the back wall and the one to her
right. The wall to her left and the one straight ahead were
uncurtained and mostly glass. Like the view she'd barely
glimpsed from the hallway, the view from here seemed to
stretch for miles. But it wasn't the view, breathtaking as it
was, that gave her pause. It was the stark simplicity of the
room. A king-size bed dominated the open space, its mod-
ern black lacquer headboard matched by the nightstands on
either side of it, and a thick black comforter still thrown
back from when Joe had gotten up this morning. A painting, something with bold slashes of red and black and white
hung over it. Except for a chrome and black leather valet,
over which he draped his suit jacket as he waited for her to
enter, there wasn't another stick of furniture in the room.

"You don't have to give up your bed for me." She stared
at the rumpled sheets, thinking he must sleep as restlessly as
she did. "I can sleep on your sofa."

Joe had abandoned his tie and loosened the first button
of his shirt hours ago. Now, crossing toward her, the second button came undone. "I have some work to do in the
other room. You'll rest better in here."

She'd rest better if he would stay with her.

"Come on," he said, taking her by the elbow to pry her
from the doorway. "You have about as much color as my
carpet. I know you're tired, so why don't you just go on into
the bathroom and get ready for bed. There's a new tooth-
brush in the top left-hand drawer by the sink. Help yourself to anything else you need." He stopped just short of
taking her into the bathroom himself, leaving her at the
threshold to turn to a huge walk-in wardrobe. "I'll get you
something to sleep in."

Pushing her fingers through her hair, grimacing as she
realized how awful she must look, she watched him pull
open a drawer in a built-in bureau. He pulled out a T-shirt,

decided against that one, shoved it back and took out another.

"You'll swim in this," he said, handing it to her. "But it's the smallest I've got."

Anything was better than what she now wore. Taking the shirt, she offered a quiet "Thank you."

"Don't lock the door. If you pass out, I don't want to have to break it down to get in. I'm coming back in five minutes to check on you."

Clutching his shirt, she gave a nod to indicate she'd understood his instructions and turned into the bathroom. A moment later, she faced the mirror filling the wall above the counter and sink.

Even through the closed door he probably heard her groan.

When she opened the door five minutes later, Joe was sitting at the foot of the bed.

"Better," he said, looking her over as carefully as a mother might inspect her newborn. Her hair, still soft and shining despite its confinement under the scarf, fell partly over the bandage above her right eyebrow. There had been no way to conceal the abrasions along the side of her face, but having washed away the last of the grime, her porcelainlike skin held a natural blush that made her look incredibly young. Or perhaps, he thought, it was the complete lack of artifice that gave her a look of such innocence. Without makeup, and wearing his too-large T-shirt, she seemed almost childlike. Yet, there wasn't anything remotely childlike about the impact she had on him.

Joe stood. His glance skimmed down the shirt he'd given her, pausing where it ended, a good six inches above her knees. She had incredible legs: long, lithe and supple—and he could too-easily imagine how they would feel wrapped around his hips. Just the thought was enough to pool heat in his groin, but he wouldn't think about that now. He needed to think about what she might need and not do anything to make her feel any more threatened than she already had tonight.

He didn't realize he was frowning when his glance settled on what looked like floor burns just below her kneecaps. If she wasn't aching everywhere already, she'd no doubt feel like she'd been hit by a truck by morning.

Aw, sweetheart, he thought, coming up to where she stood so uncertainly. I wish this hadn't happened to you.

"Did you find everything you need?"

Amanda hesitated. Joe had changed into a pair of running shorts and an old sweatshirt, the sleeves of which he'd pushed past his elbows. Focusing on the dark hair swirling over his strong forearms, since it seemed safer looking there than into his eyes, she gave him a nod to indicate that she had. She would have added her thanks had he given her the chance.

"I didn't ask if you were hungry. I don't have much here, but I could scrape up some soup or something . . ."

"You don't have to do that. Really," she added, though by rights, she should have been starving by now. The lunch she'd had with Joanie might well have been days ago for all that had happened since then. Yet Amanda hadn't even thought of food. "I just want to lie down."

He seemed relieved to hear that. Either because he didn't feel like testing what she suspected were limited culinary skills, or because he simply didn't feel like bothering with her any more tonight. Despite the conclusion, she thought he seemed a little reluctant to leave.

They stood awkwardly for a moment, Joe searching Amanda's face for some clue as to what she might be thinking. Or some hint as to how he could ease her apparent discomfort about having to stay at his place. Even if there was something he could do for her, or if there were anything she needed, he had the feeling she wouldn't tell him. She wouldn't want to impose. More importantly, she wouldn't want to be obligated. He understood both. Yet, as pale and vulnerable as she appeared, he didn't want to leave her. She still looked shaken and in desperate need of being held. Or maybe what he sensed was his own need, and that confused him even more. The need to give comfort wasn't something he was familiar with. He wasn't even sure he knew how.

"I'll be in the other room if you need anything." Any other time, any other place, he would have reached for her. Here, in his bedroom, touching her could be disastrous. "I'll check on you in a while."

He left her sitting on the edge of his bed, knowing from the rustle of the sheets that she'd crawled beneath them as soon as he'd reached the door. He hoped it wouldn't take her long to fall asleep, and that she'd be all right once she did. She needed the rest. As for himself, it would be a while before he stretched out on the long sofa in his living room. He rarely made it to bed before one in the morning, and he had reading to catch up on. He could get a lot done in the two hours before he was due to wake her as the doctor had instructed. As agitated as he felt, he'd welcome the diversion.

It was twelve forty-five when he sat down with the latest *American Bar Journal* and a copy of *Washington Week*. By the time one-thirty rolled around, he'd flipped through both, but hadn't bothered to do more than skim the articles he'd intended to study. Disgusted with his lack of concentration, determined to get something out of his efforts, he'd turned to the shortest of the legal articles to try again when he heard the faint sound of movement behind him.

He saw her first in the reflection of night-blackened glass ahead of him before he turned from where he'd sprawled on the sofa. She stood back, hesitating at the step that led from the wide hallway to the living room.

"Amanda?" Puzzled to see her awake, he tossed his reading to the coffee table. "What's wrong?"

Joe didn't wait for her to answer. Keeping his glance on her face, he crossed to her, his bare feet soundless on the thick carpet. Her fragile features were still pale, but she appeared more frightened now than fatigued. The fear was in her eyes as she hugged her arms around herself. He saw helplessness there, too, though she tried to pretend there was nothing amiss by offering a faltering smile.

The effort failed miserably. Her defenseless expression ore at him, making him feel a little helpless himself when ne realized she wasn't sure she should have come to him.

"I didn't mean to disturb you."

He ignored the implied apology, annoyed that she felt obligated to offer it. "Couldn't you sleep?"

Amanda's arms were folded around her middle. She hugged them tighter. "I was dreaming," she said, her voice as faint as it was apologetic. "The boys... they were coming after me in the alley..." Her shoulders lifted in a listless shrug, the motion seemed to dismiss what he was sure she'd just as soon forget. "I don't want to go back to sleep. If I do, I'm afraid I'll start dreaming again."

She couldn't seem to stop shaking. But the awful trembling and her sleeplessness weren't the reasons she'd come looking for Joe. Amanda hadn't even realized she'd fallen asleep until she awakened fighting the same sensations she'd felt when she'd been pushed to the pavement. But when she'd awakened, disoriented and afraid, her first thoughts were that Joe could make the fear go away. It didn't occur to her to question the phenomenon. It had simply seemed imperative for her to go to him, to seek the sense of security and safety she felt in his presence. She needed both too desperately to worry about propriety or pride.

He stepped closer, his eyes intent on hers. She didn't care that he was probably only checking to make sure her pupils weren't doing something weird. She just needed to be with him for a while.

His glance skimmed her arms, hugged so tightly against the soft cotton shirt he'd lent her. "You really should get some rest," he told her, unsettled by the sudden sheen of tears in her eyes. "You're cold."

He could feel her shivering when he cupped his hand over her shoulder to turn her around. Yet, her skin wasn't cool, as he'd thought it would be. It felt warm through the shirt. He could feel its suppleness, too, and the feminine fragility of her slender bones. But it was the tension in her body that gave him pause. He felt her shudder. Not at his touch. Incredibly, she actually seemed to welcome it as she closed her eyes and drew a deep, stabilizing breath. The trembling seemed to be the same as he had felt in her at the shelter.

Oh, Amanda, he thought, sliding his arm over her shoulder. *Why didn't you say you were scared?*

She didn't have to say it for him to know just how much she was holding in. Cursing himself for having left her alone in the first place, he drew her close. The doctor had said she might have trouble sleeping tonight.

"Let's get you back to bed." The deep breath she drew would have sounded like a sob to anyone but him. He didn't think Amanda would let herself cry. Tears only made feelings worse.

Or so he'd told himself when he was fifteen. "Do you want me to stay with you?"

"If you wouldn't mind."

"I don't. I won't leave unless you tell me to. Here." He bent then, and slid an arm behind her knees. "Put your arms around my neck."

She stiffened, startled when he'd picked her up. Then, within moments, he felt her relax against his body. Her tacit acceptance of his actions pleased him, even though he doubted that her acquiescence had much to do with him personally. She was alone and frightened. After what she'd admitted in his car, he knew she didn't have anyone else to turn to.

He was all she had.

Strangely drawn to that thought, he carried her to his room where he sat down with her among the tangled sheets on the bed. Were he a man who entertained ideas of hearth and home, he might have even been unsettled by it. But he wasn't that kind of man. He knew himself well enough to realize that he had no room for such things in his life: the demands and obligations of husband and father. He'd accepted long ago that he wouldn't be any good at either. Rather than hurt people he cared about by letting them down, it was easier to avoid involvement to begin with.

Swallowing what almost felt like regret, he leaned his back against the headboard. He pulled Amanda up with him and cradled her head beneath his chin. The light from the hallway slanted across the foot of the bed. Other than that and the glow from the city lights, which he often fell asleep to trying to count so he wouldn't have to think, the room was dark.

"Talk to me," he heard himself say, wishing he could absorb her trembling. "Tell me what happened. Maybe it'll help." Her skin felt soft, like fine satin as he slowly ran his hand over her upper arm. "Bernie says it does."

Had Amanda felt like smiling, she might have just then. Bernie believed in the therapeutic value of talking out a problem. It was clear from the way Joe attributed the solution to his friend that he didn't have a whole lot of faith in the process himself.

At the moment neither did Amanda. "There really isn't anything to say. You already know how it happened."

That was true. The attack had been quick and dirty, which didn't leave much room for details. "Then maybe you should try to sleep." He smoothed his hand over her hair, liking the soft feel of it. "You're safe here."

Had she not been trying so desperately to shake the last vestiges of the unsettling dream, Amanda would have found the assurance in his quiet words remarkable. As it was, she simply accepted him at his word because she needed so badly to absorb the solid strength of his body and pretend, just for a while, that the odd sense of security she felt in his arms was real. She did feel safe now. Tomorrow she could go back to being on her own again.

"Thank you, Joe," she whispered.

"No thanks necessary," he whispered back and nudged her chin up with his finger.

He'd only meant to brush his lips over her forehead. He didn't know why he'd wanted to do that. It had just seemed right, somehow. But when he met her eyes, he forgot all about what he'd intended.

In the dim light, her eyes glistened with the tears she refused to shed. Not knowing what he would do if they did start to fall, he lowered his head to touch the corner of her eye with his lips. He felt her lashes flutter down, the sensation like butterfly wings against his cheek. Soft. Silken. Cupping her face in his hand, he kissed the corner of her other eye, catching the tear that lingered there.

Amanda wished he hadn't done that. She felt something squeeze inside her, testing her fragile control. She didn't move. She scarcely even breathed as he carried his caress to her temples, her cheek. It was almost as if he wanted to drink her tears so she wouldn't have to let them fall. Maybe he understood that she couldn't cry. If she were ever to start, all the feelings of loneliness and hurt she'd repressed for so long would come tumbling out and she'd be powerless to stop the flow. Yet she didn't feel that loneliness with Joe. Not now. Not with him holding her.

No one had ever been so tender with her before, so exquisitely gentle. He touched her as if she were made of crystal: something precious and incredibly fragile. Even if she hadn't been so badly in need of such care, she would have been moved by his tenderness. He very nearly brought the tears she'd never intended for him to see when he drew a line of kisses along her neck where her necklace had torn her tender flesh. Yet it wasn't tenderness she saw in his expression when he pulled back a moment later.

His eyes roamed her face, questioning. Even her name was a question, when she heard him whisper it. But she couldn't answer the raw hunger she saw darkening his eyes. Not verbally.

His lips touched hers. They felt firm and cool, and for the space of a half dozen heartbeats, they even felt gentle. But as she leaned into him, kissing him back, she heard his breathing alter. What had begun as tender, slowly turned into something far more urgent.

He pulled her closer with his arms, drew her deeper into the kiss with the languid strokes of his tongue. Longings she hadn't known she'd possessed rushed to the surface, freed by the tenderness but fueled by his hunger. In her disconcerted state, she hadn't considered anything beyond needing to be with him. She hadn't questioned why that was or what he might think of it. What she hadn't recalled was that security wasn't all she felt in his embrace. She had wanted this from the moment he'd stood in her hallway and he'd turned her insides to jelly with the touch of his finger to her throat. She wanted the sense of vitality he offered, the mystery and the recklessness. She felt alive when he touched her, and she hadn't realized until she'd met him that she had been slowly suffocating inside.

Her arms slid around his neck, her body uncurling to flow against his.

Lightning. The word slammed into Joe's consciousness the moment he felt her open to him. Swift, hot and devastating, the hunger ripped through his body, splintering all his good intentions. He'd only meant to comfort her, to ease the anxiety he felt responsible for having caused. Then he'd tasted her sweetness, breathed in her scent, and all he wanted was to feel her naked beneath his hands.

His hands moved along her sides. If she would even so much as hint that she wanted him to stop, he would. He probably should, even if she didn't say or do anything. But he forgot all about chivalry when his hand stilled on her back.

She wasn't wearing a bra. He could feel no telltale strap or band beneath his fingers. All that lay between her smooth skin and his hand was a thin layer of soft cotton. His heart hammering, he moved to cover her breast with his palm and gently squeezed the tender flesh. Beneath his palm, he could feel the nipple harden and grow.

Amanda swallowed a faint moan. Or maybe it was Joe who'd made that small, hungry sound as his mouth moved over hers. She had never denied the physical attraction between them. What she hadn't realized was how powerful it was, or how quickly the heat could escalate. She could feel her body softening, straining toward him. But the contact wasn't enough, so she lifted herself back, encouraging him to slip beneath her shirt so she could feel his hands on her.

Sweet heaven, Joe thought, the wonder in the words as close to a prayer as he'd come in years. She wants this. She wants me to touch her.

With her shirt pulled up, he teased her bare breast with his fingers, greedily drinking in her soft sigh. He knew better than to want this woman, yet he wanted her with a passion that had him close to pain. All he had to do was strip off the shirt and the satiny underpants covering her delightfully round bottom and he could touch every inch of her. Any way she wanted. She seemed so desperate for him.

Desperate.

The groan escaping Joe's lips wasn't one of pleasure. It would almost have been easier to cut off his hand than it was to pull away from her just then. He wanted her that badly. But he felt sure he knew what was driving her desperation, and he couldn't take advantage of her distress. She was alone and frightened, and she'd turned to him for comfort.

He'd told her she'd be safe.

With great reluctance he drew his hands from beneath the shirt. Hoping to calm her, and himself in the process, he stroked her back as he smoothed the worn cotton over her hips. He couldn't leave her alone. Yet, to lie with her...

"Easy, honey," he whispered when, sensing his withdrawal, she started to pull away herself. "Just let me hold you. Okay?"

He felt her hesitate, but when he tucked her against his side, careful to avoid bumping her injured arm, she seemed to relax again.

He hoped she could sleep. It was doubtful that he would.

According to the digital clock on Joe's nightstand, it was eight-seventeen when Amanda awoke. She stared at the clock, then at the beige elastic bandage on her wrist when she raised her arm to push her bangs from her forehead. She closed her eyes with a quiet groan. The events of yesterday afternoon came back in a rush. But it was the memory of the early hours of the morning that brought the knot of anxiety to her empty stomach.

She was alone in the huge bed, a circumstance for which she felt enormously grateful as she slipped from beneath the sheets and headed into the bathroom. Through the six-inch gap of the bedroom door, she could smell the tantalizing aroma of fresh coffee. She could also hear Joe talking on the phone out in the other room. He'd obviously been up for a while.

When she turned on the light in the bathroom, she realized he'd been up longer than she'd thought. Traces of steam from his shower still clung to the edges of the mirror, and the air held the scent of his soap. She would have killed for a hot shower herself. She wasn't supposed to get the bandage on her forehead wet, though, and she didn't know if she was supposed to unwrap her arm. It would also be nice if her fairy godmother would show up and zap her up something to wear.

Lacking the fairy godmother, she entered Joe's living room several minutes later still wearing his white T-shirt. He was still on the telephone.

He stood at the window, wearing jeans and a pale yellow polo shirt. His broad back was to her while he instructed whoever was on the other end of the portable phone to cancel his morning appointments. He didn't move as he spoke, his focus seeming to be fixed somewhere in the distance of his panoramic view beyond the city. There had been a time when she would have expected him to be pacing by now, using the motion to relieve the enormous energies he possessed. But she was coming to know that Joe wasn't given to revealing what was going on inside him with typical outward behavior. His deceptively relaxed stance meant nothing. Even from here she could sense the tension in him.

The expression about still waters running deep came to mind. The more she discovered about him, the less she actually knew.

Her bare feet were silent on the carpet as she stepped closer. As he ended his call, she moved toward the large

U-shaped white sofa in the center of the area. Other than a chrome and glass coffee table in front of it, the sofa was the only piece of furniture in the room. As did the solitary piece of furniture in his bedroom, the sofa faced the windows.

She could understand the appeal of the lovely open views beyond those windows. It was why he chose to surround himself with such sterility, such . . . coldness . . . that she was trying to comprehend when he realized she was there.

She saw him lower the phone to his side. Hesitating a moment, as if sensing her presence, he turned around.

His glance was sharp, encompassing and brief. Sounding preoccupied, he mumbled, "'Morning," and set the phone atop a stack of magazines on the table. "I'll get you some coffee."

"I can get it. Go ahead and finish what you're doing."

"All I'm doing now is waiting for my secretary to call me back. It'll be a few minutes."

Joe stood in front of her, his hands on his hips. Up close he didn't look quite as indifferent as he was acting. "Your jaw looks a little better. It's starting to scab over. How did you sleep?"

Charming compliment, she thought and crossed her arms when she saw his glance drop to her breasts. She was wearing her bra now, but the quick heat in his eyes was a potent reminder of last night when he'd discovered she wasn't.

"I'd have slept better if you hadn't kept waking me up to check my eyes."

Heat dissipated to bland innocence. "I only woke you twice."

She remembered. She remembered, too, how apologetic he'd been and how he'd pulled her back into his arms after he'd made sure she was all right and told her to go back to sleep. Sleep had come easily then, lulled as she was by an unfamiliar feeling of absolute security.

Her smile came softly. Whether he knew it or not—or, perhaps whether or not he'd admit it—Joe was really very good at taking care of people. He kept a definite distance between himself and his charges, his emotional involvements to a minimum. She was certain he was doing the same with her. Yet last night he had taken care of her with little regard for himself, protecting her even from herself when she had allowed her need for his solid strength to overcome her own defenses.

From behind them came the muffled gurgle of the coffeepot, the only sound in the suddenly silent room. Neither one of them had moved. Neither had said anything beyond the small attempt to overlook the fact that a few short hours ago they had been in each other's arms. With no effort at all, she could easily recall the feel of his big hands moving over her body. From the slow flare of his nostrils as his glance moved to her mouth, she knew he, too, was thinking about what had nearly happened in his bed.

"Thank you," she heard herself say. "For everything you did for me last night."

She'd wanted to ease the strain. From the way the muscle in his jaw jumped, she realized she'd only made the tension worse.

"You don't owe me any thanks."

"Of course I do. You . . ."

"You wouldn't have needed any help if it hadn't been for me. If I hadn't gotten you involved in the shelter, you wouldn't have been down there to begin with."

"You didn't get me involved. All you did was show me the place."

"Same thing."

Her chin came up, her eyes narrowing. Not in irritation. Out of curiosity.

"You don't need to feel guilty on my account, Joe. I take full responsibility for my actions. All of them. It's not necessary to blame anyone. Especially yourself."

She might as well have been talking to a tree. "Do you want that coffee or not?" he asked, then left her staring at his back while he walked around the long and shining black counter that separated the living room from the kitchen.

It was as clear as the kitchen's glass table, on which he set a heavy blue mug, that Joe was going to blame himself for her being hurt, whether or not she was willing to accept his conclusion. That being the case, it followed that everything he'd done for her since last night had been an attempt to make up for it. As unnecessary as she felt it was for him to make any sort of amends, Amanda was too grateful for his help in keeping the incident quiet to push the matter any further.

"I'm glad you took me to Matthew's House," she told him, needing him to know that. "I'd never have met Lucy and LaVonne, if you hadn't. Or Sister Bernie, either." Assuming that her mug was the one he'd set on the table, she picked it up to savor the richly scented steam. "She's a very interesting woman. Not at all the way I'd have expected a nun to be."

Joe, his denim-clad legs stretched out in front of him, leaned against the counter. He didn't take her bait. Instead of commenting, he simply watched her sit down while he took a swallow of coffee and waited for her to explain what she meant.

"I realize that nuns don't usually dress in habits anymore. So it's not her jeans and sweatshirts. I think it's her attitude. She seems so...earthy sometimes."

Her cup between her hands, elbows propped on the unadorned table, she glanced idly over the rim of her mug. There were no windows in the kitchen, but the overhead lights were as bright as day. That light caught the touches of silver at his temples.

"Where did you meet her?"

Joe'd had the feeling the question was coming. Amanda had asked it before, after all. When she asked that last time, he'd hedged, unwilling to share what couldn't possibly matter to anyone but him and, maybe, if she even thought about it anymore, to Bernie.

He glanced toward the phone, wishing it would ring. He knew it would be a while before Doris could get his calendar juggled, though. No reprieve in the offing, he contemplated the contents of his mug.

"I used to live with her. When we were kids," he told her, figuring he owed Amanda that much, anyway.

"Here? In Atlanta?"

"In a place called Kettletown." He tipped the mug sideways, watching the black liquid rise toward the edge. "It doesn't exist anymore. It was torn down during a renovation. The area is called Ardmore now."

Ardmore was a bedroom community east of Atlanta. It had been a prototype for dozens of other communities that had sprung up around the state in the past twenty years. Amanda knew that only because she'd heard her father compare his own project to Ardmore as being of that same scope and purpose.

Amanda felt herself go still.

Joe wasn't looking at her. He was staring at his cup, his head bent and his jaw working.

It was with a certain hesitation that she ventured the question she had to ask. "Were you living there when they decided to tear it all down?"

"If by 'they' you mean the politicians who were bought by the contractor who saw the project as his ticket to retirement, then, yeah. We were living there."

His voice was quiet. Still, the bitterness was evident. Deep, lingering and, to Amanda, almost tangible.

"We?" she gently coaxed. "You and Bernie?"

"My mom and dad and me. Dad owned a grocery store. It was nothing but a little hole in the wall, but the old guys would sit around and play checkers..."

He cut himself off, frowning at the memory. Or maybe the frown was the result of having recalled that particular detail. "It had been his father's," Joe went on. "I suppose he expected it to be mine, though we never talked about it. But they gave him a couple thousand dollars for the business and our apartment over it and bulldozed the block." He made a sound that was half laugh, half disgust. "Hell, they bulldozed the whole damn neighborhood."

Chapter Nine

Amanda hadn't noticed the faint hum of the refrigerator. Nor had she paid any particular attention to the gurgle and hiss of the coffeepot. Now, waiting for Joe to decide whether or not he wanted to say anything more, the sounds seemed to echo in the sudden stillness of the room.

She slowly lowered her cup to the table, careful to keep the heavy ceramic from knocking against the glass top. Joe hadn't moved. Leaning against the counter, he stared into his cup as if the secrets of the universe were written on the bottom. His thoughts seemed to carry him back, away from her and into the place where he locked the darker feelings and emotions that kept him at such a distance from the people who wanted to care about him. If she said the wrong thing, asked the wrong question, he might offer nothing more. His jaw had clenched so tightly she thought his back teeth might shatter.

When his silence turned brooding, she decided she had little to lose. It seemed safest, though, to shift the focus back to his friend.

"Did Bernie's family lose everything, too?"

Joe shook his head. "Her dad worked in the mill, so he still had his job. They moved before the demolition started."

"And you went to live with them?"

He'd yet to look at her. "Not exactly."

He drew a deep, nostril-flaring breath. Then, as if coming to some sort of decision, he slowly let it out. "I moved in with them after my dad drank himself to death. Matt McPherson had been a friend of his. I didn't have anywhere else to go, so he took me home after the funeral."

"You didn't stay with your mother?"

"She'd moved out to California by then to live with her sister. I could have gone with her. She wanted me to," he added, because that was important to him now. "But I'd gotten the idea in my head that she was betraying Dad by leaving him, and wouldn't go. I didn't realize at the time that she'd gotten to the point where she just didn't know how to deal with him anymore. Dad wouldn't leave the apartment even after they'd condemned the building. He'd just sit there with his bottle."

Letting everything crumble around him, he could have said, but just the thought made his stomach clench. Joe's father hadn't been the only man to ever lose his dreams. But he was the only man Joe knew who'd let his wife walk out and left his son to be taken in by strangers because he was too weak to put up a fight. "You might say he stuck it out to the bitter end."

He looked up then, braced for her reaction to his less than illustrious background. He didn't know why he'd said as much as he had. Or why he felt it important that she know. Maybe it was because he didn't want her thinking he was something he wasn't, or that his lineage or past could stand up to any sort of scrutiny. He didn't think she would judge him as others might; hold him personally accountable, somehow, for his being born into a place one step away from the slums. From her refusal to believe what she'd first heard about his motives for helping the shelter, he already knew that she made her own decisions about people. But she was as much a product of her environment and upbringing as he had been. As he had felt the obligation to stay with his father, she obviously felt obligated to conform for her parents—to the point where, just last night, she wouldn't have sought medical help for herself for fear of upsetting her father's political applecart. That same sense of obligation would certainly preclude personal involvement with someone who'd once had to steal bread because his father had drunk away all the money.

There were some things he'd never even told the McPhersons.

He shook off his last thought, assuring himself that involvement with Amanda wasn't something he wanted, anyway. He only had to look at her to be reminded of how much power men like her father had over people's lives. It was just a pity he was suffocating his own daughter.

Defensiveness had slipped over Joe's expression like a shadow. Amanda watched the change, fascinated by what it revealed. As he had spoken, his tone had been matter-of-fact, his features completely without emotion. Some people, those who bought the reputation he'd cultivated, might believe he'd felt no regret or pain at his losses. But Amanda knew how easy it was to hide what you wanted no one to see. At least—as she was learning—from anyone who wasn't also an expert.

She'd heard far more than he'd said. Too much to let him lapse into silence now.

"How old were you when all this happened?"

"Fifteen." Joe shrugged. "Maybe sixteen."

That was awfully young to accept responsibility for an alcoholic parent. "Did Mr. McPherson make you go back to school?"

"How'd you know I'd dropped out?" His frown was swift. "Did Bernie say anything to you about any of this?"

"No, she didn't. Not about what you just told me." Not specifically, anyway. "She did say you're the reason they have the day school, and that calling the shelter Matthew's House was your idea. She never said why, though."

Now, the reason was easy to see. Matthew McPherson had taken him in when he'd had nowhere else to go. Just like the women Bernie helped. Compassion obviously ran in the family.

"It seemed appropriate," Joe confirmed. "He and his wife had hardly anything themselves, but they were always taking in strays." The place had seemed like a halfway house for the homeless, the helpless and the hopeless. "They already had seven kids of their own, plus a couple of foster children. Between all the people and the stray animals Bernie and her brothers kept bringing home, living with them was like living in a zoo."

Those memories were obviously better than the others he'd shared. At least, it seemed so to Amanda. She could still sense the tension in him, but his scowl had softened with the recollections. As self-contained as Joe was, she didn't doubt that he'd just as soon leave most of his past buried. But a person couldn't ignore something that had come to affect every day of his life.

"This is why you were so angry at the dedication, isn't it." It wasn't a question. She could still hear his ire when he'd referred to her father's arrogant disregard for people. "You were seeing it all happen again with the shelter."

The sharp sound of his mug set firmly on the counter was his first response to her statements. Crossing his arms, the gesture seeming to deliberately close her out, he pinned her with a cool, dismissing glare. "I was angry because your father wouldn't listen to a reasonable request. Not that any of it matters now. With only two weeks to go and not a prospective property in sight, there's nothing to do but hope those prayers of Bernie's work. Just don't be like her and try to psychoanalyze what I do. Okay? She drives me crazy with that crap. The only reason I do what I do is because somebody has to."

The glance he shot at his watch held exasperation. With her or with himself she wasn't sure. What she was sure of was that his reasons for doing what he did ran far deeper than what he was willing to explore. He might not want to think about it, or have anyone else point it out, but a person didn't have to possess a degree in psychology to understand at least part of what Joe was doing. There was much about this complex man that he protected too closely to trust anyone with. Maybe he didn't even trust himself to face whatever it was that truly drove him. But he'd let Amanda glimpse enough for her to understand that the shelter and school were ways of fighting a past that wouldn't let go. Having escaped the slums, he was determined never again to want. That he didn't want anyone else to go without, either, was more evident than he probably realized.

Her chair leg scraped against the gray tiled floor as she left the table to carry her coffee cup to the sink. She could feel Joe's eyes following her, though he didn't move from where he still lounged against the long counter.

"You know," she began, turning to face the barrier of his crossed arms. He'd once said she made it hard for people to know her. All he did was make it hard for people to get close. "I've met a lot of people. I've even been impressed with a few. But I've never met anyone like you."

She was always so careful of her every move. Now, suddenly tired of having to be so guarded, she didn't even think about what she was doing. Curling her fingers over his forearm, she raised on tiptoe to brush her lips over his cheek. He smelled of shaving cream and soap, and his skin felt warm to her touch. Inside, though, down deep in his soul, she had the feeling he felt very, very cold. "I think you're a very special man, Joseph Slaighter."

She pulled back then, feeling a little self-conscious because he wasn't doing anything but staring at her. "I just wanted you to know that."

It was impossible to tell what thought brought the swift flash of pain to his eyes in the moments before his expression grew shuttered. But there was no mistaking the source of his relief when he pushed himself away from the counter and from her a few scant seconds later.

She didn't think she'd ever seen anyone seem so grateful to hear the telephone ring.

* * *

Joe's call didn't take long. Neither did the one she made to a locksmith who finally showed up at her house a little before noon. Joe, taking over as he seemed so adept at doing, stayed with the man while he went through his huge ring of keys searching for a master to fit her lock, while Amanda sat in the seclusion of her back porch to avoid treating any of her neighbors who might be home to the sight of her wearing little more than a man's T-shirt. The locksmith had been curious enough about her appearance as it was.

Fortunately, despite his impolite and lingering stares, he hadn't recognized her. Amanda was as common a name as Jones, and unless a person ran in certain circles, kept up with the private lives of politicians or read the society pages, he wouldn't be likely to know—or care—that she was the governor's daughter. As far as he was concerned, the Amanda Jones who'd called for his services because muggers had taken her purse, was just another citizen who'd gotten up close and personal with one of the hazards of living in a big city. With her purse most likely emptied of its contents and residing in a dumpster somewhere, he hadn't even demanded identification to prove that the house's lock he was picking was hers. She proved that to his satisfaction by knowing the code to deactivate the security system when he finally got in. Once inside, however, she wasn't nearly as anxious as she should have been to get the shower she wanted so badly.

"Go on up," Joe told her when he saw her glance toward the mahogany staircase. "I'll stay down here and keep an eye on things. Do you have more than two doors leading outside? Or just a front and back?"

A door also led into the kitchen from the garage. It would need the lock changed, too. She started to show him where it was, the locksmith following as though he, too, didn't question who seemed to be in charge here. But Joe told her they'd find it and turned away with the same preoccupied look he'd been wearing ever since they'd left his place. The two of them hadn't said three words in the past couple of hours that hadn't been limited to whatever needed to be done next.

To Amanda, Joe's slightly brusque and businesslike manner made it seem almost as if what had happened between them last night hadn't happened at all. Or worse, that he regretted that it had—and was bound and determined to see that it didn't happen again.

Not dealing as well as she'd have liked with that thought, Amanda followed the men into the kitchen, anyway, to arm herself with plastic wrap and a plastic bag to protect what she wasn't supposed to get wet. Politely telling them that she wouldn't be long, she breezed by without so much as a glance, then headed up the stairs. She needed to create a little distance of her own. Make the attempt, anyway. As intrigued as she was with Joe, she was actually a little afraid of what she was beginning to feel for him, of how strongly she was attracted to the elements of tenderness he hid from nearly everyone else. She just wasn't very adept at letting go once she started to care.

She could certainly conceal her feelings, though. Heaven knew she'd had enough practice doing that. Or so she reminded herself in the moments before she switched gears to the worry that had been nagging at her for the past eighteen hours. She still had to keep her parents from finding out what had happened to her.

That thought was still on her mind forty minutes later, when, feeling more human, she stepped over the cans of stain and wood refinishing supplies still stacked near the top banister and headed down the stairs. Rounding the landing, she could see Joe inside the French doors that separated her entry from the living room. He was just hanging up the telephone when her bare feet hit the polished hardwood floor in the sun-filled space.

Seeing her, he folded the note paper on which he'd been writing and stuffed it in his pocket. A moment later his large frame filled the doorway. "I needed to make a couple of calls," he said, crossing his arms over his broad chest. "I hope you don't mind. The locksmith just finished," he went on before she had a chance to say a word. "He went out to his van to write up your bill."

Through the oval window on her door, Amanda could see the white van with a red key on its side panel parked at the curb. The man in the gray uniform was already coming back up her walk.

With her checkbook gone, she'd brought down a check from her desk in her bedroom. She still had to call the bank, along with a number of other places, to replace the contents of her wallet. But she could do that after Joe had gone. Now she filled in the check after the locksmith presented her with his bill, thanked him for coming so quickly and tried not to feel self-conscious when, new keys in hand, she closed the door and turned to find Joe still watching her.

"Some lady called," he said, his glance quietly approving as it skimmed the coral camp shirt she'd tucked into white cotton slacks. "She's coming over."

"You answered my phone?"

His frown was as swift as hers had been. "No, I didn't answer your phone. Your answering machine got it. I was standing right there, so I couldn't help but overhear." Having assured her that he hadn't overstepped himself, the scowl faded. "I just thought you'd like to know you were going to have company."

Amanda didn't have time to consider that Joe didn't seem to be in any hurry to leave. Her only thought was that company was the last thing she needed. With her hair freshly shampooed and the subtle touches of makeup she wore making her look more like herself, she still appeared to have been on the losing end of a fight.

Please, God, don't let it be my mother.

Refusing to feel like she was twelve years old, she told herself not to panic. "Do you remember who it was? Or what she said?"

The panic was there, anyway. If not in her voice, definitely in her eyes. Seeing it, Joe stepped aside so she could get by him. "It's on the machine."

The call he'd referred to wasn't the only one she'd received. According to the glowing green number of the digital message counter, four other calls had come in since she'd hurried out so unsuspectingly yesterday afternoon.

Dreading the thought that her parents might have somehow discovered what had happened, and that one—or all—of the calls were from one of them, Amanda pushed the bar labeled Play Messages.

The machine whirred and clicked, then played back a voice that plunged Amanda's heart straight to her stomach

To Joe, she simply went pale.

"Amanda," came the deceptively soft Georgian drawl of her mother's voice. "The Garden Society is sponsoring a tea on the twenty-seventh. It would be nice if you could attend with me. Your father is putting in an appearance at the Arts thing in Savannah this weekend and I'm going with him, so call Faith to RSVP. By the way, you never have gotten back to her about the Old Capital Celebration dinner. Jason has sent regrets, so we won't have a problem with people watching to see how you two handle being at the same function. He's been dating Senator Whitney's daughter for a couple of months now, you know. I'm sure he'd have brought her. Call me next week."

Amanda hadn't known about Jason's latest target. But the knowledge that he'd already found someone else, and her mother's typically insensitive way of breaking the news, wasn't what made her knees a little weak. What caused her to sink to the antique chair by her cherry-wood phone desk was simply relief that her mother hadn't been calling to castigate her.

Yet.

The machine emitted an electronic beep and the second message began.

"Ah, Ms. Jones? This is Cliff at the Art Store. The fixative you ordered is in."

Another beep sounded. It was followed by a hang-up, and another message.

"Amanda, honey," came a voice as sweet as sorghum. "It's Trudy. You haven't been answering, so you must be working. You know what they say about all work and no play, especially for someone who doesn't have to work to begin with. I've got to be over your way this afternoon, and I'm determined to drag you to lunch. No excuses."

"That's the one."

Amanda groaned. Then, the panic she'd put on hold hit in earnest. Trudy Wingate-Anspaugh had a mouth like a megaphone.

"I can't be here when she shows up. She'll take one look at me and call everybody she knows."

"Nice friend."

"She's nobody's friend. She's just one of those people who likes being able to tell everyone she knows you and being the first with the gossip."

Joe, appreciating her consternation with this little complication, lowered himself to the blue and white print sofa a few steps away. Sitting at the phone desk, worrying her bottom lip while she looked from the pastel painting behind him to the lilacs on her coffee table and then to the everpresent smudges on the fingers of her left hand, it was obvious she was searching for some sort of solution. And coming up empty.

"Have you thought about going away for a few days? It might not be a bad idea. At least until that heals."

Her bangs covered most of the white bandage on her forehead, and the angry red line where her necklace had been torn away was concealed by the upturned collar of her shirt. There was no way to camouflage the sore-looking scrape along her right jaw, though. Rather than touching the soft skin below it, as he could do if he were to lean over and reach out, he merely nodded toward it.

"Maybe if I don't answer the door..."

"Or the phone? Or set foot outside for a week? That's what it would be like if you tried to hide out here."

Considering how little she appreciated him pointing out what she'd already considered while staring at her jaw in the mirror, her expression was quite tolerant. "I'd definitely prefer leaving for a while. It wouldn't even be that inconvenient." Murdock's could send over whatever they wanted her to illustrate for their next campaign instead of her attending the publicity meeting to pick it up. The only other appointment she had next week was to deliver brochure mock-ups to Joanie. Those, she could mail.

"But I have one small problem." She held up her right arm with its beige elastic bandage wrapped from knuckle to mid-forearm. "My car's a stick shift."

Joe looked from her arm to her, then pushed his fingers through his hair.

"I'd been thinking how lucky I am that it wasn't my left arm that I'd hurt. I can still work and do everything else. I just can't drive anywhere." Which eliminated any number of places she couldn't leave the house to go to anyway; such as the grocery store.

From the straining smile curving her mouth—the mouth that had so eagerly sought his last night—he felt certain she didn't want to ask for his help. Knowing her as he was coming to, she probably wouldn't ask even if she choked on the question. He would concede that he deserved her reticence. That wasn't easy for him to do, but it did help him appreciate Bernie's truly saintlike patience in putting up with *him* all these years. When someone got close, he clammed up. But Amanda had gotten far closer than he'd ever intended, and he'd all but bolted from her touch. She hadn't deserved that. Some defense mechanisms just worked better than others.

Some, he'd discovered, weren't working at all.

He had few defenses against her smile; especially when it was bright like the sunshine she seemed to invite into every room in her house. That healing warmth was missing now, though. The smile hovering on her lips was too dispirited to convince him that she wasn't desperate to keep her parents from finding out what had happened.

It was amazing how easy it was becoming to read her.

"If you could drive, where would you go?"

"I can't drive, so I don't know that it much matters."

"Just humor me. Okay?"

She wasn't sure she wanted to. Though she was far from ostentatious in her tastes, all the man had to do was look around to know that she wasn't hurting financially. And she could choke Trudy by her perfectly matched pearls for that crack she'd left on her answering machine about her not having to work. The trust fund her family had established for Amanda was certainly sizable, but money didn't make a person feel useful.

It didn't make *her* feel useful, anyway. But as she considered whether he'd be put off by her family's wealth if she mentioned their getaway places, she was struck by the opposite side of that thought. It was quite possible that, for someone who'd come by his affluence completely on his own, money could make him feel very useful indeed.

"I'd thought about our cottage on Jekyll Island," she finally decided to say. Joe had known all along what kind of family she came from. It was she who had to come to grips with the legacy left him by his. "Or our hunting lodge in Kentucky. I wouldn't know if mom and dad had already promised them out to someone without checking with Faith, though. And I really don't want to talk to her right now."

The name seemed familiar to him, no doubt because he'd heard it on her mother's message a few minutes ago. "Who's Faith?"

"My mother's secretary."

"You communicate with your mother through her secretary?"

"Most of the time." She felt horribly insignificant having to do that, but she'd become accustomed to it. Or so she'd convinced herself. "It's usually easier since she keeps Mom's calendar."

The legs of the coffee table had feet carved into animals claws. Joe contemplated the claw near his left foot, thinking as he did that he was hardly in a position to criticize maternal behavior. He'd had a mother who couldn't cope. Amanda had one she had to make an appointment to see.

If theirs were the norm, it was hard telling where advertisers came up with the moms in commercials who cared so much about their kids that they agonized over what brand of vitamins to feed them.

Preferring not to think about why he suddenly wondered what kind of mother Amanda would make, he let the matter go—along with his curiosity about another name her mother had mentioned. That of some guy named Jason.

"So forget the island and the lodge. Anywhere else?"

Those were the only places Amanda could have gone without having to give a name. Because she couldn't risk running into anyone who might mention her appearance to her family—or some overzealous member of the press—any place open to the public was out of the question, provided she could get a reservation on such short notice. Those circumstances effectively eliminated all the nearby resorts and rustic-but-fashionable retreats a single female like herself could escape to for a few days of R&R.

With a feeling Bernie would no doubt call "prophetic," Joe knew his intentions to put some distance between him and Amanda were about to become history. In fact, his plans took a one-hundred-and-eighty-degree turn.

"Look." He paused, waiting for a lightning bolt to hit him with some other inspiration. When several seconds passed and nothing else occurred to him, his breath escaped in a resigned rush. "I've got this place in the Blue Ridge Mountains. The cabin's not much. I'm sure it's nothing at all like you're accustomed to, but it's isolated and it's got a view that goes on for forever. You're welcome to use it. It's only a couple of hours' drive." He glanced at his watch, doing some quick mental calculations. "I'd have to run by my office first to pick up a file and drive by a place on the way out of town, but I could have you there by late afternoon."

The magazines on her coffee table suddenly didn't seem straight enough to suit her. She stood to fuss with them. After all the circumstances he'd seen her in, Joe thought it rather unique to see Amanda flustered now.

"That's really nice of you, Joe. But you don't have to do that."

"You don't like the mountains?"

"It's not that. I love the mountains." Having aligned the magazines with a square crystal vase of lilacs, she glanced over at him. Indecision played over her face as she quickly glanced away. It always made her uncomfortable when he watched her that way, as if he were trying to figure out what she was thinking. "It's just that I've inconvenienced you enough."

The clock in the hall chimed the hour, the deep sound reverberating through the silence. He could let it go now. If he had the brains God gave a goat, he would. He'd made the offer and she'd refused. He'd done the right thing.

Brains he had. It was this odd protectiveness he'd begun to feel toward her that kept screwing things up. Joe couldn't have cared less if the honorable governor and his wife found themselves disappointed or angered or whatever it was Amanda feared they would feel. Nothing he'd heard about them from Amanda had done a thing to improve their images in his mind. Because they mattered so much to Amanda, though, and because it was she who would bear the brunt of their reaction, he couldn't just walk away.

"Do it as a favor to me then," he said, and watched curiosity enter her warm brown eyes. "I've been looking for an excuse to get up there for weeks. I really should check on the place." That was the truth, too, though he'd all but given up hope on getting there this spring. "Aside from that," he pointed out mildly, "you have company coming soon. It might be a good idea if you were gone before she gets here."

There was one more argument Joe could have used. The lawyer in him probably hated quashing it, too. He'd admitted to himself having no qualms about using any means necessary to make a point, however lacking in scruples the means might be. But he deliberately refrained from mentioning that she was a tad short on alternatives to his offer at the moment—even though she knew darn well he was

thinking it as she hurried up the stairs to throw a few things
into the suitcase he then loaded into the trunk of his car. Her
large sketch pad and canvas bag went with them, too.

Since Joe had implied she could have the cabin to her
self, Amanda didn't ask if he was planning to stay tonight
She assumed he wasn't since they didn't stop at his apart
ment for clothes or his shaving kit on their way into town
They didn't stop on the way back, either, after she'd waited
for him in the car while he'd retrieved a thick file from an
efficient-looking woman in the plaza by his office building.

"One more stop," he told her when he slid back into the
comfortable sedan. "Get the map out of the glove box and
find the forty-four-hundred block of Sullivan, would you?"

At that location was a strip shopping center he wanted to
check out for a case he'd been asked to look into. Had he
asked Amanda's opinion of it when they finally found the
building along the four-lane street, she'd have been hard-
pressed to say anything positive about it. The little shopping area had definitely seen more prosperous days.

"I just wanted to look at it." His frown echoing what
Amanda had been too polite to say, he turned the corner for
another pass. The place was a pit. "There's a highway bypass proposed a few blocks over that's got the guy who owns
this pretty worried. He says that if it goes in, the reduced
traffic along here will kill the businesses, and his tenants will
have to close or move out. Looks to me like its dead already."

Of the ten storefronts forming an L around a semipaved
parking lot, only four of the spaces seemed to be occupied.
Judging from the three cars in the lot, presumably belong-
ing to whoever was working inside, even those businesses
weren't doing all that well. The tailor's shop had a closed
sign in the window, and the Sale sign in the vacuum and
sewing machine place was so faded it must have been there
for a year. Only the thrift store had any customers in it.

Driving around a speed bump to save his shocks, Joe
pulled into the lot and parked by a light pole obliterated by
neon-colored fliers announcing garage sales that had taken

place months ago and such diverse services as pet grooming and deep-muscle massage.

Reaching into the seat behind him, he grabbed a sheet of paper from the file Doris had met him with. He'd had a feeling that something wasn't quite kosher here. "He didn't say the restaurant had closed," he muttered to himself.

Amanda, caught contemplating the defunct serve-yourself buffet on the long end of the L, turned at the sound of his voice. "Pardon?" she said, thinking he'd spoken to her.

"Oh, it's nothing." Disgusted at having had his time wasted, Joe flipped the paper into the back seat and shifted the car into gear. "He just made it sound like there were a lot of jobs at stake. All I see here is his greed."

Amanda was confused. "I don't understand."

Joe did. Too well. Someone had thought he'd be gullible enough to take on something like this just because he had a reputation for fighting City Hall. He'd go to the wall for someone if they were getting a raw deal, but this guy was strictly an opportunist—like the jerks who screamed whiplash and went for a huge insurance claim when someone barely tapped their bumper. Joe may have lacked a few scruples himself, but he wasn't dishonest.

"It's cheaper to settle a case than to take it to court. The guy who owns this just saw an easy way to make a fast buck. That bypass isn't going to make any difference one way or another to these businesses. But if he can make it look as if it will and files suit, the city would probably make a monetary settlement for lost lease income. It would be worth it to them to settle for the nuisance value alone."

Gunning the engine, he pulled past the confetti-colored lamp pole to the street, hitting the speed bump this time. With his head turned away from her to watch the bus that slowed at the stop farther up the block, his tight "Not interested" was barely audible.

Amanda hadn't had to hear him say so to know he didn't want the case. Still, she wasn't at all certain she understood his reaction. He seemed awfully agitated for a legal matter she'd have thought he'd be fairly indifferent about.

Or maybe she understood more than she'd thought.

Joe's eyes were straight ahead, his hand deceivingly relaxed on the wheel as they left the tacky little strip center behind. As she considered his strong profile, she began to suspect that what had piqued his interest to begin with hadn't been the situation with the property, but the potential lost jobs.

"I thought you worked with the bigger corporations. Working on their regulation problems and lobbying for them. That sort of thing." That was more or less what Ruben had told her—and Joe himself had indirectly confirmed the day he'd first taken her to the shelter.

"I do."

"But you take smaller clients, too?"

He didn't so much as blink. "Never. The small ones can't afford me."

"Except for those you take for Bernie, you mean?"

His glance was brief, but it revealed a kind of indecision that looked very unfamiliar on him. Almost immediately, he turned his attention back to the trucks and cars honking at each other on the busy thoroughfare.

The beautiful weather made the traffic heavier than usual for early afternoon. Being Friday, everyone on the road seemed to be heading for the freeways out of the city, intent on getting a head start on the weekend. Yet Joe's preoccupation didn't seem to be with the other vehicles.

"I don't represent the people Bernie sends me," he finally said. "I refer them to firms more suited to handling their needs."

He'd chosen his wording carefully. But not carefully enough for someone who knew more about him than he was comfortable with. He might not represent those people himself, but Amanda would be willing to bet that he had something to do with taking care of the legal expenses they incurred. The same way he saw that the shelter's expenses where always somehow met.

In Rocky's case, he provided even more. He provided moral support, and someone for the boy to look up to. Knowing Joe, Amanda felt sure he would prefer to think of his taking the boy to and from his hearings as nothing more than providing transportation.

She'd never known anyone so intent on minimizing his own efforts. She kept that conclusion to herself. Having met with his withdrawal once today already, she wasn't anxious to do it again. Whatever truce they were operating under, she wanted to keep in place.

But she also wanted whatever information she could get. "I take it that the guy that owns that strip mall back there wasn't one of your corporate clients, then?"

His frown was swift. "Have you ever heard of attorney-client privilege?"

"Sure. But it doesn't sound like you want him for a client."

"There's still some confidentiality involved."

Amanda frowned, too. But there was a smile behind hers. "If you don't want to talk about this just say so."

"Fine. I don't want to talk about it."

"Could I ask you one more question first?"

Looking very much as if he knew she was going to ask, anyway, he muttered, "Go ahead."

"How much do you think he'd sell it for?"

"He doesn't have it up for sale."

"Come on, Joe. Everything's for sale if the price is right."

She was right. It bothered him, though, to hear that cynicism from her. "Why do you want to know?"

They had entered the freeway and were traveling on one of the huge ribbons of concrete that tied itself into a bow and sent them looping off in another direction. Headed north, they would soon have the city behind them. Now the urban sprawl stretched as far as the eye could see. Tucked in among the larger areas of progress, the nice neighborhoods and the beautiful parks, were pockets of poverty

Amanda had never noticed before, never let herself really think about. Before, it had never touched her.

"I think it might have some potential for Matthew's House."

"You're kidding."

She was dead serious.

So was he. "It would cost a fortune to convert a place like that. Even if the funds were available, it would still be impossible. The zoning's all wrong. That property is zoned commercial. That means 'nonresidential.' No one can live on the premises."

"I understand what nonresidential means."

He hadn't meant to insult her. "I'm sure you do," he conceded.

"Zoning can be changed."

"Not in a week. It would take that long to get an application filed. God only knows how long it would take after that. It could be months."

She heard the certainty of experience in his voice; saw its effect in the faint tightening of his mouth. From everything she'd heard from Bernie, no one had tried harder than Joe to find them a new place. At every turn there had been nothing but dead ends or red tape.

It was no wonder he got so frustrated.

"Amanda?"

At the quiet way he spoke her name, she glanced across the comfortable interior of the car.

"Thank you," he said.

The words surprised her. So did the faint smile that so briefly touched his hard mouth.

"For what?" She hadn't done anything but add to his concerns.

Or so she'd thought.

"For caring about what Bernie's doing. For trying to help. It's good to know somebody else is thinking about it."

The feeling his words and his fleeting smile gave her was rather nice. It helped take the edge off the faint tension that permeated the atmosphere whenever they were together. At least it did enough to make silence almost companionable when he turned the radio on low to get a traffic update.

They traveled that way for quite a while, without conversation. Joe apparently felt no need for it, and Amanda didn't want to interrupt whatever thoughts he used the time to ponder. As it was, she was preoccupied with thoughts of her own. She wasn't quite as prepared as Joe had been to dismiss the potential of that near-defunct strip mall. Zoning could indeed be a problem, but the property had a lot going for it—once a person started thinking about what all could be done.

So that was how Amanda occupied herself for the first several miles, finding it rather nice to be left alone with her own thoughts while she watched the scenery go by. Whenever she'd gone anywhere with Jason, he'd always needed to be talking about something; solving some crises or working out another battle plan for his campaign. Whenever they were on their way anywhere, he'd want her to tell him everything she knew about whomever they would see at whatever function they were attending. Then, armed with that information, he'd turn on the charm when introductions were finally made. Every trip was a planning session. It didn't matter if they were going across town for dinner or to the island for the weekend. The conversation always revolved around his wants, his dreams and his plans.

She found it rather ironic that she regarded it as something of a coup whenever she could get Joe to string six words together about himself.

It was a little after two when Joe pulled into a drive-through for hamburgers. Back on the freeway, they ate them in the car so as not to waste time getting to the mountains, not talking about much of anything other than how much easier it would be if they got there before dark. They would need to stop at the little grocery store at the fork on their way up, he told her. It closed around five o'clock and his cupboards were bare. There wasn't another place around for miles.

The land turned hilly and the roads were narrower, when they left the freeway and started to climb. Even out here, still miles from the tall pines and lakes, the population had grown thinner.

The silence had fallen again, feeling different this time. Thinking she might be concerned about the seclusion he'd mentioned, Joe reached over, touching her thigh to get her attention. The way she'd been staring out the window, made her seem a million miles away.

"You'll be okay up here," he wanted her to know. Not everyone liked this sort of isolation as much as he did. "The cabin's secure, in case you're worrying about it."

He withdrew his hand, looking as if he weren't sure he should have touched her. Unconsciously putting her own over where he'd brushed against the soft cotton, she smiled over at him. "I'm not worried. I was just thinking."

"About anything in particular?"

"Yeah." The smile grew mischievous, then wistful. "I was just thinking how much fun it would be to ride these roads on your motorcycle."

Chapter Ten

Joe wasn't sure why Amanda's comment about his motor-cycle made him grin. He wasn't sure, either, why he suddenly felt just a little bit freer than he had the moment before. Maybe the phenomenon had something to do with letting go a little; with thinking about this particular moment instead of spending his mental energy on what needed to be done in the next hour or day or month. All he knew for sure was that he felt better about having offered to bring her to his mountain.

At least he did until, having left paved roads after a quick trip up and down the three aisles of the tiny country store for supplies, he finally pulled to a stop at the end of a rutted and narrow dirt road.

They had come three miles into the forest, and the sun now touched the treetops to the west in a clear blue, nearly cloudless sky. His weathered cabin sat off to the left, all but obscured by the oak and pine edging up to a gently rippling lake. It was a moment before Amanda noticed the modest

little shelter. When she did, just as he cut the engine, she
went completely silent.

He thought he'd prepared her. He remembered telling her
in her living room that the accommodations probably
weren't what she was accustomed to. He knew he hadn't
specifically mentioned that there wasn't any running water,
or that the shower was a bucket and string suspended from
a convenient tree branch. But there was a well with the
sweetest water he'd ever tasted not twenty feet from his front
door, and she could warm it on the woodstove easily
enough. Whether or not she minded standing buck naked in
the wilderness to take that shower was something she'd have
to decide for herself. Personally, he'd never given it any
thought.

There was something else he hadn't mentioned when he'd
finally made the decision to offer his place. He wasn't comfortable with the words it would have taken to tell her, but
he wanted very much for her to be somewhere beautiful so
she could forget about all the ugliness he'd caused her to see.
To him, nothing was more beautiful than the sunrise re-
flecting off the lake outside his cabin's front door.

From her silence when she stepped from the car, the sharp
retort of the door slamming echoing off in the distance, it
looked to him as if he might have made a serious error in
judgment. There was no expression on her face as she
glanced from the small brown cabin to the lake. She simply
stood by the front bumper and stared.

Apparently, she didn't see the place as he did.

Actually, Amanda saw a lot more. As she listened to the
rustle of leaves nudged by the breeze and the gentle lap of
water against the stones lining the lake, she realized that this
was more than just a place for her to hide away for a while.
This was a place of solace and peace. An escape. And she
was touched to know Joe had trusted her enough to feel he
could share this private part of himself with her. He hadn't
had to tell her it even existed.

She turned to where he stood by his car door. Oddly, he
seemed braced for disapproval.

"Did you build your cabin?"

"Part of it." He glanced toward it himself, his familiar defenses in place. The building had been little more than a shell when he'd found it. "I warned you. It's pretty primitive."

"You didn't tell me it was all so pretty." There were leaves and pine needles beneath her feet, and the clean scent of pine filled the air. "This whole place is wonderful."

For a moment he looked as if he weren't sure he should believe her; as if, perhaps, she was only being polite. Then, seeing her smile as she turned full circle, he seemed to let go of whatever had made him seem so suddenly guarded.

"Aren't you going to show it to me?"

There wasn't much to show. Or so he said as he led her across the clearing, telling her to watch her footing on the damp leaves that covered the ground. Her white flats weren't at all practical here, but she hadn't taken the time to change before they'd left her house. She had tennis shoes in her suitcase, along with jeans and sweaters. The mountain air was cool; it would only grow chillier as the sun sank behind the trees.

Joe seemed to be considering that, too, as he stopped at a lean-to next to the cabin and lifted the corner of a large sheet of black plastic from a pile of stacked wood. Seeming pleased to find the wood dry, he cradled a quartered log in his left arm and singled out a key from his key ring with his right hand.

A moment later, he'd unlocked the cabin's very solid-looking oak door. He pushed it open with his foot as he pocketed his keys. It made an arthritic creak.

Amanda was right behind him, hugging her right arm with her left more to ward off the chill than to support the mildly aching sprain. She didn't enter when he did, though. She couldn't see anything inside but black. With heavy shutters covering all the windows, not a beam of light leaked in to reveal what lurked in the corners. The waning sunlight entering the open door provided only enough illumination for her to see that Joe had turned right.

She heard the logs hit something hard, the floor presumably, just before Joe called back to her.

"Storms can be pretty nasty up here," she heard him say, his footsteps moving closer. "With the exterior shutters locked in place, I don't have to worry about replacing windows. Helps keep vandals out, too. Not that it's ever been a problem."

Looking behind her, seeing nothing but the huge lake and the trees lining the other side, she appreciated the assurance. He'd told her the place was secure and she believed him. As solid as the shutters and door looked on the outside, she had the feeling nothing larger than an atom could get in once all the locks on them were thrown.

The door had only been opened partway. It stood at a forty-five degree angle from her spot on the threshold, so she couldn't see what Joe was doing. She could hear him, though, muttering something terse. The mild curse gave way to a dull clink. Seconds later, he edged past her with another set of keys in hand and proceeded to unlock the heavy outside shutters. Once that was done, he slipped past her again and disappeared into the darkness. Moments later, pale sunlight fell across a plank board floor.

Now that she could see, she stepped inside and turned to face a wood cookstove near a short butcherblock counter. It was the window over that counter Joe had opened and he was already working on the one near a small table with two chairs. When the slatted interior shutters there were opened, enough light streamed in to reveal the bright colors of the quilt atop a double bed in the far corner of the room. Midway down that same wall was a stone fireplace, faced by a deeply cushioned tweed sofa that served as a divider between the 'living area' and the other two thirds of the room. Storage cupboards covered most of the back wall.

Having been closed up all winter, the room smelled faintly of dampness and woodsmoke. A fire would help remove the dampness, and the fresh air rushing in as Joe opened the last two sets of shutters and raised the windows brought with it the clean scent of pine. There were no curtains to flutter on the paned windows, though. Nor was there the slightest hint of fuss about the decidedly rustic interior. The creature comforts were all there; the bed, the comfortable place to watch the fire, the kitchen and table on which to eat. He even had a bookshelf near the bed filled with the divergent works of Melville, Hemingway and Clancy. What Amanda didn't see in her cursory inspection of the cozy little room was any door other than the one still standing open.

He'd said primitive.

What he'd meant, she realized, noticing that there were no faucets on the sink in the kitchen counter, was that the place came equipped with an outhouse.

"There are a few things I need to show you." Brushing off his hands as he passed her, Joe headed to the floor-to-ceiling cabinets opposite the kitchen counter. "Have you ever done any camping before?"

She hadn't. And when she told him that, he didn't seem particularly surprised. On the other hand, she didn't feel particularly inclined to tell him that it hadn't been her fault that her parents hadn't sent her to summer camp as a child. Or that she'd never been interested in it in college as had some of her environmentalist acquaintances. Her trips to the mountains had been pretty much limited to ski resorts.

As he took matches and a lantern from the shelf, Joe didn't seem to care about her lack of experience. All he wanted to know was how much he would have to explain.

When he asked her to bring the red can from the bottom shelf, she said, "I think you'd better explain everything."

So he did, and Amanda learned how to fill and light a kerosene lantern and to leave a window cracked when it was burning so she didn't asphyxiate herself. She also learned that she could drink the water from the well but not from the stream sixty feet behind the cabin even though it was as clear as crystal. She wasn't to put garbage outside, unless she wanted nocturnal visitors. And the fish in the lake made an excellent breakfast—if she was inclined to try her hand at catching one with fishing gear in the tall cupboard. She also discovered that she was right about there being an out-

house, and found herself just as ambivalent about his out-
door shower when she learned about it.

Joe's instructions were clear and concise, his tone and
manner very much like a teacher intent on making sure she
understood for her own good, as well as the satisfaction of
knowing he'd done his best to give her the tools she needed.
She might have found his pedantic approach amusing, too,
had it not been so impersonal. The companionship they'd
managed on the drive up seemed to be vanishing with every
second, and by the time he'd completed his little seminar on
the pleasures and pitfalls of roughing it, he was treating her
as he might one of his clients. His manner was businesslike,
detached, polite and, to Amanda, as disheartening as it was
annoying.

As much as she disliked controversy, she'd rather they
were arguing. At least then, he'd have to react to her, and
she wouldn't feel as if she were just another problem he had
to take care of.

Not wanting to *be* a problem, Amanda carried in her
drawing supplies by herself and set them near the table. Her
suitcase already lay open on the bed. Since it hadn't gotten
any warmer in the great outdoors, she was tugging on her
oversize black sweater when she heard Joe come back in
with the two sacks of groceries.

He frowned at her canvas bag. "I told you I'd get your
things."

"And I told you it wasn't necessary for you to bring it all
in." Ruffling her hair with her fingers when her head
popped through the neck, she tugged the long hem of the
sweater over the seat of her pants and walked over to where
he'd leaned the sacks against each other on the counter.

Ignoring her reminder, as well as her for the moment, Joe
glanced at his watch. His brow furrowed as he tried to think
of something he might have forgotten to mention.

"I think that should do it. You have plenty of kindling,"
he said, indicating a large metal bucket by the woodstove.
"So you shouldn't have any trouble starting a fire. There's
newspaper..."

"Under the bed." Her smile took the rudeness from the interruption. "You told me. Twice."

"I just want to make sure I covered it all." He glanced at his watch again, the fire he'd built for her in the fireplace catching the strands of silver at his temples when he bent his head. He seemed anxious to go. Yet at the same time, reluctant. "You said you'd never been in the woods like this before."

"I'm looking at this as a delayed learning experience."

"Admirable attitude," he muttered. "But some things are better off not learned the hard way."

"I'm not going to blow anything up. Or burn anything down. I'll be okay. Really." He looked doubtful. But then, so was she. She wasn't intimidated with having to build fires and cook on a woodstove, although she definitely wasn't crazy with the plumbing situation, but being alone up here was another matter. She felt safe enough with the daylight—what was left of it, anyway. She just had the feeling nights could be very . . . dark.

"I'll be fine," she repeated.

She reiterated the assurance because of the way he looked at her. Not with the heart-stopping sensuality she'd caught in his eyes so often. But with a slow, measured scrutiny that weighed and compared as it moved from where her bandaged wrist peeked from the cuff of her sweater to where her bangs partially hid the bandage on her forehead.

"How does your head feel?"

It was just now twenty-four hours since she'd turned into the alley by Matthew's House. Amazingly, in Joe's company, she hadn't really thought about the attack since they'd left Atlanta.

She certainly didn't want to think about it now. "It feels fine. The headache's completely gone."

"What about your wrist?"

She shrugged. "It's okay, too. It only hurts if I try to move it."

"You'll be able to handle the well all right?"

If it hadn't been for the concern behind this little interrogation, Amanda might have become a little exasperated with it. Being self-sufficient and fairly resourceful, if not exactly experienced at this sort of thing, she had already assured him that she could carry wood one piece at a time if she had to. With two full cords of oak and hickory chopped and ready to burn, it wasn't like she'd have to handle an ax herself. As for bringing in water, she was sure she could pull the bucket up from the well—something he didn't seem inclined to accept until she attempted it just to show him.

The well was only a few feet beyond the cabin. Stone lined and looking much like the pictures she'd seen over the years of any other well, it had a crossbar and a rope with which to lower the bucket. Joe took the wooden lid off and propped it against the side.

"Go ahead." With his feet planted a foot apart and his arms crossed over his pale yellow shirt, he looked as immovable as the majestic trees rising behind him. "Drop it down and bring it back up. And don't let go of the rope."

She realized why he'd added that last instruction when the galvanized metal bucket went sailing down the dark hole and the rope raced after it. As deep as the well appeared to be from the splash that didn't come until three seconds later, if a person didn't hold on, the rope would follow the bucket all the way in. Both would be irretrievable.

Pulling the bucket back up wasn't quite the piece of cake Amanda had envisioned. While the two wraps of the rope around the crossbar helped ease its ascent, when full, the bucket felt as if it were filled with bricks.

Weight wasn't the only problem. She could pull the rope fine with her left hand, but she couldn't hold it with her right to get another grip with her left to pull again. Pinning the rope between her arm and her side to hold it didn't work either.

She'd noticed a full rain barrel behind the cabin. If she used that water to wash her hair, she'd only have to use well water for cooking and to wash up. As much as she'd been intrigued with the thought of Joe standing *au naturel* in the forest, she simply wasn't that uninhibited herself.

"I guess this isn't going to work," she finally conceded.

Joe said nothing. He simply raised the bucket with a disgustingly easy hand-over-hand motion and walked, dripping water all the way, through the cabin door with it. He returned a minute later, filled it two more times, disappearing inside in between, then returned to tie the bucket back on the rope and place the wooden lid back over the well.

"There were some gallon jars under the sink. I usually use them to store fish bait, but they'll hold enough water to keep you until I get back in a few days."

Her nose wrinkled. "Fish bait?"

"The jars were clean, Amanda. You won't taste anything."

She was relieved to hear that. She wasn't sure, though, how she felt about him leaving. She'd expected it all along. But hearing him say it filled her with so much disappointment she had to admit she'd hoped all along he'd really planned to stay.

The sun was gone now, turning the trees across the lake into stark black silhouettes against a fading twilight sky. It would be another hour before dusk turned to darkness. But the dense woods growing up to either side of the narrow and rutted road he had to drive would cut the dimming light long before then.

"I'll check on you Sunday."

Amanda nodded, not quite knowing what to say. "Thank you," seemed appropriate. "For everything."

It wasn't enough. There had to be more she could say for all the trouble he'd gone to for her. More needed to be said—and not only about how thoughtful it was of him to be sure she could take care of herself up here on his mountain. What needed to be voiced even went beyond how grateful she was to him for helping her keep peace with her parents. It had to do with him and with her; with what even now, standing an arm's length apart, they weren't allowing to be acknowledged.

Something was growing between them: a sort of friend-ship they couldn't quite get to because of walls Joe kept so firmly in place. Joe might be bent on denying it, but the at-traction they had for each other was very real. She could feel it now, stirring her blood as his guarded glance settled on her mouth. It stirred the very air around them, drawing them closer even as it kept them both rooted exactly where they stood.

The call of a bird settling in for the night joined the rus-tle of leaves. An owl hooted off in the distance, waking from its sleep. The sounds were lulling, peaceful, but Amanda was aware of little beyond Joe when his eyes locked on hers.

Don't go, she silently begged.

Honey, please. Don't ask me that.

I don't want you to leave.

You know I can't stay.

The gentle breeze picked up, ruffling her hair. He reached over to touch the silken strands, to smooth them against her temple. "Go on in," he told her, his voice quiet and oddly husky. "The fire could probably use another log by now. I'll see you in a couple of days."

His hand fell, curling into a fist as he stuffed it into his pocket. Not even conscious of her movement, Amanda touched the spot he had so lightly caressed, then turned be-fore he could tell her again that he had to go. He could stay if he wanted. It wasn't as if he needed an invitation from her. Or even her permission. He'd already made his deci-sion. Having reached out twice, and twice having been pushed away, she wouldn't embarrass herself by trying to change his mind.

A hollow ache had settled in her stomach when she reached the cabin door. It was closed to keep out the winged things the firelight and the lamp glowing on the table would attract. Her fingers tightened around the handle, but Amanda didn't open the door. Instead, she turned, think-ing she'd watch him walk to his car.

He hadn't moved toward his car. Instead, his long, sur-prisingly dispirited strides carried him toward the lake lap-ping at the stones forty yards away. He stopped at the shoreline, his powerful frame a dark silhouette as he scanned the twilight horizon. A full minute passed. And another. Then, when she began to wonder how long he would stand there without moving, she saw his hand come up to grip the back of the neck.

Slowly he shook his head.

Her hand fell from the latch. Joe had told her he'd been looking for an excuse to come here. At the time, she'd thought he'd said that simply to make it easier for her to accept his offer. She had the feeling now that he really had been hoping for some reason to come. Just wanting to get away from daily demands as everyone else occasionally did, apparently wasn't enough for a man as driven as he so often seemed to be. Now, watching the dejected bow of his noble head, Amanda realized just how badly he needed the revitalizing peace he found in this, his special place.

Her footsteps were soundless as she crossed the clearing. She had provided him with his excuse to be here, but her presence was making him leave before he could even begin to enjoy its serenity.

"Joe?"

She hadn't thought she'd startle him. Yet he jerked around at the sound of his name, his surprise fading quickly to an unreadable mask.

The air felt cooler by the water. Or maybe it was apprehension that made her shiver. Crossing her arms, her shoulder hunched against the cool breeze coming across the lake, she didn't wait for him to ask what she wanted.

"I was just thinking that if you didn't have to go back to Atlanta tonight, maybe you'd stay and have dinner with me. It's already almost dark, and it's got to be dangerous driving through the woods..."

The words trailed off when he shook his head. "I don't think that would be a very good idea, Amanda."

"You *want* to go, then?"

She knew. To put it that way, she had to. Joe cupped his hand over the back of his neck, working at the knotted muscles there. The thought of leaving, of going back to the noise of the city and the cool austerity of his apartment, had him feeling like a tightly wound spring.

"No, Amanda," he said, hoping to heaven he didn't sound as tense as he felt. "I don't want to go."

"Then, don't."

"It's not that simple."

"Do you have to be somewhere else tonight?"

"Not tonight."

"In the morning, then?"

"Lord, Amanda. What is this? Twenty questions?"

She stepped back, stung by his sudden vehemence. "I'm sorry." She should have known better. Every time she took a chance on him, she encountered another wall. "I only came out here because I thought you might not really want to leave. I just didn't want my being here to keep you from staying if that was what you wanted to do."

She turned then, anxious to thwart his chance to tell her she had no idea what he wanted, because that was what his darkening expression seemed to say. She needed to escape the disquieting sensation of tension surrounding him. She hated that she could so easily feel what he did; hated even more that she felt so helpless to do anything about it.

She left him standing on the darkened shore and hurried back to the cabin with its golden light glowing in the windows. The latch gave with a dull clank and she wasted no time closing herself inside the cozy warmth. The fire had burned lower, as Joe had said it had, so she went there to get a log from the stack he'd left beside the hearth. After that, she would make a sandwich or something and find a book to stare at. What Joe did was none of her concern.

She had a log in her hand when the door opened.

Closing out the draft of cool air swirling over the floor, Joe hesitated for a fraction of a second before covering the distance between them in four long strides. He didn't look angry. But he did look determined.

He took the log she held, whipped back the screen and put it in the glowing embers himself. After adding another log, he pulled the screen together again and rose to brush his hands off on the thighs of his jeans. It was then that he faced her.

"Amanda," he began, seeming to force his patience. "I'm trying my damnedest not to make your situation any worse. You're already worried about what will happen if someone finds out what happened last night. That's why you're here, remember? I don't think it will improve your position if someone discovers you spent the weekend up here with me. I'm not one of your father's favorite people."

Amanda couldn't acknowledge how protective Joe was being of her. At the mention of her father, a too-familiar resentment surged in her chest, blinding her to Joe's concern. Usually she could quash that resentment. Not now. Whether or not Joe came out and said it, the fact that her father was the governor—a man like those Joe had come to resent so much—still clouded how Joe felt about her. Equally as disturbing was the implication in his last words. The obligations of being the dutiful daughter were now dictating how she was to feel about him.

He was right in his conclusion. Her father had already warned her to stay away from him. Their association would, at best, raise any number of political eyebrows. As for her mother—the woman whose blood was as blue as the sapphires she preferred—she would no doubt pop a vein to discover that her daughter had made such an unholy alliance.

The events of the past twenty-four hours had affected her more than she'd realized. Her composure strained to the limit, Amanda still managed to sound quite calm when she met Joe's unblinking eyes.

"How you feel about my father, or how he feels about you, isn't anything I can control. It seems I can't control much of anything, including my own life. Not that I have one," she added with an unusual trace of acerbity. "Thank you for thinking of my reputation. God knows how important it is to everyone."

Impatience was replaced with confusion. Caught off guard by her sarcasm, Joe spread his hands at his sides. "I was under the impression that guarding your reputation was what we are trying to do. I thought it *was* important to you."

"This isn't about me," she shot back. "This is about everyone else I'm supposed to mean something to."

She turned from him then, knowing she should have just kept her mouth shut to begin with. She wasn't about to bleed her heart out about what it felt like to be used; to have no one need her for herself. There were people starving in the streets. Compared to that, what difference did it make that her most attractive quality seemed to be how she could make people look, or what her connections could do for them. Heaven knew those had been the reasons Jason had been attracted to her. As for Joe, her connection to her father was why he'd asked for her help in the first place.

The new logs Joe had put in the fireplace crackled and hissed as the flames found dried pitch. In the relative quiet, Joe's voice sounded deadly calm. "Who do you mean by everyone else?"

Upset, trying not to be because it was a waste of energy she didn't have, she missed the hesitation in his question. "At the moment," she replied, hugging her arms to her as she stared into the obscenely cheerful fire, "I mean my parents. You can't imagine how tired I am of having to consider how my actions reflect on someone else's image."

The fatigue she professed was evident in the defeat that settled across her slender shoulders. He'd never considered that she might not have a choice about what she did; or that what choices she had were so severely limited. Neither had it occurred to him that her life had been completely dominated by a role she hadn't chosen for herself—until the irony of their situations began wavering into focus.

He hadn't had much choice in his role, either. Thinking about that as he watched her shoulders rise with the deep breath she drew, it seemed to him that they had both been affected by the same forces—the wages wrought by political power, and parents too involved in themselves to see, or care, how they scarred their children. It had never occurred to him, either, that Amanda Jones, with her position of money, class and privilege might be as much a victim as he had been.

He didn't know what to say. He did know, however, that he wasn't going to let her parents dictate his actions. There was a downside to that determined resolution, however. It brought him face-to-face with the other reason he'd felt it imperative that he leave; the reason that had him feeling like a caged tiger.

Ever since last night, he hadn't been able to shake the memory of how she had fitted herself to him; how eagerly she had sought him. She had fit him so perfectly and had felt so incredibly good in his arms. Sex with her was something he wanted as much as his next breath, his next heartbeat. To be confined with her in the cabin and to keep his hands to himself would be pure, unadulterated torture.

"I really had thought it better if I go." He pushed his fingers through his hair, the breeze-blown locks falling straight back over his forehead. "You're making this damn difficult. You know it?"

"I'm not doing anything. What you do is your decision."

It wasn't petulance in her voice; it was weariness. Her eyes were still trained on the fire, or he might have seen it in her expression, too. Neither of them had slept very well last night.

"Look at me." He didn't wait for her to comply. With the tip of his finger he lifted her chin toward him. "What I do will be *our* decision. Okay? If you don't mind my staying, then I will. I don't *want* to go. I just want you to understand one thing."

"What's that?"

The muscle in his jaw jerked as he withdrew his hand. "There's only one bed."

"There's a sofa," she said flatly.

"With a bad spring dead center. There's no way I'm sleeping on that thing."

"You don't have to." At the smooth rise of his eyebrow, Amanda added, "if you want to stay, I'll sleep there."

"You obviously haven't sat on it."

The droll comment was accompanied by his hands settling on her shoulders. Turning her around, he backed her up to the middle of the sofa and gave a slight push.

The moment she landed on the defective cushion Joe leaned forward, bracing himself by planting his palms on the cushions on either side of her.

"Now tell me where you want to sleep."

Amanda's breath caught. Not just at what he'd done, but because his beautiful face was mere inches from hers. He was so close that she could see the firm definition of his lips and the tiny lines of fatigue etched into the corners of his eyes. Had it not been for the spring jabbing in her backside, she'd have felt bad about how tired he looked. She was the reason he'd had such a lousy night's sleep after all. But the spring he'd referred to was about the size of a tea saucer and felt like a pointed rock.

Growing more uncomfortable by the second, she glared at him. "Would you let me up, please?"

Joe straightened, probably not as quickly as he could have, and held out his hand. She grabbed it, pulling herself up a lot faster than she'd gone down, and gave him a look that made it clear the demonstration hadn't been necessary. Joe would have disagreed had she said anything about it. The hint of exasperation in her eyes went a long way to remove the defeat that had so disturbed him. He just didn't want to consider how good it made him feel to see that hint of her old spark.

"Well?" he asked, hands on his hips.

Somewhat begrudgingly, she muttered, "We'll work something out."

Joe didn't ask what that something might be. Nor was anything else said about whether or not he intended to stay. The assumption was simply there as Amanda walked off to put the groceries away.

Following a moment later, he decided to check the cupboards to see if he had a razor that wasn't rusted and a sweatsuit or something to go running in in the morning. Some things were simply better off not being verbalized, it seemed. He'd just take each moment as it came and deal with whatever came up when it became necessary. He wasn't accustomed to doing things that way, but with Amanda it seemed he didn't have a lot of choice. So, for now, he would try very hard to keep his mind off her body and the bed dominating the far corner of the room.

He found a package of disposable razors, but the real progress toward keeping his thoughts in line came when he spotted his fishing tackle box. The thing sounded like a metal box of marbles when he set it on the floor.

Startled by the sound, Amanda turned to see Joe now pulling out some sort of net. It didn't look to her as if he intended to waste time enjoying his mountain. What struck her most, though, as she watched his large hand wrap around a fishing pole and prop it against the wall, was that he would have given up this time for her.

"Joe?" A can of soup in hand, Amanda stopped beside the rectangular gray box he'd practically dropped on the floor. He had already turned back to the tall cupboard.

"Yeah?" came his mumbled reply.

"I want...I mean..."

She cleared her throat, needing to start over, to get the words right. She wanted to thank him again, and to apologize for the way she'd acted before. He had only tried to do what he'd thought was right, and she'd only been thinking of herself. But when he turned around, he had a smudge of something black on his nose, what looked like a little witches' cauldron in his hand and a very perplexed expression on his face.

"You want what?" he asked.

"Ah...to know if this is okay for dinner." She held up the soup, eyeing the little black pot as she did. As preoccupied as he looked, her apology would be wasted.

"Yeah, sure," came his disinterested reply.

She still eyed the cauldron he held by its handle. "What is that?"

"A lead pot."

"Okay," she conceded. "What is a lead pot for?"

"I use it to make sinkers."

Of course he did. "Sinkers?"

"They're things you tie on your fishing line for weight. If you don't use 'em, your hook just floats on the water."

"I take it that's bad?"

He saw the smile in her eyes, the one she seemed to be having some difficulty keeping from her mouth. "Since the fish are usually under the water, it helps if the hook is, too."

"I see." That much, truly, was clear. It was everything else that wasn't, particularly the reason for his scowl. "Is there a problem with this particular pot?"

"The problem," he said, setting the item under discussion on the floor so he could dig around some more, "is that I can't find my lead. I thought I had a couple of bars of it in here."

"Isn't that stuff poisonous?"

"Only if you eat it. I'm just going to melt it and pour it into molds. Damn it, I could have sworn . . ."

"You shouldn't swear."

At her droll tone, he glanced back at her. She had no idea what he'd been about to say. Whatever it was seemed forgotten when he saw her smile break free.

"What are you grinning at?" he wanted to know.

With her hand still wrapped around the soup, she pointed to his face. "You have a streak of black stuff from that pot on your nose. You look like a chimney sweep."

His glance darted to his hand. Sure enough, soot from the bottom of the pot was all over it.

"I guess you rubbed it," she observed as he took a deliberate step forward. "Your nose, I mean."

With him closer, she had to tip her head back to look up at him. He wasn't smiling, but there was a definite glimmer in his eyes. "I guess I did."

He knew he shouldn't do it. Playing with fire was always dangerous, but he'd never been able to resist her smile. The fact that she was teasing him made its effect on him that much harder to ignore. After the past twenty-four hours, seeing her happy made him feel ridiculously good himself.

It was only because he knew how hard soot was to get off that he didn't use the soot-covered hand. Using his clean one instead, he curved his hand over the back of her neck and gave her a gentle tug forward.

Amanda saw his head come down, blocking out the light behind him. His lips hovered a fraction of an inch over hers, his mouth curving. "I think you're going to have it on your nose, too," he whispered and proceeded to do a very thorough job of altering her breathing.

He also did a pretty good job of altering his own. But instead of deepening the kiss when she responded, he slowly eased away—and told her he'd open the soup if she couldn't manage the can opener herself.

It wasn't that Joe didn't want to kiss her again. Or even that he was hungry. For food, anyway. It was just that if he did, there was a very good chance they'd wind up on that bed long before either one of them planned on sleeping.

Chapter Eleven

Amanda opened her eyes, stunned and a little breathless when Joe lifted his head. The teasing was gone from his expression, replaced with a feral gleam that made his proud features stark and haunting.

His glance fell to her mouth.

Powerless to move, Amanda felt his hand ease from her neck. With the tip of his finger, he touched her lower lip. It was swollen and damp from his kiss, and if he'd looked into her eyes just then, he'd have seen that she wanted desperately for him to kiss her again. But his glance followed the light, incredibly sensual touch of his finger along her lower lip. Fascinated by its fullness, its texture, something like wonder swept his expression. It was almost as if he couldn't quite believe how easily she responded to him, or how stunned he was by his own response to her. Or maybe, as she saw his nostrils flare with his deeply drawn breath, what she saw was simply his formidable control being pulled back around him.

When he met her eyes again, his hand had fallen to his side.

He reached behind him, into the back pocket of his jeans, and handed her his handkerchief. "Sorry," he said, his husky voice rasping the length of her spine.

She didn't know if the apology was for the soot he'd apparently transferred to her face, or the fact that he'd kissed her. With his expression as closed as it had become, she didn't ask. He'd just changed the subject, anyway.

He'd nodded toward the can dangling limply in her hand.

"We can heat that on the grate in the fireplace. No need to start up the woodstove."

After telling her she'd find pans in the cabinet to the left of the sink, he turned his back to her. Staring at the smooth flexing of muscles beneath his yellow knit shirt, she watched him reach for the top shelf in the cupboard. Amanda didn't see what he was after. Terribly confused, and not at all accustomed to the feeling, she turned away, too.

It wasn't relief Joe felt when he heard the cabinet door close and a pan scrape the countertop. He told himself it was, though, and for the remainder of the evening, as they both tried to ignore the tension that grew as thick as the fog that sometimes obscured the mountains, he periodically reminded himself that, as uneasy as it was being with her, he needed to be here.

Amanda hadn't mentioned it, but he knew from the way she would tense when her hand inadvertently brushed the bandage on her forehead, or an unfamiliar ache in her body would catch her movements, that she hadn't yet had time to get over what had happened to her. She was a strong woman, and he hoped what she'd experienced yesterday would be behind her soon, but he shouldn't have even considered leaving her alone. Had he let himself think about it, he'd have realized sooner that she'd needed someone to be with her. He'd made it difficult for her to ask, though. Only when she'd realized how badly he'd needed to spend some time here, had she gathered her courage and asked if he wanted to stay—and not for herself, either. For him.

The least he could do was be here for her without taking advantage of the situation. She might have insisted that it wasn't her reputation they were protecting. But he knew otherwise. Amanda cared very much what people thought of her. She especially cared what her parents thought. If she didn't, she wouldn't have given up so much of herself trying to please them.

He made it as easy as he could for her that night. After they'd cleaned up their supper dishes and she'd helped him search every inch of cabinet space for the lead he never did find, he took off to sit by the darkened lake so she could change into a nightgown made of some sort of eyelet stuff that covered her from neck to ankles—then stayed up reading until long after she'd gone to sleep.

The sunrise he loved to watch had been obscured by the mist.

Joe sat on the bank, breathing hard. He'd walked the last quarter of a mile around the lake to cool down. But he'd pushed a little harder than usual this morning and his heart rate was taking its sweet time getting back to normal.

"Must be the altitude," he groaned, and flopped, arms out, onto his back.

It wasn't just the altitude. And he hadn't pushed just a little harder. When he'd eased out of bed this morning, daring the mattress to creak and wake Amanda, he'd been hell-bent on exhausting himself.

He'd awakened to find himself curled around her, her sweet little backside tucked against him. He'd started out on top of the blankets until the fire had burned down and the cold crept through the thin quilt he'd been covered with. Still dressed, it had seemed safe enough at the time to crawl under the blanket. But he had sought her in his sleep—and woke up as hard as a post.

That was why he'd all but run himself into the ground. Lying there with her pressed against him, it had been too easy to picture himself moving his hand up to cup the softness of her breasts. He could still hear the tiny moan she'd made when he'd touched her there before. Knowing she'd liked the feel of his palm over her, remembering how she'd eased back so he could tease her nipples, had nearly made him groan out loud. Thinking about it now he almost did it again.

Running hadn't helped at all. What he needed was a few dozen laps in the lake.

A trio of ducks wheeled overhead, searching for the tall rushes on the other side of the water. Joe decided to watch them instead before heading for the cabin and the coffee his body craved. No sense going back until he was sure Amanda had had time to dress. He knew she was up. He could tell that from the anemic thread of smoke tentatively escaping the chimney.

She'd never have made it as a Girl Scout.

Amanda came to that enlightened decision as she stood at the sink, her arms wrapped around herself while she shook her head at Joe's prone form. She had put on jeans, socks, tennis shoes, a camisole, a shirt and a sweater. She'd topped that off with a flannel jacket of Joe's that she'd found in the cabinet. All those clothes, and she was still freezing. Joe, on the other hand, appeared to be wearing nothing more than a sweatshirt and a pair of fleece running shorts and he was stretched out on the damp ground as if worshiping the sun. Only there was no sun this morning. A thick, gray mist hung above the lake, cutting off the view of the trees and blocking whatever warmth a little sunshine might provide.

Shivering, she looked back to the fireplace. The fire there looked pretty pathetic, but at least the log had finally caught. Sort of. Her first two attempts had done nothing but burn up the paper and the kindling. Now, if she could just get the coffee going.

She looked up from the blue speckled metal pot to see Joe sit up and lean back on his arms. She didn't know if he was doing what he normally did when he came here—if he was enjoying his solitude—or if he was only avoiding her. He hadn't wanted her to awaken when he'd left over an hour ago. That had been obvious from the way he'd so carefully lifted his arm from where it had draped over her waist and eased himself from her back.

What was obvious, too, was that Joe was bent on avoiding involvement. Not being into rejection, she should take the hint and forget him. Failing that, she should stop thinking about him and use her mental energy on something else—such as that strip mall they'd looked at yesterday. Thoughts of its use as a shelter had been nagging at her ever since she'd seen it. Maybe when Joe came in, she'd pump him for more information about it.

The water jugs sat at the end of the counter. Moving from the window, Amanda filled the pot, a task that would have been simpler without a sprained wrist, and found the can of coffee they'd bought yesterday back in the cabinet with jars of disgusting-looking orange fish eggs. She'd just measured in the grounds when the door groaned open. Even the hinges sounded cold this morning.

She turned to see Joe close the door and met his hesitation with her own. Joe looked immediately to the log smoldering in the fireplace. He didn't move to get it going again. Instead, he headed straight to the unlit woodstove.

"It's as cold in here as it is outside." Knees creaking as if to echo the complaint, he squatted down to open the metal door below the first two burners and shoved in a log and a few pieces of kindling. He raised back up for a match from the container on the wall. After striking the wooden match, he held the flame against a straw-sized piece of kindling until it caught. "I thought the smoke coming from the chimney looked pretty thin. Did you have trouble starting the fire?"

To her disgust, the fire he'd just started immediately caught. Within thirty seconds flames were dancing brightly, throwing their heat out into the chilly room—until he closed them off with the clank of the metal door.

"No," she drawled, trying to fit the lid back on the pot with the cuffs of the flannel jacket covering her knuckles. His tone had been expressionless, neutral. The way he apparently intended to treat her. "I wanted to conserve wood."

Her flip comment drew his frown. He could see she was having trouble. "What are you doing?"

"Making coffee."

The lid hit the counter, then bounced to the floor with a clatter.

She swore.

Joe's eyebrow arched. He'd never heard her do that before. "Get up on the wrong side of the bed?" he asked, swiping up the lid on his way over to her.

She needed coffee. She needed to be warm. She needed him to stop frowning at her. "I got up on the only side there was."

The pot sat on the counter behind her. Reaching around her, he snapped the lid in place. "The stove works best for this," he explained and set the pot on one of the back burners.

A moment later he turned back and reached for her uninjured arm. Without so much as a blink, he curled his fingers around her wrist and held up her hand. The sleeve dangled over the end of her fingers.

"Where did you find this?" he asked, referring to the red flannel jacket that all but swallowed her, as he rolled up the sleeve.

"In the cabinet. I hope you don't mind, but I was cold."

"It's no wonder you couldn't do anything."

"I was managing."

"Right." With the first sleeve rolled to her wrist, he took her other hand. He was gentler this time because he didn't want to hurt her, and in a few moments that sleeve had been rolled over the elastic bandage. "I can only imagine how you'd have managed it if I'd left you here alone. You'd have had a fire going by around noon, when you no longer needed it, and you'd have had coffee by suppertime." He glanced pointedly at the water puddle on the countertop. "Spilling water like that, you'd have probably run out by morning, too."

Though Joe's tone was droll, he smiled, partly in amusement, partly in admiration. Amanda hadn't complained about any of the inconveniences she'd encountered, including having to follow the beam of a flashlight to the outhouse in the cold and dark, and Joe felt a little ashamed that he'd once thought her so terribly spoiled. She was nothing like the woman he'd imagined her to be; the woman in the newspaper articles who always appeared just a little aloof as she attended society's functions; the woman whose own engagement party had rated a half-page spread of its own.

Amanda didn't see the smile. With her focus trained on one of the innumerable little holes time had worn into his college gym shirt, she heard only the criticism. Already thinking he wasn't too pleased with having to share his space, she decided now probably wasn't a good time to ask about the strip mall.

"It won't take long for the stove to heat up," she heard him say as he turned to fill a pan with water. "Coffee'll only take a few minutes when it does. It'll get too strong if you leave it on longer than ten minutes. Okay?"

Her quiet "Okay" was directed to his back. With the pan of water on the stove, he'd pulled out a skillet and a bowl. A carton of eggs from the cool locker in the floor was set on the table, along with a bag of hash browns that had only partially thawed.

"The water's yours to wash up with. I'll take care of that when I come back in," he told her, seeming to indicate the breakfast preparations as he picked up a towel and a bar of soap. A minute later, he'd disappeared out the door with the jeans he'd worn yesterday and another, equally holey sweatshirt.

Ten minutes later he was back, wearing the jeans and sweatshirt and rubbing his wet hair with the towel.

Amanda still stood where she had when he'd left. She hadn't been there the whole time he'd been gone, though. She'd washed with the blessedly warm water as soon as the steam had started rising from it, and found herself feeling a little more human. The transformation would be complete once she had her coffee. Its rich scent filled the room, but the brew wasn't ready yet. The stove had only heated enough for it to start perking a few minutes ago.

Pulling her glance from the appealing length of his body as Joe crossed to her, she told him that.

He seemed preoccupied and mumbled something she didn't hear. With the towel draped around his neck, his damp hair sticking out in every direction, he said the coffee was done enough and grabbed one of the two mugs hanging on the rack above the stove.

Over the sound of coffee being poured, she heard him say, "Who's Jason?"

She'd just reached for the other cup, in desperate need of caffeine herself. Her hand fell. "Excuse me?"

"Jason. Part of your mother's message yesterday was something about him not going to a dinner. I just wondered who he was."

She reached for the mug again, solid blue like the one Joe had taken. He didn't seem to go much for adornment on anything. "He's my ex-fiancé."

He seemed to have expected that, but all he said was, "Hold out your cup."

She did, watching him as he poured her coffee, then sat the pot on a cooler spot on the stove so it wouldn't grow too strong.

"Mind my asking what happened?"

Had anyone else asked that question of her, she wouldn' have told them. She'd have given a noncommittal response that served to reply without giving anything away. But Joe already knew the reasons. She just hadn't told him they applied to Jason, too.

"I wanted a husband and children. Jason wanted a family that was politically correct."

"What does that mean?"

"He wanted a wife with the right voter appeal."

"No kids?"

"Oh, he wanted them, too. A boy first, then a girl two or three years later."

"What didn't you agree on? The order or the schedule?"

"In the end we didn't agree on anything."

"Why?"

The lawyer at work, she thought, thinking it must be the nature of the beast that made it so curious.

She took a sip of her coffee, then stared into her cup, much as he had done in his kitchen just yesterday morning.

"Jason was in love with the idea of being married to a prominent politician's daughter, of having the political and social connections. He liked the way we looked together, because we photographed well. He even liked the idea that I had a career because he felt that image was important to female voters. He didn't love me, though." The words had hurt once. Now, oddly, saying them didn't bother her at all. "It was the trappings he was interested in."

"You'd been around politics all your life. You had to know all that would appeal to a politician."

She knew from the mildness of his tone that Joe wasn't blaming her for having made the choice. His was a legitimate observation; one she would have made herself had she not been knocked off her feet by Jason's patented charm. They'd met at a function both had found utterly tedious and had spent the evening talking about every place they would rather be other than where they were. Unlike less imaginaive men, he hadn't sent her an elaborate bouquet of roses he next day. He'd been much more subtle than that. He'd ent a single gardenia in a lead crystal bowl. They'd sat by . gardenia bush the previous evening, and his card had said ie would never smell that sweet perfume without thinking f the lovely lady who'd spared him an evening of unadulerated boredom.

Jason Cabot was suave and sophisticated and knew exctly what to say to get what he wanted. Amanda, having vaited so long for someone to care about her, had wanted o badly to believe he'd come to need her as much as he said ie did—and not just for his career.

She watched steam curl over the edge of her cup, wonlering at her own naïveté. For as cautious as she could be, he had been so terribly gullible. In some ways she probaly still was. She wanted so badly to believe in the fairy-tale. 'I wanted to believe that it would be different for us. He promised it would be.'' The steam wavered as she released a leep breath. "I should have known better."

"You did." Joe ducked his head, seeking her eyes. "It ust took you a while to realize it. Maybe it won't take you o long to get over him now."

The statement startled her. "I *am* over him."

He didn't look like he believed her. Walking off to get the killet, snatching up the carton of eggs on the way, she heard iim mutter, "Whatever you say."

"Joe." She started after him so quickly that her coffee loshed precariously close to the rim. Slowing, she took a sip o lower the level, then sat it down next to the bowl he'd just put in front of him on the counter. "I am," she insisted. 'It's been over four months since I called off our engagement.''

"You haven't seen him since?"

"No."

"Then, can I ask you one question?"

He turned on her, looking very much like counsel for the prosecution preparing to drive home the case-winning point.

She glared up at him, not at all impressed with the Clarence Darrow routine.

"What?" she asked since all he'd done was stand there looking very smug.

"Who gave you the necklace those kids took from you?"

At the mention of the now-lost gold chain, her hand circled her throat. Just about the time his eyebrow arched as if to say "I told you so," she smiled.

"My Aunt Helena," she said, feigning ignorance of his implication. "What's that got to do with Jason?"

It struck her then, as she watched Joe's eyes narrow on her grin, that Joe's interest in Jason might have been more than just a way to make conversation. If it were possible, he almost seemed a little bothered by the existence of another man in her life.

Picking up an egg to crack into the bowl, she nudged him with her elbow. "Come on, Joe. I've answered your questions. You answer mine."

He reached for an egg, too, and shrugged. "I just thought he'd given it to you, is all. You seemed pretty protective of it, like it meant something special to you. I was wrong." He didn't seem reluctant to admit so, either. She liked that. "Okay?"

"Okay. But you weren't wrong about it being special." The necklace had been more than special, and its loss had been what angered her most about the attack. "It's tradition on my mother's side of the family to give jewelry on a woman's twenty-first birthday. My aunt knew my parents were getting me diamond earrings and that Grandfather Wadsworth was giving me Grandmother's ruby brooch. My aunt gave me a plain gold chain because she wanted me to keep my perspective. It was simple, but the metal made it precious." She smiled, remembering. "Helena said it was like the important things in life. Like friendship."

Joe hadn't cracked his egg, so she took it from him and cracked it into the bowl herself. At the rate they were going hey'd be having breakfast for lunch. "In a way, it was the most valuable thing I owned."

He reached for another egg. "How will you explain how you lost it?"

"I'll tell her the truth. She's the only person I could tell who would understand."

Joe's egg made it into the bowl, along with a bit of shell. "Is this the same aunt who taught you how to play basketball?"

"Uh-huh. She's also the same one who taught me how to play poker, hold a teacup properly and do tequila shooters."

"You're kidding."

"Not at all. The teacup lesson happened when I was nine. But she took me to Cabo San Lucas with her as a present when I graduated from college. We learned how to do a *folklorico* the same night."

"Dare I ask what that is?"

Amanda smiled at his skeptical tone. "It's a native dance. Sort of this wild, frenzied thing where you keep twirling around until you're not sure it's you spinning or the room. It was wonderful."

Joe just bet it had been. He'd have given a month's pay to see that little show. The thought of Amanda abandoning herself to the driving beat of Latin music, her skirts flying and that smile turning on every male in the place—

Clearing his throat, he picked up the salt. "You sound close to her."

"I am. But I don't get to see her anywhere near as often as I'd like. She travels all the time. Right now she's in Africa on a big-game shoot."

"Hunting rhinos?" he drawled, though it sounded a distinct possibility.

"Oh, Lord, no. She wouldn't harm a fly. She won't even eat anything that has a face. She's a photo journalist. The only thing she'll shoot with is a camera." Joe hadn't taken out the bit of shell, so she fished it out for him. "Helena's tastes are impeccable, and she insists on quality in every thing, but she loves untamed things. She says they're more honest than what civilization has gotten hold of.'' Her smile was soft, lighting her eyes. "I know for certain that she'd like you.''

They stood side by side, her shoulder a scant inch from his arm as they prepared what was apparently going to be scrambled eggs. With her attention on the towel she'd picked up to wipe her hands, she didn't see Joe's expression grow shuttered. If he was going to say anything at all, she expected some remark about her thinking him untamed or uncivilized—which, in some ways, he was. In ways that appealed to her, anyway. What she heard threw her completely.

"I'm sorry I won't meet her.''

He'd spoken quietly, as if he were genuinely sorry he wouldn't have the opportunity to meet someone he would have found most interesting. There was something else in his tone, too. That was what finally made her look up.

It was then that she saw the tightness in his expression.

"There's no reason you shouldn't,'' she said, confused. "She usually comes for the bluegrass festival in June, and she likes to meet my friends.'' Not, she'd come to realize, that she'd had many to introduce to her.

"We're not friends, Amanda.''

Behind her, she heard the crackle of freshly exposed pitch as a log in the stove broke apart. It was strange, but her heart felt a little like it had just done the same thing.

"No,'' she said, her voice subdued. Why was it every time it felt as if the barriers were coming down, she said or did something to make him throw them back up? "I don't suppose we are.''

Joe closed his eyes, calling himself eight kinds of fool as she turned away. She hadn't understood, and he hadn't meant to hurt her. It just about killed him to see the pain she so clearly tried to hide.

"Amanda, don't." He caught her arm, unwilling to let
er increase the distance he'd so unwittingly created. "For-
et I said that, okay?"

"Why? If that's what you think, then it's the truth."

"Yeah. Well, it's not the whole truth, though."

Disgusted with himself, he let her go to push his hand
through his still-damp hair. Outside the window the pale
gray fog still swirled through the trees, distorting their familiar shapes and obscuring the lake. He felt as if he were
in the midst of that fog, groping blindly for a way to explain to her something he couldn't even explain to himself.

"I don't want to be friends with you," he finally said, and
immediately knew he'd just made matters worse. He could
see Amanda's hand shake as she reached for her coffee.

"No." Covering her hand with his before she reached the
candle, he pulled her around to face him. She looked as if
he'd just struck her. She had no business being that vulnerable to him. "Let me finish. I don't want to be friends with
ou," he repeated carefully. "I want more than that. But
'm not going to make promises I can't keep just to get you
to bed."

He expected that proud little chin of hers to come up. But
she stood there, too stunned or too hurt to move.

"Damn it, Amanda," he all but growled as he reached to
touch his fingertips to her cheek. Her skin was as fine as a
baby's and felt like the softest satin. She felt like that all
over. "I want you so bad I hurt. I keep thinking about how
ou felt when we were in my bed. How you wanted me to
touch you. What I wanted to do to you. So, no. We can't be
friends.' Not when everytime I look at you, I'm thinking
thoughts like that."

Joe wasn't sure what he was trying to do. Scare her off,
maybe. Warn her, definitely. Laying it all on the line seemed
the best way to avoid any further misunderstanding, and
that's all he cared about at the moment. As she stood staring up at him, her eyes wide and her cheeks flushed, it was
certain enough that she had the picture. He'd embarrassed

her with his reminder of how she'd responded to him. Bu
while she'd swallowed hard, she hadn't looked away. She'
gone completely, utterly still.

Stop looking at me like that, he demanded, wondering :
she had any idea how she was affecting him. *You're sup
posed to tell me you understand and push me away. Don
you realize how complicated this could get?*

Amanda saw the fierceness enter his eyes. "I don't war
promises," she said, amazed to find strength in her voic
when she felt so little of it in her knees. "I'm not askin
anything of you. Except that you be honest with me. I'v
had promises before, Joe. They're just words." And Joe'
actions had spoken so much louder than any of the empt
words she'd heard before.

"I am being honest."

"Then I don't see the problem."

The fierceness turned feral.

His hand had moved to her shoulder. Now he let it sli
down her arm to her wrist. The muscle in his jaw jerked, hi
expression dark and primitive. "Is it necessary to shov
you?"

Amanda suddenly felt very warm. The stove had finall
started throwing out heat, but it was the heat in Joe's eye
that threatened to turn her blood to vapor. She knew wha
he was going to do.

"I guess you're going to have to."

Joe didn't reply, but the look that swept his face almos
buckled her knees when he brought her hand to him. Hi
eyes steady on hers, he pressed her palm to the rigid lengt
straining against his zipper.

Amanda swallowed hard and stepped closer. If he'd in
tended to frighten her off with boldness, he hadn't suc
ceeded. All he'd succeeded in doing was proving that he
wanted her. The knowledge inflamed her as surely as the fee
of him, hard against her palm. And she wanted him as des
perately as her next breath.

"Understand?" he asked, his voice strained.

He released her wrist. But it was a moment before she drew her hand away. When she did it was to touch his face.

"Joe," she said, or maybe she only thought his name. Whatever else she'd intended to say was lost.

His arm looped around her waist. Looking straight into her eyes, he slowly drew her hips against his. His head bent as she rose to meet him. It seemed she wanted to tell him she did understand, but as her fingers brushed his cheek, she was aware of little beyond the rough, nighttime stubble of his jaw and the soft heat of his mouth.

She sagged against him, breathing in the clean scents of soap and fresh air clinging to his skin as their lips parted. His hand slid down her back, splaying over her bottom to align her more intimately. With his lips playing over hers, his tongue seeking, probing, he drew her in by slow, debilitating degrees. Or maybe it was she who sought to deepen the contact. Her fingers had pushed into his damp hair, spreading over the back of his head to pull him closer. She strained against him, encouraging the provocative motion of his hips, her insides softening at the feel of his hardness seeking her through the layers of their clothing.

The first layer of that clothing came off long moments later when Joe reached between them and slid his bulky flannel jacket from her shoulders. As it hit the floor, he raised his head. His eyes glittered like black diamonds.

He held out his hand.

The gesture held a question as well as an invitation. He was making it clear that what happened next was up to her.

Slowly, deliberately, she slipped her hand into his.

For a moment Joe didn't move. He just stood there, breathing hard and looking very pagan while her pulse pounded in her ears.

You know what's going to happen, don't you?

He hadn't said a word, but Amanda felt herself nod. The motion caused his grip to tighten on her hand, sending a faint jolt through her body at its possessiveness. Even the air felt slightly electric as he led her toward the bed in the darker corner of the room.

His voice was low, his expression shadowed now that they were away from the pale light of the windows. Still, there was light enough for her to see how careful he was when he touched her sweater above the bandage on her sprained wrist. His taut glance moved from there to the collar of her blouse. "How many layers are under here?"

"Two," she said, her voice little more than a whisper. "I was cold."

She wasn't now. Despite the chill the stove had yet to remove from the air, the heat in his expression as he removed her sweater and blouse was as intense as any fire. When he drew her lace camisole over her head and slid the thin straps of her bra down her arms, that heat nearly scorched her soul. It was with something close to reverence that he spread his hand over the fullness of her breast and lowered his head to her mouth.

It didn't occur to Amanda to question what was happening. Loving Joe felt right. Necessary, somehow. Though she only now acknowledged that love was what she felt for him, the feeling had been growing even without the words. That was why she needed to touch him as he was her; why she became so impatient to feel his skin against hers. She needed to give him whatever she could to show him how very much she treasured the gift he probably didn't even know he'd given her. He was the one person she would never have suspected she could trust, but he'd proven to her more than once that he was probably the only person she could.

His sweatshirt had joined her blouse and sweater when Joe took a step forward with her in his arms. The movement pushed her backward, causing the backs of her knees to bump the edge of the mattress. With her arms curved around his neck, he followed her down, easing her onto the quilts. But he only stayed with her long enough to ease his arm from under her before he pulled back to work at snaps

nd zippers and add denim to the collection of clothes on
he floor.

He stood beside the bed, watching her face as he dropped
er panties on the pile. He was so magnificently male, so
bviously aroused, and Amanda was struck by the sheer
eauty of his hard, proud body. Seeing his hunger, she was
lso aware of her own much smaller body and reached for
he sheet to cover herself.

Joe stopped her. Pushing the sheet aside, he pressed her
rms back into the bedding. She would have shied from be-
ng so exposed, so vulnerable, but what he did touched her
oo deeply for her to be embarrassed by his frank gaze.

There was a small bruise on her shoulder. A little dime-
ized spot she hadn't noticed until he touched it with his lips
nd told her he was so sorry she'd been harmed. He found
nother bruise on the heel of her hand. He kissed that, too,
nd the bruises on her knees and a faint purple mark on her
ip bone. With his lips he touched every place she had been
urt, seeming intent on replacing the pain with pleasure.
And when he'd tended all the places where her body had
uffered injury, he turned his attentions to the places he'd
nissed.

His lips trailed liquid fire over the plane of her stomach
o the underside of her breast. Still, he kept her arms lightly
oinned, touching her only with his lips and his tongue. She
ched for him to cup his hand over her, to touch her as he
aad before, but he only continued to torment her with kisses
hat teasingly circled her nipple—until, finally, her back
arching against the exquisite sensations, he pulled the tight
oud into his mouth.

Joe made a low, guttural sound as he felt her swell against
ais tongue. He was ready to die from wanting, and the feel
of her responding to him was almost more than he could
oear. He could feel her trembling. Delicate shudders rip-
oled along her flesh as he suckled her. She was such a sen-
ual woman, and he couldn't seem to get enough of her. Her
lesh tasted sweet and felt like warm silk. He wanted noth-

ing more than to slip between her legs and bury himself inside her.

The thought was nearly enough to drive him over the edge. He was precariously close to the edge as it was.

He moved his weight over her, seeking her mouth. The taste of her filled him, consumed him. He knew he wouldn't last long. Not this time. So he pushed his hand between them, until the moans he drank from her lips turned to plea, and slid his hands under her hips to bring her to him. With her arms curved around his back, he heard her whisper his name. Then, glorying in the feel of her, he thought of nothing but the sweet oblivion they created—and the profound sense of completion that shattered the lock on his soul.

The fire in the stove had thoroughly heated the inside of the tiny cabin when Amanda awoke to the feel of Joe's fingers trailing up and down her arm. They were on their sides, the quilts in a tangle at their feet, and their legs still wound around each other's as if they woke up that way all the time.

"Hi," she heard him say, then felt his lips touch her forehead near her bandage. "I was wondering if you were going to sleep all day."

The room was brighter, the light pouring through the windows at the far end of the room, the pure light of sunshine.

Joe had slept, too. She could tell from his softened expression—and the crease the pillow had made on his cheek. She touched the faint, red mark with the tips of fingers that peeked from the beige elastic wound around them. He looked absolutely wonderful to her—which was rather the way she felt.

"Do you always lie around in bed on Saturdays?"

The lazy question drew her smile. "Only until nine o'clock. Then I weed my garden."

"Sounds as exciting as my Saturday. I'd have been at the office by now."

That didn't surprise her. What *did* was that he sounded so unconcerned about not being there.

His hand continued its journey up and down her arm. "Is there anything you want to do here?"

"The only thing I'd planned on was picking your brain."

His hand stilled. "About anything in particular?"

She smiled, tipping her head back to see him better as she tucked her arm around his waist. "That strip mall we saw yesterday. I still think there's potential there."

His tone was indulgent, but his fingers resumed their feathery caress. "Except for the zoning problem."

"Let's say we forget that for a minute. What about the building itself? It would need work, but I'm sure Bernie's ladies would be willing to do whatever was necessary to make it liveable. It wouldn't be very convenient at first, not until they could knock out some walls, anyway. But there was a restaurant there and it would probably have the kind of kitchen facilities they'd need."

The more she thought about what could be done, the more animated she became. To Joe, her face shone with the light of an angel's. "There must be restroom facilities in there somewhere, too. Showers might be a problem, but surely the plumbing could . . ."

"I hate to interrupt," he said, when what he really hated to do was kill her excitement. "But do you have any idea how much it would cost to go ripping out walls and messing with plumbing?"

Her expression was utterly innocent, the feel of her body pressed so intimately to his positively wicked. The contrasts had him barely able to concentrate.

"I'm sure we could find out."

He was sure they could. "Do you really want to talk about this right now?"

He moved against her, his eyes drifting to her mouth.

He was right. They could talk about this later. "How about after breakfast? We forgot it."

"I know." He pulled her over him, adjusting the pillow behind his head and spreading his legs to tuck around hers. Eyes smiling, he slowly ran his hand down her spine. "We got sidetracked. What were we building over there, anyway?"

"I think it was scrambled eggs. Or an omelette."

"Sounds good."

"Which?"

"You."

He kissed her then, and she didn't remember to tell him that he hadn't really answered her. Not until a long time later, anyway. Not until he'd taken his time to explore all the places he'd forgotten before, and given her a chance to learn him as well.

Joe was by turns greedy and patient, giving and demanding. In ways she felt as if he were branding her, spoiling her so that no other man could ever touch her as he had. And she knew no man ever would. He had protected her, cared for her, pleasured her, and he had touched her in the most intimate of places: her heart. Yet, even as she gave herself so completely, in the depths of her heart she knew there was a part of him she could never reach: the part that kept the love he might be capable of giving trapped forever inside him.

The part she had to face when the idyll came to an end.

Chapter Twelve

Joe had planned on heading back to the city Sunday afternoon. He didn't know how Doris had rescheduled his appointments, but since he already had a full calendar, he had the feeling he was about to face the week from hell. Yet when it had come time to leave, he'd been sitting on the shore with Amanda, trying to teach her how to fish, and time had gotten away from him. Laughing at her squeamishness when she'd refused to thread a worm onto her hook, he carried her back to the cabin and to the bed that never did get made. Then they'd sat in front of the fire as night closed in around them, talking in low tones about nothing in particular—until she'd brought up the strip mall again.

Joe knew she wanted to help. But the mention of what she thought that property would be good for brought the familiar knot of tension back to his stomach. Until that moment he hadn't realized how much he'd relaxed; how completely he'd lost himself in her. Acknowledging that

startling accomplishment required that he also acknowl
edge the realities he'd temporarily escaped. He could do tha
when he left here, though. The battle was half lost already
but he didn't want to ruin what peace remained of the eve
ning by having to explain how much time and work woulc
be wasted checking out a property they had no hope of get
ting in time. So, as Amanda had sat by his side, he'd told he
that he wanted to forget about problems while they were
here: the shelter, his work, what had happened to her. Anc
she'd seemed to understand when she'd said nothing else
about it—until five minutes before he was ready to go at six
o'clock Monday morning.

"Are you sure you want to do this?"

Joe directed the words to her back as she closed her suitcase and checked around to make sure she hadn't forgotten
anything. She was leaving with him, or so she'd announced
when they'd gotten up half an hour ago.

Turning in the middle of the room, she offered a hesitant
smile. "I'm sure," she said, sounding oddly uncertain despite her insistence otherwise. "Look. You can barely see
anything."

He didn't tell her that was probably because the light was
so lousy as she tilted her face up for his inspection. Yet when
he pulled her closer to the pale light coming in the window,
he had to admit that three and a half days had made a definite difference in her appearance. The swelling had disappeared from her jaw, and the fading redness and scratches
had been covered with makeup. She'd changed the bandage
on her forehead to one of the flesh-colored ones they'd
picked up at the little country store. By combing her bangs
straight down, the deeper abrasion there wasn't even noticeable. The bruises on her knees were covered by long
slacks, and most of the elastic bandage on her arm was hidden by her long-sleeved sweater. She wouldn't want to run
into anyone she knew close-up, but from a distance, he had
to agree she didn't look too bad.

"It's up to you if you want to go back now. But it's not like there's any rush. You've got your work here, and I could come back to get you in a few days."

That was true. She did have her work and a nice safe place to stay while she protected herself from prying eyes ... and her parent's potential disapproval. While she protected herself from life in general, she forced herself to admit. But while she was busy living in her little glass box, time would be running out for the only real friends she had. "There's something else I have to do."

"What?"

"You asked me not to talk about it here."

"You're not still thinking about that strip mall, are you?" Seeing her smile falter, he knew she was. "I already told you it won't work. It would take months to get . . ."

Cutting himself off, Joe shoved his fingers through his hair. He saw no reason to repeat what he'd already told her. She'd heard him the first two times. The woman was smart enough to have grasped the details. The problem was that she was so stubborn.

She was also getting deeper into his life by the second.

There seemed only one way to end her preoccupation with his idea. "Look. I'll ask the owner if the property's for sale. All right? Even if it is, I'm sure he'll want way too much for it. If it isn't for sale, there's nothing else to discuss."

She didn't appreciate that he'd focused only on negatives. "You won't even give this a chance."

"That's because I've been through this before, Amanda." He didn't want to lose patience with her, but she truly had no idea what she was dealing with. She couldn't pick out a piece of property for a homeless shelter as if it were a car or suit or something else that had caught her eye. "I don't have time to waste on a wild-goose chase. If I thought there was a snowball's chance in hell of that place working out in time, I'd look into it. You know that. But we don't even know if the guy wants to sell it."

"So ask. If he does, I'll talk to him."

"*You* will?"

"Why not? I won't bother you with anything unless looks like we can work something out." She hesitated, h voice growing quieter. "I need to do this, Joe. At least let m try."

Joe swore, but only to himself. What she asked was pe fectly reasonable. And her request really wasn't his to den He understood about needing to try. God knew he'd bee doing it all of his life.

"Suit yourself," he told her, pushing his hands into h pockets to keep from reaching for her. He was already la as it was. "If he's willing to talk, I'll have my secretary s it up for you."

Since there didn't seem to be anything else to say on th matter, he pulled her suitcase from the bed and headed o to the car. Amanda watched him walk out the open doo then, frowning, went to get the keys to lock the exterio shutters. She should feel good about having won his agree ment. That was what she'd wanted, after all. But instead o feeling as if she'd accomplished something positive, she fel a definite twinge of anxiety.

She'd felt it beginning last night: Joe's slow and subtl withdrawal from her. Or maybe, she told herself, what sh felt was simply her own insecurity. The closeness they share was a precarious thing. Something she was afraid to lose an afraid to trust. It was too new, too fragile to withstand th words it would take to talk about it. So she kept her anxi eties to herself as they left his cabin and his mountain be hind—and tried to believe everything would be all right a the tension Joe had shed in the mountains crept back int him with every mile they got closer to town.

He didn't stay when he dropped her suitcase in her entr a couple of hours later. Knowing how anxious he was to ge to his office, she didn't expect him to stick around. What h did do was turn her knees to wax with a kiss that effectively